VOYAGE IN THE KEYS
A LOGAN DODGE ADVENTURE

FLORIDA KEYS ADVENTURE SERIES
VOLUME 15

Copyright © 2022 by Matthew Rief
All rights reserved.

No part of this book may be reproduced in any form or by any electronic or mechanical means, including information storage and retrieval systems, without written permission from the author, except for the use of brief quotations in a book review.

This book is a work of fiction. Names, characters, businesses, places, events and incidents are either the products of the author's imagination or used in a fictitious manner. Any resemblance to actual persons, living or dead, or actual events is purely coincidental.

Edited by Eliza Dee, Clio Editing Services
Proofread by Donna Rich and Nancy Brown (Redline Proofreading and Editing)

LOGAN DODGE ADVENTURES

Gold in the Keys
Hunted in the Keys
Revenge in the Keys
Betrayed in the Keys
Redemption in the Keys
Corruption in the Keys
Predator in the Keys
Legend in the Keys
Abducted in the Keys
Showdown in the Keys
Avenged in the Keys
Broken in the Keys
Payback in the Keys
Condemned in the Keys
Voyage in the Keys
Guardian in the Keys

JASON WAKE NOVELS

Caribbean Wake
Surging Wake
Relentless Wake
Turbulent Wake
Furious Wake

Join the Adventure!
Sign up for my newsletter to receive updates on upcoming books on my website:

matthewrief.com

Acknowledgements

First and foremost, I'd like to thank my longtime editor, Eliza Dee (clioediting.com), who has once again gone the extra mile. Smart, insightful, and with the heart of a teacher, Eliza has been editing these adventures since the first book and has played a pivotal role in their success. I consider myself incredibly fortunate to work with her.

I'd also like to thank my proofreaders, Nancy Brown (redlineproofreading.com), and Donna Rich (donnarich@icould.com). They're both sharp-witted, skilled, and possess superb eyes for detail. I couldn't imagine publishing a book without them.

A special thanks as well to Fred Anderson for generously taking the time to help me with the sailing details in this book. Fred's years of experiences out on the water have made him a treasure trove of knowledge, and his assistance proved invaluable.

ONE

The two men were forced at gunpoint across the dark beach.

Their wrists were duct-taped. Their mouths gagged.

Streaks of moonlight broke through the shifting midnight clouds, glowing silver across their tattered, blood-soaked clothes.

They were prodded over the fine sand and onto the planks of an old dock. Strong arms shoved them onto the deck of a brand-new thirty-foot offshore fishing boat.

Then, without a word, the four shadowy apparitions retraced their steps back to the shore, leaving the two prisoners huddled at the stern. The captives sat in silence, weakened from the beatings they'd suffered, as the boat's lines were cast. Its dual Mercury engines fired up, and it peeled away from the pilings, rapidly accelerating to over forty knots. It motored three miles out into open ocean, then the engines died and all went silent.

It was a still evening. Barely a whisper of wind. And it was warm and ominous.

"I'm only going to ask one more time," a man said, striding from the cockpit and standing over the two bound captives.

He wore a ski mask. And held a six-inch knife in his right hand.

Kneeling, he hovered the razor-sharp black steel blade over the prisoners, then used it to slash their gags free.

"If you cooperate," the masked man continued, coming back to his feet, "I will show you mercy. If not, well…"

"You can go to hell," one of the captives spat, his voice shaky.

He was the younger of the two bound men. Had dark skin and long hair kept in a ponytail.

"Quiet, Emilio," the other captive, a plump middle-aged man, gasped.

"To hell with that," Emilio rebutted. "You criminals aren't getting anything more from me."

The masked man remained silent. Observing intently. Preparing.

"I don't know who you are and I don't care," Emilio continued, the battered man struggling to get the words out. "You won't get a peso more from me. There's nothing you can do."

The masked man stood perfectly silent and still.

Like a statue. Staring at the defiant prisoner. Then a crude smile formed on his face.

"Emilio here thinks there's nothing I can do to sway his mind." He turned to the shadowy forward part of the boat. "What do you think about that, Diego?"

With the uttering of the name, a massive muscular man appeared from the shadows.

With big paws for hands, he grabbed Emilio and heaved him to his feet. Forced his arms all the way above his head and secured them to a metal loop in the hard top. Then he tied a harness around his waist and tightened a black lifejacket over his neck. Knotted it snug so it wouldn't come loose.

The masked man's smile broadened. He could see fear sprouting up in his captive's eyes. The man's pulse pounding as the anticipation and fear grew.

Once Emilio was secure, the hulking man withdrew a switchblade, the menacing edge glistening under a sliver of moonlight.

"This is your last chance," the masked man said.

When there was no reply, Diego sliced a gash across the prisoner's left wrist and then his right. Emilio cried out. A high-pitched shriek like a dying animal. His eyes bulged and blood flowed out from the cuts.

Shaking in pain, he struggled to break free, but it was no use.

Another man appeared from the shadows and tightened rubber tubes around Emilio's wounded limbs to pinch the veins just upstream of the lacerations. Not to stop the bleeding. But to control it to a steady trickle.

Then Diego hoisted Emilio back down, forced him aft until they reached the transom, and clipped a metal cable to the harness secured around the prisoner's body.

The masked man stepped forward, and Emilio looked up and cried out, "You sick bastard!"

The broken, pain-riddled yells echoed across the void surrounding them.

"You think that's sick?" the masked man said. "You haven't seen anything yet."

The leader of the group leaned back and landed a strong front kick into Emilio's gut. The tall captive stumbled backward, then lost control and flipped over the transom, splashing into the dark sea.

He thrashed and yelled and cursed, the lifejacket keeping him afloat as Diego payed out cable using a manual winch. The current pulled Emilio until he was thirty feet behind the stern, then Diego locked the cable and cracked open a massive cooler. Grabbing a chum cage that was prepacked with fish guts, he tied it to the stern and hurled it over the side. The smelly entrails splashed into the water and were dragged halfway between the boat and Emilio as Diego fired up the engines and crawled them along at four knots.

The bound man continued to yell out violently as he was dragged through the dark sea. Observing intently, the masked man eyed his watch.

It didn't take long. The smell of the innards, combined with Emilio's blood and quivering body, soon attracted a twelve-foot tiger shark.

The masked man smiled, then heaved the other captive up so he could watch the action.

What began as a few sporadic cries swiftly turned

gruesome. Sharp, primal shrieks of intense pain filled the air. Terror took over the helpless man's face as the predator nibbled at first, then circled back for full bites.

Then a second shark appeared. And a third. Each making intermittent strikes. Ripping off chunks with razor-sharp teeth.

Emilio turned frantic, his wails resounding, then dying off uselessly on the empty horizon.

At first, he tried to fight back. Then the pain and blood loss became too much and all he could do was cry out desperately.

Five minutes later, the captive was finished in a final excruciating crescendo. Then the remnants of his body were fought over—torn apart and ripped to shreds right in front of their eyes. Leaving only the lifejacket and bits of the harness behind.

"Now," the masked man said, "I'll be gracious and make my offer one more time."

The short middle-aged man stared at their rippling wake. His mouth agape. His eyes shellshocked. His clothes soaked in sweat.

He nodded vigorously. "I... I'll give you whatever you want." The words stumbled out. Rushed and laced with fear.

Diego brought over a computer connected to a powerful Wi-Fi signal booster. After the transfer of funds was complete, the cable was coiled up and the bloody remnants of the harness and lifejacket were tossed into a trash bag.

"You made a wise decision," the masked man said.

The prisoner fought to catch his breath, still shaking from the terrifying sight he'd just witnessed.

"Who are you?" the terrified captive said. "At least show me your face. I deserve that much after giving you everything I own."

The leader of the group turned, grabbed the top of his ski mask, and slid it off.

"No..." the prisoner gasped. "No, how... how could you?" He wheezed and tilted forward, nearly toppling over. "You conniving, backstabbing, ba—"

The leader silenced his captive by removing an Obregon .45-caliber pistol and aiming it at the man's head.

"You... you promised mercy."

"Yes. I promised mercy," the leader said, giving Diego a look.

The giant strode forward and secured a line of dive weights around the man's ankles. Once they were snug and knotted in place, he stepped back.

"And I'm a man of my word," the leader added.

He gave another sinister smile, then pulled the trigger. The bullet struck home, and the captive lurched backward, tumbling over the transom. Dead before he'd splashed into the water.

His corpse sank like a rock, bubbles trickling up as he vanished into the dark abyss.

Diego approached from behind and said, "We're still short, boss. Short by a large margin."

"Enough."

"Bu—"

"Utter another word and you join them," the leader snapped, waving his pistol.

As the colossal man retreated back, his boss stared out over the water.

Diego was right.

He was short—had a mountain to climb before he'd be out of the mess. But it didn't matter. It didn't matter the cost.

He'd kill as many as it took, and he'd come out on top. He always did.

TWO

My adversary had me beat.

I was a sitting duck, and we both knew it.

"Beg for mercy," my daughter said, pointing her foam sword at me, "and I'll give you the honor of a swift end."

I stood unarmed at the bow of a fifty-foot catamaran, holding onto the forestay and leaning over the crossbeam, the surf spraying over me as we pierced along the infinite blue. My cutlass, which had been knocked from my grasp moments earlier and blown aft in a gust, was twenty feet away. Wedged between mounted stanchion supports amidship.

"Ange, little help," I called out.

My wife sat on the foredeck, her bare feet and long sun-kissed legs gleaming under the afternoon sun.

Her blond hair tied back, she wore denim shorts and a loose white button-up. Despite my pleas for help, her head remained buried in the pages of a worn copy of *Kon-Tiki* she'd found in one of the saloon lockers.

"Crying for help won't save you now," Scarlett said, shuffling forward and pointing the tip of her weapon just inches in front of my chest.

I shot my wife another look, and she lowered her sunglasses, glanced up at me with her vibrant blue eyes and called out, "You got yourself into this mess, Dodge."

I turned my attention back to my opponent.

I got myself into this mess, I thought, replaying my wife's words and knowing that if I was going to make a move, it was now or never.

Scarlett shot me a devilish smile, the tall, athletic sixteen-year-old gearing up for her finishing strike.

My mind ran wild. Calculating. Her position. Weight distribution. Arm placement. Sword length, stride length, and distance between us. Then my surroundings and my position. All in a flash that came as natural to me as breathing. Second nature.

Scarlett called out, lunged forward, then thrust the tip toward me.

I tightened my grip on the forestay and pulled, swinging myself around and whirling out of the weapon's path just as it stabbed, puncturing nothing but air. Going with my momentum, I darted across the trampoline, swiftly unshackled the code zero halyard, and leapt onto the dolphin seat.

Holding tight to the line, I spun around, eyeing my daughter who I'd barely managed to fake out. "You will always remember this as the day that you—"

I didn't have time to finish Sparrow's famous line. With my agile daughter closing in on me again, I launched myself over the side, soaring out over the open sea in a large sweeping arc. I let out an ecstatic cheer from the exhilarating rush as I swung all the way to the stern, landing onto the starboard swim platform.

Releasing the halyard, I sprang forward toward my fallen weapon. My daughter was fast, reacting on the fly and reengaging just as I seized my cutlass. We went back at it, like two buccaneers of old. Slicing and spinning our way to the port side and then to the stern, each throwing and blocking strikes on the way.

After parrying one of my attacks, my daughter vaulted onto the edge of the transom, then came at me with a strong two-handed overhead strike. I blocked the attack as she landed on the afterdeck, our two swords locked in place.

"You've lost a step, old man," she joked.

I tightened my gaze. Gave a barely noticeable smile. I'd been taking it easy on her, but it was time to teach her a lesson.

Shifting left briefly, I rocked back to the right, swiping my weapon free. With her weight and strength pushing forward, she stumbled, then fought to regain herself against the port rail. She came back with two wild, erratic swings, and I managed to land a strike to her dominant hand, sending her weapon to the deck.

Before she knew it, she was staring down the length of my sword, the tip hovering just over her chest.

I grinned at her. "You were saying?"

My tough, stubborn, competitive daughter's face scrunched up. Then she looked around. I could see her mind at work, fighting to come up with something. Anything.

I blinked as something caught my attention at her back. Movement. A distant splash.

Then my mouth dropped and excitement rushed through me as I realized what I was seeing.

It was just a moment. A brief letting down of my guard.

It was all Scarlett needed.

She dropped and rolled. Grabbed and swooped and swung, slashing her foam blade across my side.

"Huzzah!" she yelled, then struck me with a merciless second blow, right into my heart. "Your crusade was futile."

I laughed and held up my hands. "All right, Scar, you win."

She let out a villainous cackle and pointed her chin to the sky. Held her sword high over her head. "There's nothing better than the sweet taste of victory."

"How about witnessing something spectacular?" I said, turning and gazing over the port rail.

She lowered her weapon, stood like Captain Morgan with one foot up on the transom, then shielded her eyes from the afternoon sun.

Just as she focused out over the water, the magnificent, colossal creature returned, breaching with a powerful blast and rising halfway out of the Gulf before colliding into the surface with a rumble and spray of bubbling water.

"That's incredible!" Scarlett gasped, shifting

closer to the edge.

Ange, hearing the distant grumble and our daughter's reaction, scampered over as the whale recovered, exhaled a powerful surge of mist from its blowhole, and breached again, this time soaring even higher before gravity pulled its enormous body back down.

"What kind of whale is it?" Scarlett asked.

I'd already swiped the binoculars from the helm station and had them focused on the marine mammal.

"Looks like a humpback," I said. "Or should I say, two humpbacks," I corrected as a second, slightly smaller whale made its presence known, letting out a burst of air that formed a cloudy pillar.

Breathless at the sight, the three of us watched the two bus-sized creatures as they made their way along the Gulf, breaking free in intermittent gasp-invoking displays of power.

As the whales moved on, Scarlett turned back to me, then scooped up my foam sword and handed it over. "Time for round two?"

I chuckled. "I think you mean round twenty."

Our daughter had discovered the two foam weapons in her guest cabin locker that morning, and we'd been going at it seemingly all day.

Ange leaned over and checked the time on my watch. "It's two already?"

"Time flies when you're living your best life," I said.

"Come on, Scar. Dad made breakfast, so we got lunch."

The two ducked through the sliding glass door and scampered into the galley, leaving me alone in the cockpit. After reattaching the code zero halyard to the dolphin seat, I returned to the helm. Reaching up to the hardtop, I stretched my six-two frame and ran a hand through my short dark brown hair, a smile materializing on my face. Gratitude overtaking me and freedom empowering me as I gazed out over the empty horizon.

There's nothing like being out to sea, especially under sail. Surrounded by nothing but blue. The sensation can make you feel like the loneliest person on the planet. And the most present, all at the same time. A place where it feels like time itself doesn't exist. Not out there. The rippling sea indifferent to it. Ancient.

I stared awestruck at the sight familiar to the eyes of our ancestors thousands of years back. The mystery of distant, faraway lands calling. Beckoning. Drawing forth men from all stations and status with the same fervent zeal.

The horizon held nothing, and everything, all at the same time. An empty stretch, promising possibility. Mankind has been striving to articulate the sensation of the vessel on the open ocean for millennia. But the phenomenon goes far beyond the senses. It strikes a chord in the fabric of our being. Holds us tight in the present moment while also revealing the expanse of eternity.

I could think of few things more innately romantic or liberating. Given sufficient time and supplies, you can go anywhere. It's the ultimate freedom—offering daring souls the ability to take their pick between all three hundred and sixty degrees of horizon.

I turned and gazed at our wake and the long stretch

of blue beyond its widening and dissipating imprint.

The past.

It flashed in my mind like a torrent.

A recent series of deadly encounters that had nearly done me in. And weeks of court proceedings resulting from serious charges against me. Accusations. Lies.

In the end, the truth had prevailed. We'd won the day and I'd kept my life and freedom.

But even victories leave their wounds, and the reputational beating I'd been served at the hands of locals, major news networks, and keyboard warriors alike hadn't healed with the ruling. Not completely.

After the brunt of the storm had subsided, it had soon become clear that an escape from it all was needed. Time and space. Room for healing and regrowth.

We were right in the middle of planning a trip when, just a couple of days ago, a unique opportunity had presented itself.

Chris Hale, a man whose family I'd once saved, had returned the favor in impressive fashion. The successful lawyer based out of Miami had defended my freedom in court and then, months after the proceedings, had called to explain how he and his family weren't able to take their annual sailing trip and ask me if I knew anyone who could charter their catamaran to Mexico on short notice. I'd jumped at the chance.

Call it fate or serendipity. Either way, I couldn't imagine a better way to escape from everything for a little while.

We'd set sail the previous day, right at the start of

Scarlett's winter break, heading from Key West to the island of Cozumel. Though we'd barely been at sea for twenty-four hours, I was already feeling the mental clarity that sailing the open ocean provides.

I snapped out of it as Ange and Scarlett returned topside, carrying a bowl of lobster salad and cans of coconut water.

Just the sight of them put a smile on my face.

The only thing better than gliding freely under sail in open water is doing so with good company. The best company.

"Looks delicious," I said, eyeing lunch as we gathered around the topside dinette.

Formerly Miss Angelina Fox, Ange and I had met during a vastly different chapter of our lives. We'd both been mercenaries back then—her a Swedish heiress with a troubled past who, through years of training and travel and conflict, had become one of the deadliest women in the world, and me a trained fighter fresh out of eight years in Naval Special Forces.

Though we both strived to maintain our edges, both physically and mentally, our new lifestyles had opened up time for other, more conventional pursuits.

One of Ange's was cooking, my smart, hardworking wife devouring cookbooks and spoiling us with her tantalizing results.

For lunch today was a succulent lobster salad with fresh steamed lobster coated in a blend of mayonnaise, diced celery, chopped chives, and lemon juice. The perfect concoction of flavor was combined with sliced avocados and rested on pillows of butterhead lettuce.

In typical Ange fashion, she knocked it out of the park.

We lounged in the shade while savoring the food and soaking in the sights and sounds, Scarlett unable to stop talking about both her victory in our duel and the magnificent show the two whales had put on.

That evening, we ate dinner in the galley before heading topside with armfuls of pillows and blankets. Piling a mountain of soft comfort on the trampolines, we sprawled out and gazed up at the ocean of stars, the twinkling lights appearing so big and so close we felt we could reach, outstretch our fingers, and grab them.

When it got late, we wandered down to our cabins. The interior of the elegant sailboat was nothing short of spectacular and surprisingly spacious, the marvel of maritime engineering custom made by the South African–based St. Francis Marine.

After saying goodnight to Scarlett, Ange and I snuggled in the cockpit for half an hour, then I took the first watch, letting her sleep for four hours before we switched places. By the time it was my turn to hit the sack, I crashed onto the queen-sized bed in the master cabin, passing out moments after my head hit the pillow.

We sailed for another two days, spending our time lounging and napping, reading, eating, and having intermittent dueling and workout sessions. We also rigged and secured two fishing poles and trolled off the stern, managing to reel in a few cobias and mackerel to keep the fridge stocked.

Sticking to a southwesterly course ever since we'd passed the Dry Tortugas and the outstretched fingers of the Keys, we rode the easterly trade winds, the persistent December gusts growing stronger and surpassing fifteen knots for a good chunk of the journey.

The powerful winds came in handy when we took on the substantial currents of the Gulfstream as we sailed through the narrow stretch of water between the Yucatan and Cuba that offers the only sea link between the Gulf of Mexico and the Caribbean Sea.

The Yucatan Channel is also a major lane for freighter traffic, the behemoths chugging along in both directions and keeping us vigilant as we closed in on our destination.

On the morning of the third day, after we'd traversed just over four hundred nautical miles, the northern tip of Cozumel appeared on the horizon. Scarlett spotted it first, our enthusiastic daughter holding on tight and standing barefoot on the bowsprit while belting out, "Land ho!"

The narrow stretch of limestone rose up out of the horizon, the Punta Molas Lighthouse piercing the sky above a stretch of green hugging a rocky coast.

We sailed along the northwestern curve, running parallel to the fin-shaped edge of the island while keeping our distance from the shallows. The waters garnishing the shoreline were perfect—that idyllic transition of crystal clear to vibrant turquoise to rich cobalt.

We rounded the northwest point, and the untouched coast abruptly transitioned to waterfront hotels and beach clubs.

Furling the sails, we powered up the cat's dual 57-horsepower inboards and motored into Puerto de

Abrigo Marina. We called ahead, and the marina manager guided us into Chris's slip. After tying off, we met with the harbormaster and customs agent. Both were friendly and complimented the sailing beauty.

"I wish," I said when they implied that I owned it. "She belongs to a good friend of ours."

"That's right," the marina manager said. "Mr. Hale. That's the better way to do it anyway. Have a friend who owns a boat. After all, a boat is just a—"

"Hole in the water to throw money into?" I said, finishing the popular expression.

The man chuckled, and we wrapped things up. I didn't mention that I had my own decent-size hole in the water moored back in Key West.

"I'm sad to be leaving," Scarlett said when I returned to *Wayfinder*.

She and Ange were below deck, doing a final check and tidying up before we disembarked for good.

"But this island doesn't seem so bad," she added.

Ange and I both laughed.

"Cozumel is one of the most beautiful islands in the world," I said. "And it offers some of the best diving you'll find anywhere. I think you're going to fall in love, kiddo."

THREE

After locking up, we hauled our stuff to the shore. The marina was nearly packed full—all those fortunate liveaboarders who'd descended to exotic latitudes, following the sun and warmth. We hailed a cab, the white sedan with red stripes across its sides squeaking to a stop along the curb. An enthusiastic local in his early twenties hopped out and helped us with our bags.

"Where you heading?" he said in perfect English.

"Barracuda," I replied.

He nodded and we piled in, Ange and Scarlett in the back and me in front. The driver introduced himself as Armando and he had a rosary hanging from the rearview and a picture of a beautiful woman and baby.

He put the little engine in gear and shook us onto the road, gassing south.

"You mind?" I said, grabbing the window lever.

He flipped off the AC and I rolled it all the way down, resting an elbow on the frame. After spending three days breathing in the freshest fresh air, the inside of the taxi felt stuffy.

He skirted us along the coast, passing by a line of tall resorts before the waterfront flattened out to a wide walking path along a seawall and an occasional beachfront bar. Then downtown came into view. A sprawling boardwalk. A spread of restaurants and gift shops and bars. A wide-open square with a fountain in the middle. And the ferry terminal on our right with three different-colored walk-on ferries shuttling tourists back and forth.

"Where are they coming from?" Scarlett asked.

"*Playa*," Armando said.

"We might have to day trip there," I said. "Lots of ruins on the mainland. And cenotes."

I fell silent for a moment as Ange explained to Scarlett what a cenote is. With the car stopped to let a crowd of tourists flock across the street, I gazed to my right at the line of taxis near a pullout at the entrance of the ferry terminal. I counted half a dozen uniformed Mexican soldiers with M16s slung across their chests.

"There a war going on I don't know about?" I said.

"It's just a precaution," Armando said. "Usually just two there to make visitors feel at ease. But given recent events, the security's been upped."

Ange leaned forward. "Recent events?"

The crowd passed, and Armando zipped us

onward, passing by more shops and restaurants on the left and empty coastline with docks and a big replica pirate ship tied off.

"A local disappeared last week," Armando explained. "Then two more disappeared just a few days ago."

I raised my eyebrows at him. "Disappeared?"

The guy held up his right hand and snapped his fingers. "Poof. Just gone. Vanished without a trace. Or a word to anyone. No one knows… well, someone knows."

"I didn't think Cozumel experienced cartel violence," I said.

"We don't."

"Then what do you think happened?" Ange said.

He shrugged. "We know what happened to the first guy at least. He turned up near Playa Bonita yesterday, or so I heard. Just a corpse, though. Undistinguishable at first, you know. A week in the open sea will do that."

"Who were the three?" I said. "Did you know them?"

"A little. They were all locals. Nobody's targeting tourists, so feel at ease." He chuckled. "They pump too much fuel into our economy."

We passed by the busy cruise ship terminal, but most pedestrians were using the walking bridge. A short moment later, Armando braked to a stop in front of an orange hotel with "Hotel Barracuda" painted in silver cursive over the entrance.

Armando hopped out and helped us with the bags.

"Fifty pesos," he said.

I slid out my wallet. Instead of a fifty, I pulled a

hundred halfway out of the worn leather.

"You happen to have change?" I said.

The man smiled and nodded. Reached into his pocket.

"An honest driver," I said with a grin. Then I pulled the hundred the rest of the way out and handed it to him. "Keep it. You got a card?"

Instead of change, he pried out a white card with the company logo and number. He jotted his own number down with a ballpoint pen.

"Call anytime, my friends, and I'll be there. Welcome to Cozumel."

He threw a friendly wave, then drove off.

"What was that about?" Scarlett said.

"I'll tell you later," I replied, then we hauled our stuff inside and checked in.

I'd booked two queen rooms, and the receptionist gave us an adjoining pair on the second floor. They were simple units, nothing over the top, but they both had balconies overlooking the water. Lapping waves and Spanish pop music filtered in with the refreshing breeze as I pushed open the sliding glass door.

"Of all the places you could've booked," Ange said, looking around, "I'm curious why you booked this one."

"Nostalgia, mostly."

"You've stayed here before?"

"Years and years ago. Just for a few days."

"Come on," Scarlett said, having already changed into her swimsuit and holding up her GoPro. "Look at that water. It's perfect and it's calling my name."

We swung by a nearby dive shop to get Scarlett a new mask, her old one having taken a dip on the trip here, then hit the beach.

We stepped out onto a spread of scattered tables and lounge chairs, palm trees, and palapas covering a blanket of white sand. Right beside the hotel was No Name Bar, which served food and drinks to your beach chair and had a small pool complete with a swim-up bar. At the northern edge of the hotel was a tiny dive operation, its lights still on and its doors open and facing the sea.

The place was calming by the second as we claimed a trio of beach chairs beside the seawall.

"You guys arrived just in time," a middle-aged man to our right said.

He was with his wife, and the couple lounged while reading and whittling away at a mountain of nachos. They looked so comfortable that I suspected they could've been right there all day. Maybe all week.

"We were just gearing up for the cruise ship Olympics," the man explained, taking a sip of his beer.

I chuckled. "What time do the games begin?"

"Those two monsters shove off at five," he said, pointing the neck of his Dos Equis toward a Royal Caribbean and a Carnival cruise ship moored at the end of the pier just to the northwest. Both looked like they could accommodate an entire town. "With the reported traffic jam near the gas station, it's bound to be a good show."

"The cruise ship Olympics?" Scarlett said as we set our stuff down.

"A routine spectacle here in Cozumel," I explained. "Held a few times a week. Foot races in flip-flops against the clock with high stakes."

She still looked confused, but I brushed it off.

"You'll see for yourself," Ange said with a smile.

Scarlett took in the scene while she and Ange slid out of their dresses.

"This place is something else," our daughter said.

"It is," I said, then pointed out over the water. "And you see that swim platform bobbing out there? There's a surprise on the seafloor beneath it."

"What is it?"

I fished out her new mask and handed it over. "Let's find out."

I pulled off my shirt and kicked off my sandals, and the three of us headed for the small concrete pier with a big orange arch at the end.

"Plenty deep here," I said when our feet reached the edge. "Just watch out for divers."

Seeing that the perfect translucent water was devoid of people, I leapt off the side headfirst and splashed into paradise. The girls followed, and we donned our masks, then raced out toward the swim platform roughly a hundred feet from shore. The water was teeming with colorful life. And Scarlett quickly pointed out a triggerfish, a rock beauty, and a passing school of brown chromis.

Just down the coastline, we spotted trails of underwater statues and artificial rock formations. We weaved around a few of them before venturing out and reaching the floating square. The chain holding the platform in place stretched down and was clasped to a block of concrete twenty feet down. I followed the girls closely and made sure to get a good view of their faces when they realized what was resting on the bottom. Scarlett's eyes grew big and a trail of bubbles danced up from her mouth. Lying on the seafloor was the wreckage of an airplane. While exploring and swimming the remnants of the craft, I spotted a unique, vibrant streaked tropical fish that was all too familiar.

We surfaced and Ange and Scarlett climbed onto the platform to catch their breath.

"That's incredible," Scarlett beamed. "How long has it been down there?"

"I'm sure one of the workers would know," I said, then I turned to gaze toward shore, shielding the sun from my face.

Seeing that the dive shop's doors were still open, I let go of the corner and turned my body. "I'll be right back."

"Remember what time it is," Ange said, gesturing toward the cruise ship pier. "You don't want to miss it. And this looks like the best seat in town."

I tore headfirst through the water and made good time back to shore. Sloshing out onto slippery rocks, then climbing the beach stairs, I made a beeline for the northern edge of the property. There were two guys inside the small dive office, both sporting the same white shirts with their operation's logo on them. I quickly put my family down for a two-tank dive the following morning, then glanced at the pole spear resting in the corner.

"You've got some unwanted visitors hanging out under the plane," I said. "Mind if I borrow that?"

They laughed and handed it to me. "We close in thirty. Just bring it tomorrow if we're gone. Watch out for the spikes, and see you in the morning."

I hiked back across the sand, splashed into the water, then returned to the platform. A couple minutes later I had two lionfish impaled at the end, managing to spear one right after the other.

After showing off my catches to the girls, I swam back to shore with the two colorful fish skewered at the end of the spear, holding it up like a warrior returning home from a victorious battle. A few passersby watched, intrigued, as I climbed out of the water. One of them was a young waitress.

"You mind having the cook grill us up some catch of the evening?" I said in Spanish while giving a friendly smile.

She grinned, nodded, then grabbed the spear and motioned toward a vacant table out on a spit of land overlooking the water. "Thirty minutes."

"Perfect," I said, then added in a round of margaritas and coconut waters.

I reminded her to be careful with the spines, then turned back toward the pier. Threading through a group taking pictures, I leapt into the Caribbean and made it back to Ange and Scarlett as the nearest cruise ship blew its horn.

"Just in time," Ange said.

"You guys still not gonna tell me what's going on?" Scarlett said.

I pointed toward the base of the pier, where a chubby sunburned guy was bounding as fast as he could toward his ship, a folded towel in one hand and a jam-packed shopping bag in the other.

Scarlett stared at the guy, then turned to us. "Why is he running? They're not gonna…"

"Leave without him?" Ange said. "You bet they

will."

"They've got a schedule to keep," I said.

"So what do they do if they don't make it?"

I shrugged. "Buy a plane ticket home. Happens more often than people think."

We watched as the guy picked up his pace following the blowing of another, louder horn. Then a family appeared. Three little kids. Mom and dad both with armfuls of various beach stuff, both willing their kids to move. When they were a quarter way to the end, a local pedaled a four-person bicycle into view, swooped them up, and scooted the family the rest of the way.

"Now that's a businessman," I said, bobbing my head as we observed his lucrative venture.

We watched as a few more groups made the trip, all hustling and hoping their ship stayed put a little longer. The husky guy made it, nearly passing out when he reached the gangplank. The family did as well. And though many clearly arrived a little late, the captain was apparently feeling generous.

We watched as the massive lines were cast, smoke plumed from the smokestacks, and the ships motored expertly away from the pier.

"Looks like all winners tonight," I said.

Scarlett brushed her wet hair from her face. "Amazing how many there were."

"People lose track of time," I said with a shrug. "Happens to all of us. Actually looks kind of fun and exhilarating."

As the floating cities ventured off in various directions, they left the sea before us open and empty. I peeked at my dive watch. With fifteen minutes before our dinner would be served, we free dove twice more down to the plane while Scarlett recorded with her camera, then relaxed back on the swim platform and watched the horizon as the sun burned low. It was already shaping up to be a magnificent one, and we sat in silence, reveling in it all.

"You don't want to film it, Scar?" Ange said.

Scarlett kept her eyes to the west and smiled. "I'll record the next one. I just want to enjoy it. Really savor it."

And we did. Every frame from brilliant, sky-consuming beacon to ember. And as the orb bid adieu, the majestic glow of its wake splashed across the western sky. Striking pinks and reds that shifted darker and darker. Then the light went out. The night took over. And in an instant, the breeze felt ten degrees cooler.

I glanced over my shoulder. Our table was set, and the waitress was just coming out with our drinks. She threw a wave, which I returned.

"Come on," I said, sliding back into the water. "Last one back's a rotten conch."

FOUR

The next morning, we shared an early breakfast at Jeanie's next door. We ordered rounds of coffee and juice, followed by our entrées. While waiting for the food to arrive, I woke up with a morning dip, leaping into the water less than twenty feet from our table. The Caribbean was calm and refreshing, revitalizing my senses following a restful sleep.

I swam around a bit, then climbed up the ladder to shore and rinsed off with the restaurant's outdoor shower spigot. I was back at the table just as our food arrived. We wolfed down a large fruit platter filled with freshly sliced cantaloupe, watermelon, and pineapple, along with plates of eggs and toast, waffles, and huevos rancheros. We had a long day ahead of us and would need the energy, though we made sure not to gorge ourselves.

While we ate, a group of tourists showed up and were put through a brief orientation by an instructor under a shaded palapa beside us. The seven visitors were going to be led on an underwater expedition in front of the restaurant, exploring the trail of statues while breathing inside helmets with surface-supplied air hoses.

At first glance, I noticed that the equipment looked old and poorly maintained. And there was only one instructor. It struck me as odd. In my experience, tour operators in Mexico were usually top-notch, especially in popular tourist areas like this one. It was an accident waiting to happen.

We finished up, returned to our room to gather our stuff for the trip, then reached the pier minutes before a boat with the dive operator's logo pulled up to it. A wiry local in his thirties named Benny welcomed us aboard, and we nestled into a bench seat with four other tourists. There was the middle-aged couple from the previous evening and two brothers from Houston who were about Ange's and my age. It was a fun group. And we got to know each other a little bit while motoring south to the first dive spot.

While we chatted, Benny's radio crackled to life. The dive operator stood in the cockpit and said something I couldn't hear to the guy at the helm. Then he turned to address the group.

"We've received reports that the current's running wild at Santa Rosa," he said, referring to the popular wall and planned first stop on our trip. "So we've decided to dive the wreck first. Current should ease a bit by the time we're ready for the second dive. Plus, most boats head out to the reefs first, so we should have the wreck mostly to ourselves."

No one questioned the decision. These were some of the best recreational scuba divers in the world—professionals who dropped beneath the waves at least twice a day nearly 365. They no doubt had thousands of dives under their belts. And they knew their underwater paradise as well as most people know their own backyards.

We continued past the southern cruise ship pier, motoring beside three shiny behemoths. Then the shore gradually shifted from solid hotels and restaurants to sporadic resorts and villas to mostly greenery. Heading out in the morning felt like being part of a fleet heading off to war. There were at least two dozen dive boats all cruising toward the clusters of dive sites.

"This is Uno," Benny said, introducing us to an athletic middle-aged man. "He'll be our other divemaster down there. You know why they call him Uno? Because he's the best diver in the world. And when and if he ever retires, I'll be the best diver in the world, so you're all in good hands."

He gave us a quick brief, going over our planned bottom time, a succinct description of the site, current, and other basic information. He emphasized that the important thing was to stay within sight of the two staff in the water, and not to penetrate into the wreck without their supervision.

Then he gave us a quick history of the ship. Built in Florida, the hundred-and-eighty-foot-long *Felipe Xicotencatl* was commissioned as a minesweeper in World War II. After being decommissioned, she was eventually sold to the Mexican Navy, where she was renamed and spent thirty-seven years patrolling the Gulf of Mexico and Caribbean in various operations before being retired in 1999. She was sunk as an artificial reef and dive attraction a year later, and wide-eyed visitors had been exploring the site ever since.

We arrived at the site just as Benny wrapped up his history lesson, then we all donned the rest of our gear and shuffled aft to the swim platform. I was the last one off, following just behind Scarlett and Ange.

After they'd both splashed in, Benny leaned over beside me. "You're the divemaster, right?"

I nodded.

"How many dives?"

"A thousand give or take. I lost count years ago. And I did a dive or two back when I was in the Navy."

The aquanaut grinned. "You want to explore inside the wreck, just give me a signal."

"Eel still in residence?"

He laughed. "Yeah, and big as ever."

"I'll stick with the exterior."

He shrugged and clipped a reel of distance line to my BCD. "Just in case you change your mind."

Once ready, I shuffled to the edge and took a big stride, splashing into the Caribbean in a torrent of bubbles. The chaotic white cleared away, revealing the dark, ominous wreck perfectly visible through the translucent water. The group bobbed on the surface a moment, then Benny and Uno signaled for us to descend.

We vented our BCDs, the air bubbling out as we

sank. The crew having tied off to the bow mooring buoy, we faced the wreck head-on as we dropped down, the details of the vessel emerging like a ghost ship.

The current subsided at depth to a comfortable flow that was easy to swim against as we released the line and finned along the deck. The surfaces of the vessel were coated in thick colonies of sponges and coral. And a barracuda swam right by our group, circling back and watching us carefully.

Keeping with the group, Ange, Scarlett, and I pushed along the base of the superstructure. It was hard not to imagine the vessel in her heyday. American sailors from the Greatest Generation shuffling up and down the ladders while they chugged around the South Pacific, sweeping for mines.

While passing over the bunkroom, I pointed toward an opening where a green eel was poking its head out. Its intense, piercing eyes locked onto us, and it bared its rows of needle-like teeth.

We passed by a large group who'd descended from a dive boat tied off to the wreck's stern, the dozen or so divers led along the starboard side of the wreck by what appeared to be a lone divemaster. The sight caused me to do a double take. Then a triple. That many patrons for one divemaster was asking for serious trouble, and I hoped that I'd just missed the second staff diver as we glided over the wreck.

Continuing along, we looped around the stern, then made our way back along the opposite side, taking in the sights and the perfectly clear water surrounding us.

Returning to the bow, we used Scarlett's camera to

take videos of us along the main deck and just forward of the ship. Benny signaled for us to hand him the device, and he snapped an up-to-date Dodge family photo, managing to catch the entire wreck in the frame behind us.

Once we'd seen the whole exterior and had our underwater fun, Benny and Uno pointed their thumbs skyward, and we gathered and kicked smoothly for the surface. After a safety stop, we let go of the line and broke out into the blazing sunshine.

As usual following a dive, Scarlett beamed and couldn't stop raving about all we'd seen and done as we climbed back aboard the dive boat. We removed our gear while telling our favorite highlights from the dive, and looking at the pictures on Scarlett's camera.

Once free of my gear, I chugged a bottle of water, wolfed down two granola bars, then turned to Ange and Scarlett and motioned to the roof. "I'll be up top if you need me."

Peeling off the upper half of my wetsuit, I lumbered to the cockpit. Grabbing a ladder, I heaved myself up and sprawled out on the roof, my feet dangling over the side. I closed my eyes and breathed slowly and deeply, meditating to the slow rhythm of the water and the lapping waves against the hull.

I happily lost track of time—then a powerful, sharp yell jolted me from my relaxing slumber. I snapped up, shielded my eyes from the sun, and scanned east toward the source of the sound. It'd come from one of the other dive boats floating over the site. A big, pale-skinned guy was grilling a woman in a pink wetsuit as he fished her out of the water and pulled her up onto the stern of their boat.

We were far off, but the woman looked visibly shaken and the guy continued to berate her, his words traveling clearly over the water.

"If you can't follow basic instructions, then you and your kid shouldn't be out here," he barked.

The guy then leaned over and hauled a boy out of the water as well. He looked maybe twelve and had a bright green wetsuit. The moment he was on the boat, the woman wrapped her arms around him and pulled him away from the angry operator.

I leaned over the front edge of the roof. Benny, Uno, and the captain were watching the scene and shaking their heads. I focused on the interaction and was a second away from requesting to cruise over so I could have a word with the guy when the commotion died down. The woman sat and removed her and the boy's gear, and the other operator helped calm them down while the big guy charged forward frustratingly.

Clearly I wasn't the only one angered by the interaction, because Benny had his phone pulled out, and he was contemplating calling a number.

"Who's that?" I said, pointing toward the guy.

The three men looked up at me, then shrugged in unison.

I turned back to look at the boat again. It was cramped. Over a dozen divers practically spilling out of the gunwales. And I only counted two operators.

"That operation was bought out five months ago," Benny said.

I held my gaze on the boat and said, "By who?"

"Some guy named Beauchamp. Rich real estate guy. He's buying all sorts of stuff on the island. Dive operations, restaurants, gift shops."

"Trying to force out the locals," Uno snapped.

"The gringo drives the only Cadillac on the island," Benny said. "Cruises around all the time like he owns the place and everyone who lives on it. Snobby kind of guy. His spoiled son's even worse. He drives a truck bigger than this boat. Can't miss either of them."

"Their boat seems a little overloaded," I said.

"Everyone was fired when they were bought. It's all a foreign crew. And even most of them were laid off recently, or so I heard."

"Laid off? Isn't this peak season here?"

Benny held up his hands. "It's a puzzle."

"It's only a matter of time before something happens," Uno said in Spanish. "It's too few staff. Can't watch everybody down there."

"Let me guess, this Beauchamp guy also bought out that little surface-supplied tour at Jeanie's?" I said, remembering how the tour had looked like an accident waiting to happen.

Benny nodded. "Along with many other places. They're even trying to buy us out." He laughed. "Nobody's got enough money to make us sell, though."

I remained stoic up on the roof, watching the other boat closely. Waiting for the big, short-tempered guy to make another move. He didn't. And it appeared as though things had settled down by the time Benny called out that we were heading to the second site.

I climbed down and sat beside Ange and Scarlett. Gazing over my shoulder as we motored farther south, I kept my eyes on the other boat while playing Benny and Uno's words over again in my mind.

FIVE

Though the first dive had been spectacular in its own right, the second kicked it up a notch. From the moment we broke the surface, the extraordinary underwater world below us showed off in dazzling form. Sprawling, intricate reefs teeming with fish among the forests of coral heads. An abundance of life and color. Unbelievably vibrant colors ranging from bright reds to rich blues and purples, blending together to paint a scene too magnificent for any artist to capture.

We descended into the magical world. No matter how many dives I go on, no matter how many times I suit up and dip beneath the waves, I'm always awestruck. For me, there's nothing like dropping down into the underwater world and taking it all in. Being in the moment and witnessing the calm and beautiful wonder of it all.

With our senses overloaded, we descended along the edge of the wall, leveled off our buoyancy, and watched the world drift by. The current was still strong at what felt like nearly two knots, so we kept pretty close, with Benny up front with the main group, then Scarlett, Ange, and me taking up the rear with Uno.

I did a 360 take of my surroundings, the rich blue turning turquoise as it neared the shore and transitioned to blackness in the deep waters at my back. The ledge was sheer, dropping off to an abyss over three thousand feet deep.

Peering through my mask in the direction we'd come, I watched as over a dozen divers descended nearby. It was hard to tell, but it looked like the same group we'd seen back at the wreck site—the overly loaded boat and the dive operator with the short temper.

I observed the group carefully for a moment, still feeling like one divemaster to twelve patrons was a dangerous ratio in any conditions, but especially with the currents so strong.

A series of rhythmic tings drew my attention away from the group and back ahead. Ange and Scarlett had dropped down into a wide gap between the coral and under a school of grunt fish. It was Scarlett who'd gotten my attention by tapping a carabiner attached to her camera to her dive cylinder. When I looked their way, she pointed toward a loggerhead turtle fluttering along over a fan coral branch. The carefree creature swam along, its shell sparkling in the late-morning sun as it ventured right between us, then swept down over the ledge.

I caught up to them, doing a barrel roll as I dipped under a bridge in the rock while Scarlett filmed with her GoPro. Then she handed over the camera and I filmed the two of them as they did tricks of their own. We saw a spotted eagle ray next, then a large black grouper, and a line of spiny lobsters hiding out in a crevice.

Uno, who'd been staying back, finned up to us and pointed into the entrance of a cave at the seafloor. He motioned for us to follow, and we did eagerly. There were a lot of caves and crevices in the rock and coral. Most were small and flooded with light from all directions. But a few were dark with no end in sight. He led us into a dark one, the current dying away momentarily as we pushed deeper into the darkness. He switched on a dive light and shined the way, pointing out more lobsters along with a spotted drum fish. Scarlett got good footage, then we rounded a corner and popped back out of the darkness.

The dive was panning out to be one of my all-time favorites as we traversed over the coral jungle, then curved back along the ledge. Ange and Scarlett took the lead again, and as we wrapped around a tower of rock and dropped toward a patch of sand, Scarlett froze, then turned back, bubbles spilling out of her regulator as she flashed a big smile. She pointed ahead at a nurse shark resting on the bottom in the shade beside a jutting rock. The rest of the group were just finishing up admiring the creature as we drifted in. We kept our distance but managed to get great angles of the shark. As Scarlett filmed it, the creature decided to move on and rose up before flapping its tail fin and leisurely swimming south along the brilliant white seafloor.

The rest of the group were getting ahead, so Uno gestured for us to pick up our pace. The girls did as he instructed, but I stayed put a moment longer, unable to peel my eyes off the graceful creature. It swam effortlessly, its light tan skin catching the light before it vanished in a wink beyond the reef.

With my body turned back, facing into the current, I noticed that the other dive group had nearly reached me. The bulk of the group were to my left, hovering over the bottom in a spread-out unit with the divemaster at the forefront. They were in line with me when I noticed movement, bright color, and a flash of reflecting light ahead and to the right. It was the woman in the pink wetsuit—the one we'd watched get grilled by the divemaster at the other site. Her back was facing me, and she was kicking frantically. Panicking. Fighting to beat the current any way she could. Her body scraped against the coral thirty feet ahead of me, and despite her efforts, she tumbled with the flowing water.

As she dropped, I spotted a second diver just beyond her. Smaller and wearing a bright green wetsuit. It was her son. I caught barely a glimpse of the boy, saw sheer panic in his eyes as he lay rooted in the current, stuck between the coral and rock and struggling to break himself free. A fraction of a second after he came into focus through my mask lenses, his regulator came free and the current wedged the hose in the crevice, making it impossible for him to retrieve his primary air source. And my eyes bulged as I realized the yellow hose and mouthpiece of his backup second stage were snagged behind him, leaving the boy trapped on the seafloor with only the air in his lungs.

SIX

Life turns on a dime. One moment you're blissfully floating, enjoying the moment. The next, a life-or-death situation slams into you like a runaway freight truck.

Instinct took over.

A hundred observations and calculations went through my mind in a split second. The product of being put in deadly every-moment-counts situations time and time again.

The boy was stuck and his regulator was out. Panic and terror were setting in. What little oxygen remained in his lungs was rapidly depleting. His mother was too far to get to him. And the divemaster and rest of the group were already long gone.

With no one else nearby, I needed to get to him. It

was clear that if I didn't find a way to reach him, he'd die.

The current continued to carry me onward at close to two knots. There was no way in hell I could buck that kind of current and traverse such a great distance with a BCD and tank strapped to my back.

With no time to waste, I unstrapped my gear and sucked in a deep breath. Then I pulled out my regulator, released my BCD, and tore headlong toward the boy. He was thirty yards away from me, easy. And progress was barely noticeable. I kicked and kicked with everything I had, willing my body forward.

Then I reached ahead and grabbed hold of the jagged rock. The sharp edges bit at my hands but I ignored it, muscling myself onward from corner to corner like I was scaling a wall. The water rushed into me. And the boy continued to shake and struggle, his precious air bubbling out of his mouth and dancing toward the surface. He had seconds at most before he'd pass out. Before he'd breathe in involuntarily, filling his lungs with seawater.

My own lungs began to throb as I pressed onward. I tried my best to conserve my air, but the exertion made it impossible. Needing to do something to expedite my approach, I pulled myself down into the cave Uno had shown us. The lighter current made the going easier, and I managed to swim through the blackness by feel alone.

Just as I reached the opening, my leg struck a tip of fire coral, and the sharp corner sliced a shallow gash across my left calf. I fought back the pain with a wince and continued, kicking out of the opening and pulling myself toward the boy.

He was no longer shaking. His body was going motionless, resigned to its fate. I grabbed him with two hands, planted my heels in the rock and tried to yank him free. It was no use. His gear, which was way too big for his small frame, was wedged tight, and his air hose was kinked securely in a narrow slit.

I grabbed his straps and tore them free, the Velcro cracking. With the world around me beginning to fade, I pulled the boy free of his gear, then held him tight and kicked off the bottom. The surface seemed like it would never come. And the clouds and darkness closed in. I was right there—right on the verge of blacking out. I'd blacked out before. I knew the sensation. The incessant throbbing lungs, the fringes of darkness closing in.

Fighting to hold on as the world brightened, I exhaled the expanding air from my lungs, kicked with all I had, then broke out of the water. I forced in deep breaths at first, my eyes wide and my pulse pounding with newfound vigor as oxygen pumped into my body and coursed through my depleted veins. I coughed, then squinted at the lifeless face of the boy in my arms. I tapped his cheek and spoke firmly and splashed water. Nothing. He was motionless. Not breathing.

I put my thumb and index finger to my mouth and whistled, a sharp steady tune that tore across the surface. Turning around, I spotted our dive boat about two hundred yards away. I yelled out and thrashed and whistled again and again until the boat was flying full speed straight toward us.

Despite my attempts to revive him, the boy was

still motionless by the time the boat idled beside us. The helmsman tossed a ring, then dragged us toward the stern and helped me lift the boy out onto the deck.

I was just preparing to perform CPR when the boy coughed violently. His head tilted back and water spurted out. His eyes flashed open, big and full of fear. He coughed for what seemed like half a minute, managing to clear the water from his lungs, then breathed frantically.

"Deep breaths," I said, helping him sit up. "Deep and calm. You're all right."

He fought for precious air, then shook, and tears streaked down his face.

"Everything's fine," I said, holding him tight. "You're all right. What's your name?"

"Sebastian," he said.

"I'm Logan. Nice to meet you, Sebastian. Though I wish it were under different circumstances."

"I… I couldn't see anything. I was trying to get free, I felt my lungs screaming at me. Then I felt nothing after that."

He'd blacked out. And if he'd reached the surface seconds later, I doubted he would've made it. I'd read too many stories of even experienced freedivers blacking out and dying, some just a few feet before they reached the surface.

The helmsman brought over some soda to help calm the kid's nerves a bit. Then we removed his gear. He had nasty cuts to his arm and thigh, which we began bandaging up while Ange, Scarlett, and Uno all surfaced nearby.

The helmsman cruised over and picked them up, and Ange rapidly climbed aboard and helped me out.

A woman's screams suddenly tore across the air. I peered over the port gunwale to see the boy's mother floating a hundred yards away, breaking down from thinking she'd just lost her son.

"Blow a whistle to get her attention, then let's pick her up," I said. "His mother's over there having a heart attack right now."

Scarlett blew her whistle and waved at the woman. Then Sebastian crawled up and waved at her as we closed in and helped her aboard.

Frantic, she threw off her gear and darted across the deck, falling over her son and wrapping her arms around him. I let out a breath and sat on the bench behind me, taken aback by her level of emotion.

"I'm all right," he said. "Thanks to Logan."

He pointed toward me and his mom looked up. "How can I ever repay you?" she said, looking up at me with tears welling up in her eyes.

Feeling the fatigue from the extreme adrenaline-fueled exertion, I gave a slight wave of my hand. "Don't mention it."

We motored over and picked up the rest of our group, with Benny climbing up last. Then the other dive boat roared over, stopping suddenly and idling right beside us. The big guy stood in his wetsuit, scowling at us with sunglasses on.

"What the hell's going on?" he shouted.

The woman turned into an enraged mama bear, snapping her head to stare daggers at the man. "What happened is that my son almost drowned under your watch."

The guy paused, then raised himself higher on the side of their boat so he could get a better view of

Sebastian, who was lying down, his arm and leg bandaged up.

The man grunted and shook his head. "If he'd stayed close to me like I instructed, this wouldn't have happened."

"You asshole," the woman shouted. "My son almost died because of you."

"No, he almost died because of him. Him and his stupidity."

I'd heard enough. With Ange helping to care for the boy, I rose to my feet and took a step right, eyeing the big guy across the water.

"What the hell do you want?" he snapped.

I stared at him for a good ten seconds, then grabbed a line, held it up, and tossed the other end into his gut. He barely caught it, then tied it off and I pulled them in closer. Once the gap was short enough, the big guy stepped over, standing tall, casting a shadow over the woman and her son. I took a half step closer to him, putting him within arm's reach.

"This was his fault, lady," he growled. "We had to end the dive early because he was an idiot. And you're lucky that—"

I interrupted him with a solid punch to the center of his face. His sunglasses shattered. His head snapped. And he groaned, spittle spraying from his mouth as he collapsed over the port rail.

SEVEN

Seeing what had happened, the other worker on the boat beside us hopped over as well. He landed near the bow and stomped toward me, his right hand in a fist. Ange rose and stopped him in his tracks, snatching his left arm and forcing it into an unnatural position behind his back. In about half a second, the guy went from all mean and tough to completely at the mercy of my wife, begging for her to loosen her grip.

"I'm not getting back on that boat," the woman exclaimed, still cradling her injured son. "I can't be with these two anymore."

"We'll take you both," Benny said. "And we'll rush you over to shore. I've just called an ambulance to meet us at a nearby dock."

I heaved the big unconscious guy over onto his

boat, then helped carry the woman and her son's things over to ours.

"I'll ride back with them," I said, eyeing the dozen tourists on the other boat. "Make sure these people get back safely."

A noticeable wave of relief washed over the patrons aboard the cramped dive boat. Ange and I exchanged knowing glances.

"All right, ladies and gentlemen, this is your new captain speaking," I said, hands planted firmly on my hips. "My name is Logan and I'll be taking over command of this boat due to… oh, take your pick of reasons."

Then I sounded off a quick overview of my experience and credentials, including my time in the Navy, where I'd received advanced training in special forces small boat operations and stepped away as a chief petty officer. I rarely bring up my resume, but given the circumstances, I wanted the passengers to know they were in good hands. It seemed to work as the group relaxed a little as I turned forward.

Ange released her hold on the other worker, then he glared at her before jumping back over to his boat.

"I'm captain of this boat," he said, stretching the arm Ange had nearly broken.

"Not anymore you're not," I said. "And if you've got a problem with that, you can take a nap alongside your buddy."

A few of the nearby divers chuckled as I settled into the cockpit. Benny and the others took off, banking sharply and facing the bow north. I waved to Ange and Scarlett, then surveying the cockpit, I grabbed a clipboard with a list of names.

"They're all aboard, idiot," Shorty said.

I read them off just in case, having heard too many stories of divers accidentally being left behind during trips. Fortunately and somewhat surprisingly, the two boneheads had done something right. All names were accounted for.

"Hold on," I said, firing up the engines.

The engines had some surprising zip for a vessel of its purposes. Dual 365-horsepower inboards, from the feel and sound of them. We made good time back, and I dropped each of the groups off at their respective docks.

"All right, where's home for this, bozo?" I said once the deck was clear of divers, tapping a hand on the instrument panel.

The guy's scowl mutated into a smile. "Puerto de Abrigo. Just up the coast."

"I know the place."

"Wait until my boss hears about this," he said with a satisfied chuckle.

"Beauchamp, right? Feel free to tell him what happened for me. While you're at it, tell him he needs to hire more personnel. And he needs to fire the two of you."

"Oh, I'll tell him what happened all right. He'll be very interested. I'm sure he'll want to meet you."

"Great. I enjoy making new friends."

I eased back from the dock, then turned south.

The guy shook his head in confusion, then looked at me like I was an idiot. "I told you we're at Abrigo."

"Yes, you did."

"Then why are you going this—"

"To drop me off. You think I'd waste money on a

cab on account of you two?"

"Then why'd you ask?"

I smiled. "Now I know where you guys are."

I pulled up to a short pier a quarter mile north of Barracuda, right at the edge of the downtown boardwalk. Hopping off, I gave the guy a quick left-handed salute, then cut to shore and climbed over the wall to the sidewalk. In my peripherals, I could see the guy still standing on his unmoving boat. Staring at me. Anger brewing on his face.

Ange and Scarlett were already back when I returned, having traversed the four blocks in ten minutes, and passing what felt like a hundred people trying to convince me to buy a necklace or T-shirt.

"The boy all right?" I said, settling into a shaded chair beside them.

"He's fine, thanks to you," Ange said. "Paramedics took him to the hospital, though, just in case."

"Holy crap, Dad," Scarlett said, leaning over and staring at my left calf.

I had a decent cut and a thin trail of blood trickling down, nearly reaching my foot.

I brushed it off. "Guess I'll never learn my lesson with fire coral."

Ange grabbed a first aid kit from the Dive Paradise office and cleaned the wound, then wrapped a bandage snug around it. Fortunately, it wasn't deep enough to require stitches, but I'd likely have another scar to add to my impressive collection.

"It sure is a good thing you saw that boy," Scarlett said. "How did you? He was so far back."

I shrugged. "I was watching the nurse shark you

pointed out. He ventured deeper, then he was right on the same line as the boy."

The same waitress from the previous evening came over.

"You three keep busy," she said with a smile. "Can I bring you anything? Lunch just started."

We ordered plates of grouper tacos and steamed shrimp. When she left to fulfill the orders, Ange fished out my phone from my backpack. "You have two missed calls."

I checked the screen and saw they were both from Chris Hale. Sliding on my sunglasses, I strode to the corner of the seawall and thumbed the call button. Chris answered on the second ring.

"There he is," Chris said in his articulate, confident voice. The same one he'd used to plead my case back in Key West while I was on trial. "I talked to the manager at the marina. Sounds like you made it just fine."

"Shoot, I meant to call you."

"No worries. Cozumel has a talent for distracting. Trip all right?"

"Weather was perfect. Sorry you had to miss it."

"I'm glad you all were able to enjoy it at least. The marina manager said you weren't staying on *Wayfinder*."

"We booked a few rooms downtown. At Barracuda."

Chris laughed. "Well, it's time to upgrade. I've got a place all ready for you that I think you're all gonna like a little more."

"I appreciate it, but we're really fine here."

"Just go and check it out. After your helping me

out chartering the boat down there last minute, and not to mention your saving my family's lives years back, it's the least I can do."

"Where is it?"

"'Bout ten miles south of you. Near Playa Mia."

"We'll need to rent a car, then."

"I'll take care of that as well. You guys just sit tight. I'll try to get a vehicle delivered by noon."

I checked my watch. It was already eleven.

"It's too much, Chris," I said. "We're really fine here."

"Just go and check it out. Then make up your mind. I'll message the villa's address."

Villa? I thought after we ended the call.

I pulled off my wetsuit, then rinsed it down and carried it over to the dive office.

"Sorry about the tear," I said, handing it back to the guy behind the counter along with two thousand pesos.

"What's this for?"

"A new one."

The man shook his head and handed it back. "Benny called. Told us what happened. Told us what you did. Please, we can't accept that."

I thanked him but slid the notes under a folder resting on the counter anyway as I turned and headed back out. I rinsed the salt off my body, then dried off under the sun beside Ange and Scarlett.

"What did Chris want?" Ange said.

I told them about the place he'd set up for us.

"A villa?" Scarlett said, her eyes lighting up.

A four-door Jeep Wrangler pulled up in front of the hotel entrance a couple minutes after twelve. The driver climbed out, handed me the keys, and smiled as he told me everything was already taken care of. All I had to do was sign a few papers, then we loaded up and were off.

I drove us south beyond the hotels and between lines of expensive walled-off houses. Then we passed more hotels and resorts, along with the other cruise ship terminal. Our destination was another ten minutes down the coast, just a few miles from where the island began to warp toward its southern edge.

The address Chris had given me took us to the entrance of a beautifully maintained complex. I rolled us past an ornate fountain and stopped at the gate as a guard popped out from his shack.

"Dodge family, checking in," I said.

He nodded and smiled. "Welcome, Dodge family."

He pressed a button, the gate rose, and I drove us into what was quite possibly the most expensive compound on the island. The buildings looked brand-new and were well spaced for each unit to have privacy. The patches of grass looked like they belonged at Augusta, and the hedges, trees, and bushes had to require a small army to maintain.

We parked in the assigned space, then headed for the tile staircase. Our unit was on the second floor of the building closest to the water, and when I turned the key and eased open the door, I was instantly blown away. We stepped into a spacious room connected to a big kitchen with granite countertops. There was a sectional couch in the main living space, an ample dining table, and a big sliding glass door leading to a balcony. In the corner, a Christmas tree was set up, its lights plugged in and its branches coated with ornaments.

It had two bedrooms, the master with a king and the spare with two queens. And two bathrooms with walk-in showers and dual sinks. The balcony was huge, with its own private hot tub and a view overlooking the property and nearby sandy beach. A stone path led to a pool that was just up from the surf and offered sweeping views of the water. The grounds were quiet and serene, lacking the passing cars, music, and rowdy tourists of downtown. And I felt a wave of relaxation wash over me just from being there.

"Only question is which to do first," Scarlett said. She had one of the biggest smiles I'd ever witnessed plastered across her face. "Pool or beach?"

"Why not both?" Ange said. "Pool, then beach. I'm guessing the sunset here will be spectacular."

Safe to say, I didn't need to ask my wife and daughter whether or not they wanted to switch abodes. Though I liked the Barracuda, there being something enjoyably charming about the place, I'd just walked into the garden of Eden—that is, if the biblical paradise had included its own sandy beach and warm tropical water.

The place was also gated and had guards stationed. I wasn't worried about the two guys I'd encountered earlier that morning. But if they did want to find me, it wouldn't be difficult. Considering Cozumel's size, the odds of staying hidden weren't exactly in my favor.

Scarlett found a big flat remote and pressed a button. Her jaw dropped as a massive flatscreen TV whirred up out of a long bookcase. "Jeez, how rich is

Chris's family anyway?"

"He's a great lawyer," I said. "And he lives in Miami. So sky's the limit, I guess."

She pressed another button on the remote, then a motorized sunshade dropped down from the ceiling, covering the windows.

"Well, I'm sure glad you saved him years ago," she chuckled.

After deciding to move in, I offered to do a grocery run. There weren't many restaurants on this part of the island, and I was missing Ange's cooking.

"You two stay here and enjoy the pool," I said. "I'll meet you down there."

They both made laughable attempts at offering to come along, and I assured them I was fine. Scarlett planted a kiss on my cheek, then Ange moved in. I swept her off her feet and we locked lips for a moment of pure bliss.

Returning to the Jeep, I drove back north to Mega, the biggest grocery store on the island, and filled a cart with various essentials. Then on the ride back I swung by Guido's Italian restaurant and grabbed three dinners for takeaway. After carrying the groceries back and stowing them in the refrigerator of our new unit, I peeked out over the balcony and saw Ange and Scarlett splashing and laughing in the pool.

Excited to join them, I changed into swim trunks with all the dexterity I could muster, then used the restroom. A stack of magazines rested in a stand, and I began leafing through the first one, which was a local diving publication I'd never heard of before. Brisking my way through, I stopped at a page with a story about a local dive captain who claimed to know the location of a lost shipwreck.

I washed and dried my hands, my eyes fixated on the lines of text. Apparently the captain, a guy named Mick, had stumbled upon the wreck months earlier while spearfishing. The local, who owned Lucky Divers, claimed that the wreck was located just off the eastern coast of the island, in an area known for rough seas and fast currents. The man was locked into a political battle with both the Mexican and Spanish governments. Both sides were claiming ownership of the wreck and its contents, and neither were willing to shell out anything to Mick and his team.

It was a common story—one I'd heard time and time again. Treasure hunters forced to keep the location of their discoveries secret for years until some sort of salvage rights agreement could be reached.

Countries could argue all they wanted about who owned what beneath the sea, but if they couldn't find it, what good did it do?

The story ended with Mick being firm on his conviction to keep the location hidden—that was, until he could win his case and at least procure the rights to a percentage of the haul.

I remembered years earlier when I'd discovered a wreck near the Marquesas Keys. Though I'd only managed to secure a one percent finder's fee, it had been more than enough to set me up for life if I was smart. Most treasure hunters go their whole lives without ever getting so lucky.

Having lost track of time, I snapped out of my trance, stowed the magazine in my nightstand drawer, then headed down to the pool.

I splashed in beside the girls, then swam over and leaned against the pool wall, peering out over the beach.

"Thanks for the early Christmas present, Dad," Scarlett exclaimed, propping herself up beside me.

I looked at her, confused, then turned to Ange.

"I thought we were gonna tell her together," I said.

Ange shrugged. "She saw the pamphlet just before we came down. I had no choice."

While thinking about what gifts to give Scarlett, and preferring to give experiences rather than material goods, we'd gone through a list of top things to do in Cozumel. One of them was a pearl farm tour where visitors could witness the process firsthand and purchase custom-made pearl jewelry. The whole thing sounded right up Scarlett's alley.

We hung out in the pool for another ten minutes, then headed down to the sea for some snorkeling, spotting a school of enormous pompano around the pilings of a nearby dock. Tiring out in the water, we sprawled out on beach chairs under small palapas. I heated up and brought down the pasta, and we ate while watching the sun sink.

After finishing up, I stared out at the water and, for a brief moment, imagined a body washing ashore.

It started small. Just a tiny poke in the fabric of the reality of the moment. Then it tore and spread until the thought blossomed into a clear mental image.

It was lifeless in the lapping surf. Facedown. Flesh gnawed by marine life.

Then I blinked and the image flashed away. The beach before me was pristine and calm and empty, and there was no corpse.

But a body did wash ashore, I told myself, remembering what the cab driver had said the previous day.

Just across the island. Someone had been murdered, and others were missing. Presumed dead as well. And as I gazed out over the paradise before me, I couldn't help but wonder who was responsible and why.

EIGHT

The next morning, I rose just before the sun. Sliding into shorts, I kissed Ange on the forehead, then swiped my dive mask and headed barefoot out the door. Waking up early and exercising is a habit I formed back in the military, and one I'd maintained as best I could. I've always liked the feeling of rising before the rest of the world, seeing places empty and without distractions. It's also a good way for me to get a feel for new places—to explore a little and feel comfortable in new surroundings.

I got my workout in by wading into the calm morning water and swimming along the shore. The underwater world was calm and lively, the water warm but refreshing. There was a soft breeze that provided just the right amount of fresh air.

After the swim, I showered off using the outdoor spigot beside the pool, then headed up to the unit. I was about to whip up some mango waffles for breakfast when Ange suggested trying out a spot she'd found online.

"It's got incredible reviews and it's just down the street from where we're meeting the pearl farmers," she said.

We loaded up just after eight and drove north. With no cruise ships arriving that day, the town was empty and quiet. It was a near-straight shot to the restaurant, with only one turn just past the diver statues on the Malecon, then less than half a block inland.

As usual, my wife's intuition was spot-on. The food at Jolly was incredible. We ordered up plates of omelets, eggs benedict, and one of the best breakfast burritos I'd ever had. And they had fresh fruit juices and great coffee.

After eating and downing two cups of joe, we stepped out into the morning sun. It was already eighty degrees and there wasn't a cloud in the sky.

I reached to climb into the driver's seat of the Jeep, but Ange stopped me.

"It's just a few blocks," she said. "I think we're fine to stay parked here."

Rarely one to pass up a coastal stroll, we shouldered our stuff, locked up, and headed for the waterfront.

It was incredible how different the place looked without all the tourists. It was like a different town entirely. We cut across to the wide sidewalk running between the seawall and lapping surf and the road.

Peering ahead, I spotted our destination just up the shore. Glancing at my dive watch, I saw that we'd make it a few minutes early.

"So what's this place like?" Scarlett said, referring to the pearl farm.

"Don't know," Ange said.

Scarlett looked to me and I shrugged. "We've never been there."

"Awesome," she said.

"You bring your camera?" I asked.

It was a dumb question. Our passionate daughter hadn't gone many places without it since we'd gifted it to her.

She patted her bag. "And extra batteries."

The thundering sound of a big diesel engine filled the air at our backs. I looked over my shoulder and spotted a black, lifted, big-tired truck roaring along the waterfront, heading toward us.

It slowed as it neared, the powerful engine quivering the frame. Thick black smoke plumed out from the exhaust pipe as it matched our speed. I stared at the driver's-side window. It was tinted pitch black, along with the rest, giving me no image of the inside.

"Mom, Dad?" Scarlett said, a tinge of worry in her voice.

"Just keep walking," I said.

I was closest to the road, blocking my wife and daughter. Watching the sidewalk with my peripherals, I held my stare at the driver's-side window. Hope for the best, plan for the worst. If the window slid down and anything other than a face and empty hands appeared, I'd make a move.

But the window didn't go down. The hulking mass of metal kept right with us for a good ten seconds. Felt like an eternity. Then, without notice, the driver hit the gas. The engine protested, fumes plumed out, and the tires squealed. The truck took off at a blistering pace, then braked hard and cut inland, vanishing from our view.

"I thought locals here were supposed to be friendly," Scarlett said.

I blinked and turned to focus on the pavement, ahead. "Something tells me that wasn't a local."

I remembered what Benny had said the previous day—how the foreigner named Beauchamp drove a Cadillac and his son drove a big truck. How I couldn't miss them.

"There they are!" Scarlett said, pointing toward a small dock jutting out from a parking lot and running parallel to a boat ramp.

Tied off at the end was a white thirty-foot openbow with twin outboards and the pearl farm logo and name painted on the hull.

We strode across the lot, passing a waterfront restaurant on our way to the dock. A man and a woman greeted us. They were friendly and excited and welcomed us aboard.

"Our other group canceled, so it looks like you three are in for a private tour today," the woman, who introduced herself as Rosa, said.

Scarlett beamed at that, and they quickly shoved us off. I was excited for the day ahead but couldn't help stealing a few glances toward the shore as they motored us away from the dock. There was no sign of the truck on the nearby road as we cruised north through the calm morning water.

"Where's the farm?" Scarlett shouted over the wind and engines.

"About fifteen kilometers north of here," Rosa replied. "We own a private stretch of beach near the north point. 'Bout forty-five-minute cruise."

It was a nice boat ride, even better weather and calmer seas than when we'd pulled in with *Wayfinder* two days earlier. We passed by the rusted shipwreck, then the pilot turned east toward the untamed part of the island.

We passed Isla Pasion, then the scenic trip ended at a remote, picturesque beach.

The hull sliced into the powdery sand, and we hopped off. Sloshing to shore, we gathered under a beachfront palapa with pictures and texts posted, showing glimpses of the farm's evolution over the years.

"We're very new," Rosa explained, "opening in 2001, and we're privately owned."

They went on to explain how it was the only pearl farm in the entire Caribbean. They cultivated *Pinctada radiata*, also known as the Atlantic pearl oyster, which was considered almost extinct in the Caribbean, so their farm aided preservation in the region. They also explained the unique methods they'd created for cultivating the oysters, having designed their own anchoring systems, collectors, and towers.

Then they led us inland to a yellow-painted structure on stilts where they implanted small shell beads into the mature oysters that acted as the nucleus so pearls could be created.

After the lesson, we climbed back into the boat and they motored us just offshore. We donned our snorkel gear and splashed down, catching our first glimpse of the farm. Rows of metal cages chained to the bottom were laid out before us. Since the site was spread out, they had us hold on to a rope and be dragged through the water while we took in the underwater world, an activity they dubbed "speed snorkeling."

They gave us more history and details regarding the different structures and showed us up-close glimpses of the oysters, from the small ones just starting out to the more mature ones that routinely created their pearls. The snorkel tour wrapped up with a visit to a life-sized underwater statue of the Virgen de Guadalupe.

After we took in the entire farm, they brought us back to the beach and we sat in plastic chairs in knee-deep water while enjoying ice-cold beer and soda. Then we returned to shore for burgers grilled under the shade of a palapa right on the beach.

"You guys sure know how to show visitors a good time," I said, biting into the juicy burger.

Scarlett had a big smile on her face that hadn't left since we'd arrived. For an adventurous girl who loved the water, loved learning, and loved meeting nice people, it was a perfect way to spend an afternoon.

"Like your present, Scar?" Ange said.

"Best gift ever," she declared.

I watched as Rosa approached with a narrow hardcase.

"Well, it's about to get even better," I said.

Rosa smiled at us as she set the case on the table,

then cracked it open.

"At a special request from your parents, Scarlett," she said, "you get to choose."

She revealed a spread of laminated images of various pearl jewelry. Then she opened a smaller container, revealing a dozen pearls of varying shapes and sizes.

Scarlett looked to her mother and me, her jaw slack. Then she rose and admired the pearls. "They're amazing."

"Part of your gift, Scar," I said.

Ange rose and rested an arm over her shoulder. "You get to pick the pearl and the type and style of jewelry."

"It's all handmade here on the island," Rosa explained. "Crafted by a talented local artisan. You pick what you want, and it will be ready by Christmas."

Scarlett's excitement simmered, and tears welled up in her eyes. She turned to Ange and me, then dropped into us, her arms wrapping around us. "How did I get so lucky?"

"We're the ones who're lucky," I said.

She wiped the streaking tears from her face, then calmed a bit and scanned over the pearls. She spent five minutes admiring the lustrous white spheres and poring over the different styles of jewelry.

"I like this one," she said, pointing at the image of a simple necklace design with a silver chain.

"A good choice," Rosa said. "And the pearl?"

Her hand hovered over the spread, and she plucked a medium-sized one that was nearly perfectly rounded. "This one will fit good. If it's set in this position, this side forward, it will be perfect."

Rosa smiled. "You're a natural."

She set the pearl aside, then circled the necklace on the laminated sheet with a dry-erase marker and closed everything back up. We finished our food while joking around and exchanging stories with our newly made friends. They told us why they'd decided to open up the farm, an endeavor that they'd undertaken primarily at their own expense. And we told them a little about what Ange and I did, or at least used to do, for a living.

"What kind of contract work did you two do?" Rosa asked.

Ange and I exchanged glances, then I said, "Work of a classified nature."

That only served to intrigue them more, but we managed to finish our meal without divulging too much information about our past lives. When the tour was over, Scarlett hugged them, thanking them for everything. Then we climbed back onto the boat, sad to have to end one of our favorite experiences we'd ever had.

NINE

The boat ride back was soundtracked by jokes and laughs, and smiles all around. I joined in the good time for most of the trip but turned stone serious when I gazed ahead toward the dock. The lifted pickup truck was back. It was parked along the side of the road, maybe thirty yards up from the entrance into the lot, and right beside where the road dropped down to the boat launch. There was a guy who appeared to be in his early twenties, messing around on the wharf with a young woman. The kid was tall and heavyset, and he had pale skin and short ginger hair that stood out like a spotlight under the afternoon sun.

I observed the two carefully as we approached the dock. The girl was average height and had olive skin and long, dark auburn hair. She was wearing a Hooters waitress uniform—orange short shorts and a white tank top. The guy was grabbing at her and her clothes, and the young woman appeared to be laughing, but it was borderline harassment. And as we motored closer, I could see she was clearly uncomfortable.

"Why can't that good-for-nothing disappear?" one of the workers said in Spanish.

"You know him?" I said.

"Unfortunately, yeah," Rosa said. "That's Warren Beauchamp's son. Same name. Same misogynistic personality. Same good-for-nothing behavior."

Ange shielded her eyes from the afternoon sun. "Who's the girl?"

"Dorothy Flanagan," Rosa said. "She's lived on the island most her life."

Just as we were pulling up to the dock, the young guy yelled out angrily, cursed, then reached for the local girl's butt as she darted away from him, the woman partly laughing, partly terrified.

"Punk kid's spoiled rotten," Rosa said. "He gets away with all sorts of crap all the time 'cause his daddy has money."

I narrowed my gaze at the two, then Ange stepped over and shot me a look that said "Be smart and think your actions through."

This was Mexico. And though the vast majority of its inhabitants are some of the kindest, honest, most hardworking people you'll ever meet, there are always exceptions. And I had a strong feeling that I was likely eyeing one of those exceptions.

We thanked the team for an unforgettable

experience, then strode to shore. As we approached the young man and the girl, he grabbed the woman by her shorts and yanked them down, nearly pulling the fabric down to her knees. She squealed and spun and slapped the guy's hand away. As she tugged her shorts back up, he cursed at her again, then whacked her across the face with a strong backhand that knocked her to the pavement.

"I own you!" the punk spat. "Don't forget that."

I picked up my pace instinctively and turned to Ange again. This time, her furrowed brow, intense eyes, and flaring nostrils shouted something else—that if he touched the girl again, he'd be residing in a hospital bed for the foreseeable future.

The young woman scrambled to her feet. Ange raced over to help her while I cut between them and the punk.

"Hey, stay out of this, asshole," he said, shoving a finger into my face. "This is none of your business."

I ignored the punk and inspected the girl as Ange helped her to her feet.

"Are you all right?" I said.

She gave a brief nod, then the kid stepped closer to me. Just a half step, but a foolish one. One that put himself within arm's length of me.

"Didn't anyone ever teach you to treat women with respect?" I said, staring him down.

The man bellowed. Shook his head. "I can do whatever I want to her. She works for me. Does what I tell her to do. Hell, I own her." He lowered his sunglasses. "Who knows, maybe one day I'll own these two as well," he added, eyeing Ange and Scarlett. "Play my cards right. Never know."

Ange stormed forward, and I cut her off. Pleaded with her to let me have this one. She relented, stepped back, and continued to look over the local girl.

"That's right, keep your girl on a leash," the kid spat.

"Is that your way of thanking me?" I said.

"Thanking you for what?"

"For saving your life." Before he could reply, I added, "Because my wife could've ended you just then. Now it's time for you to apologize to this woman."

He laughed, the noise coarse and painful to the ears.

He had a sick way about him. Like he'd lived his entire life doing whatever the hell he wanted with no regard for others.

"Just get lost," he spat. "Before I lay you out. This is none of your business."

"So lay me out already," I said casually. "Tick-tock. I'm waiting. Don't have all day."

The punk was silent. Thinking about it. It wasn't the speediest process I'd ever seen.

Since he was just standing there tongue-tied, I eyed Ange, then motioned toward the lot. Her arm still wrapped around the scared girl, she and Scarlett ushered her away.

"Hey," the punk said, sliding over to cut them off and pointing a finger again. "I said this is none of your—"

When the finger was a foot in front of my face, I snatched it and yanked down. Not enough to break the bone, but enough to be painful. And sure as hell enough to kick the punk's anger up a few more notches.

He grunted and clenched his jaw, clearly trying to downplay the pain in his extremity, then made a weak attempt at retaliation by throwing his other hand my direction. It was balled up in a tight fist, and the knuckles missed me by about a foot as I forced him the opposite way and down to the pavement.

His kneecaps struck the hard surface. He had his back to me now, his finger still gripped tight in my hand. It was the easiest takedown I'd managed in recent memory. I wasn't surprised. The kind of guys who hit women don't generally put up a good fight when dealing with someone their own size.

"What do you want?" he snorted, his tone going from retaliatory to agreeable in about a second.

He was waving the proverbial white flag like his life depended on it.

"First, like I said, it's time for you to apologize to this woman." He hesitated, so I pulled tighter. The bone was close to breaking. A little twitch and it would give. Sudden and painful. Easy. Like cracking a carrot stick. And he had nine more I could choose from after.

"All right, shit, man." He sighed and looked up toward the girl. "I'm sorry. Now let me go."

"That was first. There's more." I crouched down and spoke sternly into his ear. "You leave now. And if I see you do anything like this again—hell, if I even hear about you treating anyone like this again—I'll find you. Understand? And when I do, you'll beg me to only break a few bones."

It was a solid threat. Not too over-the-top, but severe enough to get the point across. I doubted the punk had been spanked or punished in any way in all his years of existence, so I was needing to dish out twenty-something years' worth in one encounter.

"Understood?" I said, roughly pinching the nerve at the base of his neck with my other hand.

He shook and groaned. "Understood. Damn, understood, man. Just let me go already."

"Last thing. Give me your wallet."

"My wallet?"

"You heard me."

He slid out a brand-new thick leather number. It was full of mainly credit cards and condoms. I grabbed five thousand pesos in cash from the main slit, then dropped it back onto his chest.

"This woman needs a taxi," I said, handing the money to the girl. "I think it's the least you can do."

I let go and left him lying there on the dirty pavement. He jerked around, grabbed his wallet, and eyed me angrily. I stared at him while ushering Ange, Scarlett, and the local girl toward the road. He pocketed his wallet, sat up, then did something that made me question his sanity.

He smiled. A big, borderline psychotic smile. Then he clapped his hands dramatically.

"Well done, Logan Dodge," he said slowly. "Well done."

I continued to stare at him as he rose to his feet and flexed his fingers in and out.

"What did I tell you, boys?" he added, raising his voice. "I knew he'd fall for it."

Four guys stepped out from behind an old trawler resting on the hard. I recognized two of them instantly. The big guy and the long-haired whiner from the dive boat I'd commandeered the previous day. The other two were big as well. Clean-cut and well dressed. Hands already in tight fists, like they couldn't wait to bash their knuckles into me.

"That's right. I know who you are," Junior said. "You know why? Because this is my island. And I know everything that happens on my island."

He wore a weird, proud look on his face as the four other guys closed in. Like he'd just pulled some kind of fast one on me. Like he had me beat or something.

If the guy was smart, he'd have brought ten of his buddies along. If he had that many. Ten would've done the trick. Unarmed and outnumbered by that kind of margin, they'd have had me beat.

But just the five of them? And with Ange at my side? They'd be lucky if they landed a single blow between them before they were all incapacitated.

"Not so tough anymore, are you?" Junior said, stomping over. "Beg for mercy and we might not bash your brains in in front of your wife and daughter."

Suddenly, a short chubby man in flip-flops and an apron rushed over from the nearby restaurant.

"Hey, break it up," he said in Spanish. "Or I'm calling the cops."

"Shut up!" Warren barked. "Or I'll shut your crummy place down."

"Don't call the police," I said calmly, catching the man off guard. "Call an ambulance. These five are going to need a ride to the hospital."

"We have our own ride, idiot," Junior snapped.

"You come at me again, and you won't be able to

drive."

Junior snorted. "Some people are just too stupid to know they've been bested."

He stepped closer and the other four closed in even tighter, creating a circle around me. In the process, two of them put their backs toward Ange. A big mistake.

She let them perform the maneuver around me for two reasons. One, it put Scarlett and the other woman out of the crosshairs. And two, she liked being underestimated. I liked it too. It was always enjoyable seeing the surprise on an unsuspecting troublemaker's face when they realized that Ange was nothing short of a force of nature. A raging hurricane disguised as a calm sunny day.

Junior laughed again—this time slow and drawn out. Real dramatic. "You're severely outnumbered." The guy stiffened taller and pushed his shoulders back. "This is your last chance to beg for mercy, pal."

The level of false security was off the charts. Like a herd of goats taking on a pair of lions. Tricked into thinking that numbers were all that mattered. Gravely mistaken.

"All right, Roman," Junior said to the big guy I'd put to sleep the previous day. "You're up."

"Why don't you just leave him alone?" the local girl cried. "He hasn't done anything to you."

"You pipe down, Dorothy," Warren snarled. "This tourist has it coming. He needs to learn that there are people you don't mess with."

I nearly grinned at that.

At least the punk got one thing right.

He nodded to the big guy again. The hulk of a man

stepped forward. He brought his right hand from behind his back, then released a three-foot length of chain, the metal links tinging as it straightened. Then he eyed me like a ruthless killer.

"Time to pay," he snarled.

He lunged his bulky frame forward, jerked back the chain, and whipped it toward me in a wide arc. I sprang right, and the chain whooshed through the air less than a foot in front of me.

Reacting faster than I'd expected, Junior jumped backward, and the improvised weapon struck the pavement between us, clanking uselessly. With the big guy bent over and briefly exposed, I grabbed him by his right arm and drove a knee into his breadbasket. The blow burst the air from his lungs, and he let go of the chain, letting it coil up like a snake at my feet.

As his upper body hinged forward, I jammed my elbow into his temple, striking the same spot I'd hit the previous day. Before he went lifeless, I grabbed him mid-body, lunged forward, and shoved him toward the seawall. His body flailed over like a fish and he splattered facedown into the low-tide muck.

The over-the-top finishing move was partly for show. To send a message. Even against your biggest and meanest, that's what I'll do. Leave you facedown and unconscious in the smelly mud.

I'd hoped it would cause the others to question their actions. Ideally they'd wise up enough to back off and run. But the message apparently hadn't been clear enough.

"I like a challenge," Junior said, feigning composure. He motioned to the three others still on their feet. "He can't take us all at once."

Junior came at me next. He'd clearly had some training. His footwork wasn't terrible, and his initial strike was decent. He faked a kick, then bobbed back and forth briefly before jumping and rearing back for a punch. Before he could throw the tight fist forward, I sprang and plowed the top of my forehead into his nose. The thick bone of my skull landed with a smack and a crunch. The punk shook backward with a coarse grunt, then tripped and landed on his side, his bloodied face buried in his hands.

The three others who came at me from behind were rapidly whittled down as Ange made her move. She went after the next biggest guy first, tripping him up with a sudden slide kick that used his forward momentum against him, and he crashed hard onto the pavement. As he fell, she pounced on another, jamming a heel into the side of his knee with an audible, cringing break.

While Junior staggered to his feet, dazed and with blood flowing out from his shattered nose, the final guy managed to get me in the side with a haymaker as I turned to engage him. I rolled with the punch, but the force rippled up my body and caused me to wince as I snatched him by the elbow, spun, and levered his arm down over my shoulder. The bone broke, then his body came with it, tumbling over me and crashing onto the ground to a stop against the seawall, not quite enough force to send him into the mud with his buddy.

With his little band of troublemakers battered and crying out in pain and his face half-coated in thick red, Junior spat and yelled, then charged at me again.

He threw a series of off-balance jabs, and I managed to snag a wrist, manhandle him around, and grip his right index finger.

"You're a slow learner, aren't you?" I said, holding him in place and causing him to groan as I forcefully threatened the same finger again.

I glanced over at Ange and the two men at her feet.

"You idiot," Junior spat. "You're a dead man, you know that? Do you have any idea who my father is? We own this island. You're a dead man."

His declaration was punctuated by his reaching for a knife sheathed under his belt. He tried his best to stab me with it, but I swiftly forced him down, ripped it free with my other hand, and tossed it into the water. Then I cracked his finger with a short quick jerk.

"Dammit!" he hissed, fighting back the pain.

His body shook and his breathing was erratic. He spat a gob of blood, then cursed me again.

"You want me to break another, punk?" I said, gripping the next finger in line.

Finally, some morsel of sense made its way into his brain and he shook his head.

The distant whine of a siren caught my attention. I focused down the waterfront and spotted an ambulance barreling our direction, its lights flashing like mad. It was followed a hundred yards back by a lone police car.

I dropped lower and spoke into Junior's ear. "You come near me or my family again and I won't be so merciful, understand?"

His enraged eyes scanned over his broken tribe, then rested on the guy lying unconscious in the muck.

"You call this merciful?" he snorted.

I nodded. "Far more so than you deserve. I've dealt with guys like you all over the world. Guys much better than you. Guys who actually know how to fight. And I no longer have to deal with them because they either learned their lesson or they're dead."

He just glared at me, tongue-tied. Then he coughed again and looked at me expectantly as the ambulance drew near.

"Apologize to this woman again," I said.

He did so. Half-heartedly at first, then with more sincerity as I tightened my grip on his finger.

The ambulance braked to a stop, and I rounded up the little pack of miscreants and had two of them help the unconscious guy who was coated in a thick layer of smelly grime. Two paramedics hopped out and aided the injured men into the back. The professionals eyed me with equal parts confusion and fear, then calmed down when the cop car pulled in. It stopped less than ten feet from me and two officers scooted out.

The driver was a middle-aged man, medium height, with a decent build and a serious face. The guy in the passenger seat was younger, tall but thin as a rail.

They both hovered their hands over their service pistols and eyed me like I was a coiled-up cobra that could strike them at any moment.

I held my hands out, stayed silent. Ange was the first to speak.

"This girl was being harassed," she stated articulately and confidently. "My husband intervened, then the five of them attacked him."

"It's true," the man from the restaurant said, reappearing out of nowhere. "I saw the whole thing. These people were attacked by the young Beauchamp and his friends. But they beat the crap out of them. You should've seen it. I've never witnessed anything like it."

The older of the two officers, whose name tag said Ramirez, relaxed and eased his hand away from his holster. Then he turned to watch the ambulance as the final injured thugs were loaded up. Junior's demeanor had shifted noticeably since the cops had arrived. The punk was silent and hunched over, but as he climbed into the ambulance and the doors were shut, his bloodied face peered through the glass, and we made eye contact. He stared, holding his hostile gaze until the vehicle fired up and flew back onto the road, heading south.

Officer Ramirez turned back to me, then nodded. "I wish I'd seen it. I'd have paid to see that."

His words caused me to loosen up as well. "Why is that?"

"Kid's got an attitude problem. Gets under a lot of people's skin around here." His gaze shifted to the woman in the Hooters getup. "Are you all right, Dorothy?"

"I'm fine, Luis," she said. Then she glanced at Ange and me. "Thanks to them."

The guy from the restaurant gave a solid account of all that had happened. And after a few questions, Officer Ramirez flipped shut and pocketed a small notebook. "Looks like a clear case of self-defense. But be warned, the Beauchamp kid might press charges."

"If he does, we'll be filing charges as well," Dorothy snapped.

Ramirez nodded, then folded his arms and eyed me again. "Off the record, thanks. Someone needed to teach that kid a lesson."

"You can't?" I said, raising my eyebrows.

"That's a dream, but no, I can't. Too much money behind the scenes. Even law enforcement heads can be greased, leaving our hands tied at times."

"You've never spoken out about them?" Ange said, listening in. "Or fought against corruption here?"

He smiled half-heartedly. "Why do you think I'm nearly fifty and still a sergeant? There are guys here in their twenties who outrank me."

He slid his sunglasses back on, nodded another thanks, then turned away from me. He made it one step before I froze him with my words.

"You think they have anything to do with the murders?" I said. He turned back around slowly, and I added, "Beauchamp and his boys?"

He eyed me quizzically. "For a tourist, you're sure taking an eager interest in our affairs."

I shrugged. "I hear things. Hard not to be interested when murders are involved. About a dozen long-running crime shows will attest to that."

Ramirez thought for a moment, then said, "It's possible. But not likely. Beauchamp and his crew of investors have been here for over six months. No complaints against them but petty stuff."

"Is striking a woman considered petty?"

"This is the first time I've heard of him going that

far. Plus these three disappearances. If you must know, all were linked to cartel involvement in their past. That's much more likely. There are thirty thousand homicides every year involving the cartel in Mexico. Just another day at the office for them."

Ramirez's radio crackled to life. He stepped away as he replied, then turned back to us and straightened his uniform.

"Thanks for cleaning this up, Luis," the restaurant worker said. Then he turned to us. "You guys have a free meal whenever you like."

He stepped back across the lot, then Officer Ramirez approached Dorothy. "Would you like a ride home?"

"I'll be fine, Luis," she said, still clearly fighting back emotions after what had happened. "Thanks for everything."

Both officers climbed back into their squad car and pulled out.

We walked Dorothy to the road, then I motioned down the sidewalk. "We'd be happy to give you a ride somewhere."

Dorothy agreed, and we walked in silence back to our parked Jeep and she climbed into the back with Scarlett.

"Why were you with that guy if he's such a jerk?" Scarlett said as we cruised toward downtown.

Dorothy cleared her throat. "He offered me a ride. Dumb move on my part. But his dad's my boss, you know?" She paused a moment. "Besides, it was hot out and I figured what could really happen. Guess a lot could."

We drove in silence the rest of the way. She didn't

need to explain herself to us or anyone. She'd done nothing wrong. No, Beauchamp Jr. and his band of troublemakers had managed all of that.

I braked to a stop along the curb beside the Hooters back entrance.

"You going to be all right?" Ange said, leaning back over the center console.

Dorothy was still slightly distraught, but she was handling it surprisingly well. She was clearly tough.

She let out a deep breath. "I'll be fine."

"Take this," I said, handing her a slip of paper with my cell number penned onto it. "That guy or his friends try anything else with you, you call me, understand?"

"Thank you," she said, her eyes welling up with tears again. Ange handed her a tissue and she swiftly dried them up. "If there's any way I can repay you. I know it's not much, but my dad owns a dive shop in town. We could give you all free dives or gear or whatever you need."

I waved a hand at her. "No need, really."

"We're just glad you're safe," Ange said.

She smiled at us, then scooted out and shut the door behind her. I slid back into drive, and accelerated us back onto the main road, continuing south. Scarlett, who'd been uncharacteristically silent since we'd left, chuckled as we passed the ferry terminal.

"What is it, Scar?" I said.

"I was just thinking about how the whole reason we left Key West was to escape the madness." She smirked, then added, "I guess it followed us."

TEN

Once back at the villa, we immediately hit the beach. We needed to relax after the ordeal, and for me, a good snorkel session was the perfect medicine. We spent two hours at the beach, then showered off and headed back up to the unit. Having swung by the grocery store on our way home, the three of us tried out a new recipe for pasta carbonara that Ange had found.

We joked around while cooking, reminiscing about how much fun we had at the pearl farm while boiling the noodles and sizzling the bacon, mincing garlic cloves and shredding parmesan. Then we enjoyed the fruits of our labor, savoring the meal on the balcony while the sun set between dancing palm fronds.

For dessert, I blended up some homemade cookies and cream and strawberry shakes. And after dinner, we microwaved a bag of popcorn, then settled into the couch. It was Ange's turn to choose what to watch, and she picked an episode of one of our favorite shows, *The Office*.

One episode quickly turned into three. And though the evening and comedic relief had calmed all of us down, Scarlett still seemed off.

"You're not worried?" she said when we asked what she was thinking about.

I shrugged. "About what?"

"Those guys from earlier. I know you two taught them all lessons they won't be forgetting anytime soon, but you're not worried they'll still try and retaliate somehow?"

"No," I said, not giving it much thought. "But what good does worrying do anyway? I'm on a beautiful island with my beautiful wife and amazing daughter. We have a week of vacation left. I'm not going to waste one second worrying about some punk and his friends. After all, like I told the guy, I've faced off against much more formidable opponents than him."

Scarlett bit her lip. "What about hoping for the best, preparing for the worst?"

"You can be prepared without worrying," Ange chimed in. "In fact, worrying negates preparedness. It throws you off. Like they're in your head, messing with you."

"Your mother's spot-on," I said. "If that punk finds us and decides to try something again, we'll deal with it then."

She hugged us goodnight, then headed off to bed. Ange and I stayed up a while longer, venturing back out to the balcony and sipping from a bottle of tequila while listening to the distant waves crash, both of us relishing the cool evening breeze.

"That was quite the move you did today," I said, smiling as I gazed into her sparkling sapphire-blue eyes. "You took down that one guy with a single move."

"Amazing what leverage can do. And you weren't so bad yourself." She fell silent a moment, then said, "You sure you're all right to stay here?"

"Why?" I chuckled. "'Cause a couple of idiot wannabe tough guys started trouble with me?"

"You think Officer Ramirez is right? That Beauchamp isn't likely connected to the missing persons and that they're gang-related?"

I pinched my bottom lip and thought that one over for a moment. "I don't know. I agree that it's not likely they're connected, though. This Beauchamp guy's a businessman, and killing locals doesn't seem like a particularly good business move. And like Ramirez said, tens of thousands of cartel-related homicides a year. So if I were a betting man, that's where I'd place it." I studied my wife as she looked out over the water. Seeing that she was still feeling slightly uneasy, I added, "But regardless, let's stay close for a while. Let those punks simmer a little after our little fight today."

She nestled up tighter, and we polished off most of the tequila. Covering ourselves in a Mexican blanket, we fell asleep right there, lulled by the rumbling waves and passing breeze.

For two days we didn't leave the resort, the three of us managing to fall headlong into full vacation mode. We swam and snorkeled along the shore, basked in the twenty-degrees-north parallel sun, and napped on the beach chairs. We took long walks along the surf, our toes sinking into the wet sand, the powdery pebbles dissipating under the arches of our feet with each receding wave.

I whipped up pancakes and French toast for our breakfasts, and we prepared steak, chicken, and various seafood meals on the balcony grill. As much as I liked Barracuda and the downtown scene, Chris had been right. This was a more effective place to clean the slate—to get away from it all and ground ourselves securely in the things that really matter. Our mental and physical health, our relationships with each other, and renewing our sense of childhood wonder.

We spent Christmas morning huddled around the tree and opening gifts to a steady stream of Bing Crosby, the Beach Boys, and the King of Rock and Roll. It was a simple affair, just a few small presents each.

Scarlett got to see her pearl necklace for the first time, Rosa from the pearl farm having dropped it off in a box and bag the previous day. It was a beautiful piece of jewelry. The 6mm pearl drop she'd picked out was set in a leaf-shaped pendant and polished to a radiant shine. A thin silver chain flowed through the bail, its ends held together by a tiny lobster clasp. Seeing where the pearls had come from added an extra dose of special to an already incredible work of art.

Ange opened her gift next. I got her an overnight spa package in Key Largo, along with pajamas and a basket of bath salts and lotions. Then she blew me away with an unexpected gift.

Tearing away the wrapping paper revealed a small white jewelry box. I slid the top away and inside was a fancy silver dive watch with an orange dial.

"You recognize it?" Ange said, her smile big and bright as she anticipated my reaction.

I grinned uncontrollably as I pulled out the marvelous timepiece. "Of course. Ange, this is incredible. I've always wanted one of these."

"I know. Try it on."

It was a Doxa SUB 300T—the same dive watch worn by Clive Cussler's famous adventurer protagonist, Dirk Pitt. I inspected the intricately crafted piece of machinery like it was a diamond pulled up from the earth.

I removed my watch and replaced it with the new one, tightening it over my left wrist. My old dive watch was efficient and durable, and we'd been through a lot together over the years. But Doxa was a hell of a lot easier on the eyes. I'd never pulled the trigger on one over the years, always knowing that I'd want to baby it given its cost.

"It looks good on you," Scarlett said.

Ange cleared her throat. "If you only want to wear it when we go out, I understand."

I leaned over and threw my arms around my amazing wife, planting a kiss on her cheek. "I love it."

We spent most of the rest of the day outside, walking the beach looking for shells. Instead of snowmen and sledding, we built sandcastles and went paddleboarding.

That evening, we had a video call with our island family back home in Key West. Most of the gang were gathered at Salty Pete's. Pete Jameson, the proprietor and a good friend, wore a Santa hat that paired well with his beard. He walked us through a sea of familiar faces, then handed the phone over to Jack Rubio, my oldest friend who I'd been running around exploring the Florida Keys with since we were kids.

"House is coming along good, bro," he said, referring to our rebuild. During our recent aggressive interactions with illegal arms dealers, one of the criminals had set fire to our old house. With me and my family miles away on a boat in the Gulf, I'd only been able to watch via security cameras as the home I'd owned for nearly four years went up in flames. I was glad to hear that the new construction was coming along nicely.

"The crew took advantage of a nice stretch of weather and put the frame up early," Jack added.

"And there's someone here who's exploding with excitement to see you," his girlfriend Lauren said.

Jack angled the camera down, revealing our yellow Lab, Atticus, shaking his tail like mad and lunging for a closer look at the phone.

The three of us greeted our dog animatedly, then I said, "Pete let him inside?"

"Shush," Lauren said, holding a finger to her lips. "We just let him in for a quick bite and to say hi."

Jack walked us through a few more friends at the Christmas party, everyone dancing and singing and spreading the holiday cheer.

"I found a new lobster honey hole the other day," Jack said. "So it's got our names on it when you get back."

I laughed, finding it hard to believe that there was a square foot of underwater real estate in the Lower Keys that Jack had never seen before.

Pete grabbed the camera again and said, "When are you three coming back? The island just isn't the same without the Dodge family."

"We'll be back on the third," I said. "Not sure we could stay away much longer than that. We're not the same without our island family either."

Pete nodded. "Let me know what time and I'll have Oz fire up a feast fitting for your return. You staying safe down there? Staying out of trouble?"

We fell silent a moment, then Scarlett's expression as she glanced at me told our old friend maybe not.

Pete laughed. "Well, try and have a normal vacation, all right? If that's possible. I'll send you over my handbook if you like. Rule number one is thou shalt always have a drink in thy hand."

We laughed, then he held the camera up high and we waved to the group, then ended the call.

The living room fell silent a moment as Ange closed the app.

"You know how they say there's no place like home?" Scarlett said.

Ange and I both nodded.

"And there's no place like Key West," I said. "It sure has a way of drawing you in." I eyed the sliding glass door, revealing the palm trees, sandy coast, and tranquil stretch of Caribbean. "But I think I can manage it here for another week."

I love my island home. It was the only place I'd ever called home, really. Growing up with my dad in the Navy, I moved around every three years or so. Then, when I was eighteen, I'd signed up as well and served eight years. Even after I'd gotten out, I'd spent just over half a decade bouncing around from here to there, working various mercenary jobs around the globe.

I'd lived in Key West for nearly four years now, not including the three years I'd spent there as a kid. But despite its hold on me, recent events had left a sour taste in my mouth, and I didn't feel quite ready to head back yet. I was glad for the extra time to heal the mental wounds—wounds that often never heal.

We watched the sunset on the balcony. Then we ate a Caribbean-themed Christmas dinner, complete with jerk chicken, homemade macaroni pie, freshly baked rolls, and rum cake for dessert. The smoky, spicy flavor combined with a special sauce we'd purchased downtown made it some of my favorite jerk chicken I'd ever eaten.

Then we played dominoes and drank homemade eggnog while digesting the meal. After a couple intense games, we ate popcorn while watching *It's a Wonderful Life*, my personal favorite Christmas movie and one of my favorite movies of all time. There was something about James Stewart I'd always been fascinated by, even as a boy. The incredibly successful all-American actor and distinguished military pilot had a way of lighting up a scene and animating his character in a way that made George Bailey feel like a real person.

It was a perfect ending to a perfect day, and one of the best Christmases I'd ever had. When the movie ended at just past ten, we said goodnight to Scarlett, then Ange and I fell asleep in each other's arms.

ELEVEN

The day after Christmas, a familiar sensation began to gnaw at me. I rose early. Ran. Swam. Made breakfast. Then the three of us hit the beach. We snorkeled for over an hour, then napped for another, then lay in the quiet of our beach chairs just up from the surf.

Feeling relaxed and rejuvenated, I propped up onto an elbow. Ange and Scarlett were both absorbed in their books. Ange was reading Robert Louis Stevenson's *Kidnapped*, and Scarlett was absorbed in *Brian's Winter*, the sequel to Gary Paulsen's highly successful *Hatchet*, which he'd written by popular demand.

Ange had always loved reading. In fact, she'd been leafing through an old paperback when I'd first approached her what felt like a lifetime ago. Her love of the written word had quickly rubbed off on Scarlett.

I could get lost in the pages of a good MacDonald or Cussler novel with the best of them, but the familiar sensation gnawing at me was difficult to ignore.

It was the faint yet tangible initial traces of boredom. After four days of double shots of swim, eat, nap, repeat, I was feeling antsy.

I was about to ask the ladies what the plan was for today when I stopped myself and observed them both a moment. They were both the definition of contentment. Pure bliss and happiness on their faces. They were already following through on their plans for today.

I leaned forward and stretched my arms high up over my head while sweeping the beach with my eyes from end to end.

"I think I'm gonna head into town," I said, grabbing my towel and rising to my feet. "We're out of frozen fruit for the smoothies. You two need anything?"

Ange chuckled, lowering her book just enough for me to see her radiant eyes. She adjusted her long, tanned legs, crossing them with the opposite knee on top in a smooth action, her perfectly smooth skin glistening with sunscreen polish under the afternoon rays.

"Now there's the Logan Dodge I know and love," she said with a cute chuckle. "We're out of fruit? Really, that's what you're going with?"

"What do you mean?"

"You can't sit still to save your life. Not for long anyways. You've never been able to."

"Caught red-handed."

"Not me, though," Ange said. "I think I could stay right here until the end of time and be perfectly content with that."

"Maybe someday I'll be more like you," I said.

"Well, since you're going out, we could use some more eggs as well."

"And donuts," Scarlett said. "We're fresh out of those."

"We never had any to begin with," I said.

She grinned. "Exactly. So we're really out of them."

Ange and I laughed.

"Just don't go beating up any more troublemakers," Ange said.

I sauntered barefoot to the outdoor shower and rinsed off before toweling dry. Grabbing my phone and keys from the unit, I threw on a T-shirt and skipped down to the Jeep. I pulled out of the complex, heading north with the top down, the sun warming my skin and the fresh breeze gushing past. While relishing the perfect afternoon and the freedom that a solo-driven vehicle with a full tank of gas provides, I switched on the radio and a familiar tune streamed through the airwaves with barely a crackle.

I grinned as I remembered the last time I'd ridden in a Wrangler while listening to "We're an American Band." It had been nearly four years ago, while cruising in rural Mexico with an old Navy buddy, looking for a lost treasure and trouble near Sierra Gorda.

The memory brought back a smile that didn't leave my face until halfway through the song. During the final chorus, I spotted a dirt road cutting inland to the right. Feeling a little mischievous, I ignored the wooden sign that said it was for official tours only and rumbled onto the pothole-ridden path.

I blared the radio as I bounced and riled up clouds of dust, cutting with the sharp turns. Summiting a sharp precipice, I roared down the other side, splashing through a murky puddle and spraying mud across the frame.

After thundering across the terrain in utter freedom for five minutes and seeing no one else, I decided not to test my luck and cruised back to the road. Just after I pulled on, a line of dune buggies motored past me, heading the opposite direction. I smiled and hit the gas harder, flying back north in my newly mud-coated off-roader.

I dialed the radio down and relaxed in the seat. It wasn't long before the city appeared, then the southern cruise ship pier, and then eventually Mega supermarket on my right side.

Instead of pulling into the store and picking up the items I'd come to town for, I continued along. No particular reason. No particular destination in mind. Just antsy and curious and wanting to take a look around the place. There were no cruise ships in port, so the island was relatively quiet, with many of the shops closed and just a handful of tourists walking the city streets.

I turned inland just before the ferry terminal. Taking my time. A leisurely drive. Observing everything around me. Taking in the architecture, the landmarks, the people. Paying attention to the ever-shifting smells as I passed by different restaurants. Chili at one corner, cinnamon at the next. Then sizzling chicken and beef, and fresh tamales. All mixed with the pervading ocean breeze.

Cozumel was set up like a grid, with main roads running east to west through a sea of alternating one-ways running north to south. I turned down a quiet one-way a good six blocks from the waterfront. The town was different there. Less flashy. Restaurants with entrées about a third of the cost of those along the water. Less polished up and more authentic, complete with old plastic furniture, poor AC, and feral cats joining you for the meal.

A quarter mile along, I spotted a faded yellow sign that said Panadería La Camelia. Remembering what Scarlett wanted me to pick up, and preferring to support a small local business if I could, I braked along the road behind a delivery truck and next to a tower of scaffolding where they were renovating an old building.

I powered down the engine, then locked up. Not that it mattered with the top down. Shutting the door, I took a moment to admire the vehicle's new paint job. Splatters of dirt streaming up along the panel like an exploding firework. Mud already drying and caking onto the frame under the Mexico sun.

The bakery was open. I was greeted by a young woman at first, and then an older woman who appeared from a back room. Both wore aprons and smiles as I strode in and looked through a glass display at shelves of sugary treats.

Being an amateur among artists, I asked for their

recommendations, which they eagerly gave. Fresh glazed donuts, churros that were still warm, and a stack of caramel apple taquitos. I picked up some freshly baked bread as well, filling every inch of a cardboard box, then paid. It was beyond reasonable, so I doubled the sale with a tip into a small jar on the counter.

They thanked me, and the young woman held the door open as I strode out. I took two steps back out into the sun, then stopped mid-stride.

Peering up across the quiet street, I spotted a dilapidated dive shop wedged between a private residence and a laundromat. The sign above the door was faded, but I was able to make it out.

I paused a moment, then glanced down at the fresh pastries in the box. Doing a one-eighty, I headed back into the bakery and asked if they could hold on to them for a bit.

The older woman nodded and grabbed the box. "I'll keep them behind the display. You come back when you're ready."

I thanked her again, pushed outside, and strode across the street. Before reaching for the worn brass knob, I paused again. Looking up, I stared at the name of the dive shop once more, then gazed up and down the street and laughed softly.

"What are the odds?" I said to myself.

Of all the places I could've entered, I went into that bakery. Right across the street from this particular dive shop.

The inside was similar to most dive establishments I'd visited before. It was small, but not cramped. To the right were a counter and a glass case with rows of dive knives and masks and various other essential gear. On the walls were rows of fins, framed underwater photographs, a map of the island, and a big Irish flag. There were also old memorabilia and black-and-white photographs, and an impressive replica of an old wooden galley on a corner table. The place bore a striking resemblance to Pete's back in the Keys, though it was a miniaturized version. The room was cut in half by a curtain. And, to my surprise, there was a tiny makeshift bar built from pallets to my left with two worn stools.

"Hello?" I said.

A metal tool clanked onto a table beyond the curtain, followed by hushed voices.

"Have a seat," a man with an Irish accent said. "I'll be right out."

The hushed voices returned as I claimed the closest barstool. Resting my elbows on the worn counter, I scanned over the pictures. One was old and grainy, of a guy with a young girl wearing scuba gear and giving a thumbs-up at the stern of a boat. The girl looked vaguely familiar, and as I tilted my head and focused, trying to place her, the curtain parted and a man appeared.

He was nearly my height, tanned, and wore cargo shorts and a faded Hawaiian shirt. His sparse, partly gray hair made me guess that he was at least ten years my senior.

"Can I help you?" he said.

I gestured my head toward the mini fridge behind the counter. "Can I get a beer?"

He eyed me quizzically, then laughed. "A hundred bars within a stone's throw of this place, and you came here for a beer?"

"Can you make it two?"

He shuffled behind the counter with light steps. Seeing him closer up, I noticed an impressive number of scars up his arms and legs, along with an abstract tattoo around his left forearm.

He grabbed the beers, popped the tops, and set them on the counter. The labels were green with text that read "Of foam and fury."

I nabbed the closest one, finding it surprisingly cold, and took a sip.

"Galway Bay," I said. "First time seeing that in Mexico."

The man raised his eyebrows, then said, "Probably the only time you will."

I took another drink, then set it on the counter. Looked up toward the pictures, then the map of Cozumel, indicating dive sites along the southwest part of the island.

"Actually, I didn't just stop by to sample your Irish brew," I said. "I'm looking to go on a dive."

"With us?"

I nodded.

"Usually we only take out our guests. We run a small hostel just next door. But of course you're welcome to join us. You got your own gear?"

"Not on Cozumel I don't."

He nodded, then walked across the room and pulled a laminated sheet from behind the counter. Returned and set it down in front of me.

"Our rates."

They were a fraction of what I'd seen elsewhere on the island.

He turned to the map. "Where are you looking to dive? Santa Rosa Wall and Palancar Reef have been especially lively lately. And there are also deeper, more challenging dives depending on your experience level."

I paused a moment and cleared my throat. "Actually, I'm looking to dive the eastern coast." I waited, observing his expression as my words resonated. Then I motioned toward the other beer. "That one's for you by the way."

He narrowed his gaze, a variation of the quizzical eye he'd shot me moments earlier.

He grabbed the beer, took a slow sip, then shook his head. "No dive sites on the eastern coast. Not with us anyway. The current's far too strong. And the surf is wild and unforgiving. The winds temperamental." Then he shrugged. "Not to mention the viz is less than ideal and tends to change on a whim. And there's not a lot to see anyway. Only a couple operations in town do organized dives over there."

I fell silent, downed a few more sips of the ice-cold beverage, then wiped my mouth with the back of my hand.

"I've heard otherwise," I said, eyeing the map again. "I've heard that there's at least one interesting thing to see."

I stared into his eyes. Watched as the lightbulb flicked on in his head.

The man looked away and chuckled. "Ah, and the true purpose of the curious impromptu visit is revealed." He went quiet for a moment. "You read the article."

"I did."

"And… you believe me? You know everyone around here, including the author of that piece, thinks I'm making it up. Or delusional. Or both. But you believe it?"

I shrugged. "I don't have any reason not to."

"Why? Why do you want to see it?"

It was the big question. And his gaze visibly narrowed as he awaited my response.

"Curiosity, really. I just happened to stumble upon the magazine. Never read it before. Then I found the piece and it intrigued me. Then I was just walking out of that bakery across the street and saw this place. Figured it might be a sign, right?"

The man rubbed his chin. "There's not much to see."

"I imagine so. A wooden ship, couple hundred years submerged in corrosive saltwater. Strong currents and surf to boot. And marine life taking their toll. I imagine there isn't much aside from the occasional cannon, bit of pottery, and a whole lot of ballast stones. And even those will be spread out."

He smiled. "You have experience salvaging wrecks?"

"A little."

"Well, I hate to bust the bubble of your moment of serendipity, but I'm the only one on Earth who knows where that wreck is. And… for the foreseeable future at least, I intend to keep it that way."

"Then why do the interview? Why put the info out in a magazine?"

He took another swig from his beer. "First of all, *Yucatan Divers* isn't exactly *Nat Geo*. I think they've got a subscriber base about as impressive as my paltry bank account. Second, I had to do something to raise my credibility."

"Politics."

"Exactly. This whole thing is one big political tennis match. I was trying to up my stock in the battle for a percentage of the haul."

I knew how that was. When we'd found the *Intrepid* at Neptune's Table about twenty miles from Key West, everyone had wanted a piece of the pie. Spain had claimed ownership. So had Mexico. And the States, of course. Hell, even Cuba had tried, given that the vessel had set sail from Havana before picking up its haul. Then there were even the descendants of those who'd perished aboard during the storm. And the list went on and on.

In the end, we'd gotten off lucky. Though we'd only received a four percent finder's fee, which we'd split four ways, we hadn't been held up in legal battles for years. And one percent of a galleon's haul is enough to set up most people for the rest of their lives, provided they don't need luxury cars or mega mansions.

I finished off the rest of my beer, then gave it a final attempt.

"No chance I could take a look at it?"

He shook his head. "Sorry. You seem like a nice enough chap. But no. Keeping it hidden is far too important to me. I'm sure you understand."

I nodded, then dug out a hundred pesos from my pocket and placed it on the counter.

"Thanks for the beer. And your time. If I ever return I hope to see a picture with you in front of a stack of chests on that wall."

He laughed. "If that happens, I sure hope I'm not still hunkered in this little corner."

I slid off the stool and headed for the door. As I reached for the knob, the curtain opened again. I thought it had been the man leaving, but a woman's voice filled the air. A familiar woman's voice.

"Logan!" Dorothy exclaimed.

I turned as she dashed across the space. Just as I focused on her, she leapt forward and threw her arms around me.

"I'm so glad you stopped by," she said, loosening her grip. "I hoped you would."

The owner and I both looked confused, then it hit me.

"This is your—"

"My dad, Mick Flanagan," she said. "And this is our dive shop."

The word *serendipity* jumped into my mind again.

Mick still looked confused, so Dorothy said, "Dad, this is Logan Dodge. He's the guy who saved me last week."

"You're the one who taught young Beauchamp a lesson?" he said, striding over.

I nodded and he extended his hand. We shook, and he squeezed tight and smiled broadly. Placed an arm around me.

"I can't thank you enough for looking after my daughter. Why didn't you mention it when you walked in?"

"I didn't realize this was your place," I said to her. "I just recognized the name of the shop from the article. Like I said."

"Well, are you looking to dive?" Dorothy said.

"Dad, I told him we'd take him and his family out free of charge."

"There's really no need to repay us. Truth is I enjoyed giving that punk a lesson in manners."

"Nonsense," Dorothy said. "We'll take you all out. Then have dinner here. I'm gonna get the schedule and we'll work out a time that works for you."

Mick held up a hand, thought for a moment, then grinned. "This one's gonna be off the books, Dorothy." She tilted her head back, eyeing her father skeptically. "We're gonna take Logan on a dive off the eastern side. There's something I want to show him."

TWELVE

"You're doing what?" Scarlett exclaimed, her mouth agape as she lowered her sunglasses.

After leaving Lucky Divers, I'd grabbed the box of goodies from the bakery, stopped by Mega to pick up some groceries, then headed back to the unit. Ange and Scarlett were still right where I'd left them. Sprawled out on their beach chairs just up from the surf, their faces buried in books.

I told my wife and daughter again that, barring weather and current conditions, I was diving a wreck off the eastern coast the following morning with a new acquaintance.

"Can I come?" Scarlett pleaded. "Please, please, can I come? I've never dived anything like that before."

Few people have, I thought, feeling the excitement of the upcoming dive brewing within me.

"Sorry, Scar, but he's only allowing me to go. He's keeping its location a secret for the time being."

"What kind of a wreck is it?" Ange said, propping up onto an elbow.

I shrugged. "It's all a big mystery. But hopefully I'll find out tomorrow."

Scarlett folded her arms and buried her chin into her chest, causing me to chuckle. "Don't worry, Scar. Someday, I'll take you diving to a real shipwreck. Scout's honor." Seeing she was still bummed, I slid the box of pastries out from under my towel. "But in the meantime, does this make up for it?"

Her expression did a rapid one-eighty, and she lit up, bounding over to me. She grinned from ear to ear as I held them out to her, and she and Ange opened and gazed into the box like a pirate who'd just discovered his long-lost treasure chest.

I sprawled out beside them, enjoying their reaction and gazing out over the water. A deep, romantic excitement sparked, then burned intense within me.

A lost shipwreck? I thought with a grin, unable to imagine a more effective remedy for my restlessness.

"I've got the day planned for us tomorrow anyway, Scar," Ange said after savoring a big bite of glazed donut. "We're diving Palancar Caves. The place looks incredible, and you can get some good footage. Then we're getting a fish pedicure after at the club just down the beach from here."

"A fish pedicure?" our daughter said, raising her sunglasses.

Ange smiled. "You'll see. Little ticklish at first,

but it's surprisingly nice."

We spent the rest of the afternoon on the beach, then whipped up homemade pizzas for dinner.

I had trouble sleeping and woke early. Well before the sun. Excitement for the day ahead fueled my actions as I performed an easy workout on the beach then had a light smoothie and toast breakfast. There are a number of things that really light me up on the inside, but few compare to the prospect of diving a recently discovered wreck.

I kissed Ange on the forehead, left a note for her on the counter, and was on my way to town by six. I had plenty of time, so I took the long way, cruising south at first. Soon, the thick foliage and occasional resort or villa to my right opened up, revealing nothing but mostly barren coastline as the road wrapped around and I rumbled north along the eastern coast of the island. The wind howled, and thundering waves smashed against the jagged limestone coast. Just off the surf, large rollers battered into each other and whitecapped, and I could see the powerful swirling currents from there.

It was a beautiful, magnificent sight. The shoreline was a night-and-day difference from the tranquil shores on the western side of the island. This was the hard side. The battered side. The side that fended off the mature waves charging from the Caribbean, the brunt of most of the storms, and the currents of high seas. I've seen a lot of angry coastlines in my time, and this was right up there near the top. It wasn't difficult for an observer to see why dive charters stuck to the western side.

The route swiftly became one of my favorite

drives. A barren coast broken up by the occasional stretch of beach and the small handful of scattered restaurants and beach bars.

It took less than thirty minutes to reach the point where the paved road cut inland at a ninety-degree angle beside Mezcalito's Last Frontier.

Once in town, I pulled into the same marina where I'd moored *Wayfinder* when we'd arrived. It was already in the mid-seventies, and I felt every degree as the rising sun peeked through the rows of structures.

Mick was already there, hauling gear alongside his daughter and a young man I hadn't seen before. I parked, then greeted them and helped with the rest of the gear.

"Logan, this is Rico Espinoza," he said, introducing the young man, who I pegged at maybe nineteen.

I shook his hand, then Mick added, "Rico's my first mate. And he'll be piloting the boat for this dive while the three of us drop down."

He was medium height and lean, with a baby face. A local who I soon learned had lived his entire life on Cozumel.

Once everything was ready, we climbed aboard an old twenty-seven-foot Boston Whaler with a pair of 250-horsepower Evinrude outboards clamped to the stern. It had a fully enclosed cockpit, a small flybridge, and a cramped cabin Mick had converted into gear storage. *Craic of Dawn* was painted in faded green letters on the side, along with their company name and shamrock logo. It was aged and far from spacious, but experienced. Time-tested. The kind of vessel that had likely spent tens of thousands of hours on the open water.

"We'll do the brief out on the water," Mick said.

He scanned around the marina. There were only a couple people in sight, and maybe one within earshot, though none of them were paying us any attention.

"Away from curious eyes and ears," Mick added.

Dorothy chuckled. "Not that it matters. No one believes it exists."

"Why do they think you'd lie about something like that?" I said.

Mick shrugged as we untied the forward and aft lines. "Attention, I guess. I don't know. There's just not a lot of wrecks found anywhere near here. With the way the old Spanish trade routes ran from Veracruz and Portobelo to Havana, Cozumel's out of the way, so it wasn't likely this ship would end up here."

"But it did," I said.

"You bet it did. And you're about to see it."

We shoved off and Rico fired up the engines. Soon we were cruising north, following the same line the pearl farmers had taken the previous week.

"I drove across the island and checked the conditions already this morning," Mick said. "I was there at four thirty. It's necessary with dives on the eastern shore. Things look pretty good, but they can change quickly, so we'll gauge it again once we're there."

Just over an hour into the trip, we neared the northern tip of the island. We were greeted by the white-and-red-striped Punta Molas Lighthouse, sprouting up out of the flat, rocky landscape. It was like a switch was flicked as we wrapped around the corner. The mood of the current and waves turned in an instant, and the small boat began bouncing up and down with the swells.

Mick laughed. "Welcome to the east side."

"More like the moody side," Dorothy corrected.

Following the coast four miles south, we motored past Castillo Real, an impressive Mayan structure built right along the water.

Mick began scanning the shore intently as we motored along, making sure no one was watching. It was remote and empty, but he explained that it was common for fishermen to cast along the thundering surf.

"Today's a cruise ship day, so that's good," Rico said. "Seven pulling in, I think."

"Not a lot of people take days off on cruise ship days," Mick explained. "So less chance of a curious local on shore spotting us and wondering what we're up to."

Upon Mick's order, we donned our wetsuits and prepped our BCDs.

"Blindfold on," Mick said, handing me a black bandanna.

Mick had already explained how he was willing to show me the wreck but wanted to keep its location hidden.

"You saved my daughter, and I'm grateful," he'd said. "But we've still only just met you, so we've gotta take precautions."

I smiled momentarily, thinking over the irony. I'd been blindfolded before over the course of my life, but never willingly.

Grabbing the bandanna, I tightened the cloth over my eyes, turning the world around me pitch black.

I listened intently as the engines shifted their tone. It was subtle, but Mick had clearly given the order for Rico to up our speed. Another fifteen minutes passed, then the young man throttled back.

"All right," Mick said. "We'll drop in here. But do me a favor and keep that on for the time being."

"This isn't the part where you have me walk the plank, is it?" I joked.

The three of them laughed.

"Don't worry, Dad's dramatic sometimes, but harmless," Dorothy said. "Besides, I saw what you did to those guys last week. I'm sure you could take all of us on, even while blindfolded. No offense, Dad and Rico."

"All right, easy on the ego jabs," Mick said. "And everyone listen up. Here's how this is gonna go down."

Mick gave the unique instructions for the dive and I followed along while listening to the world around us. The wind felt like it'd picked up, but I doubted it would affect our dive much.

Once we were all clear on the plan, he went over it again, just to hammer it home. Mistakes are amplified underwater, and that's even more so the case in a rough area. On Mick's signal, Rico eased back on the throttle even more.

"All right, keep us steady here," Mick said.

The young skipper did as instructed, matching the current to keep the boat in place while the three of us strapped on our BCDs. Mick offered to help and was surprised when I managed to don it without trouble.

Little did he know, this was far from my first time strapping into scuba gear while blindfolded. Back at BUD/S, not only had we often been blindfolded during the notorious pool phase of our special forces training, we'd also been jostled around underwater, had our gear torn off, and even been attacked time and time again. I could don dive gear blindfolded in raging surf with one hand if I needed to.

I hung my mask around my neck and strapped on my fins. Then I slid on a pair of gloves, and Mick handed me a dive light, which I strapped around my wrist. We took posts on the gunwales, and I kept the bandanna over my eyes until Mick gave me the all clear.

Yanking off the fabric, I blinked the bright world around me into focus. I was seated on the starboard gunwale, and Rico had the bow pointed south into the current, so all I could see beyond Mick and Dorothy on the port gunwale was a long stretch of empty blue Caribbean.

Following Mick's instruction, I kept my head forward, securing the mask over my eyes. On the count of three, we fell backward. The rush was electrifying, the wild Caribbean swallowing me up and cooling me off as I submerged. Entering negatively buoyant, I sank ten feet before leveling off and checking on the others. When we all gave the OK sign, Mick stabbed a thumb toward the bottom, and the three of us vented more air from our BCDs.

The visibility was slightly better than I'd expected, offering a good fifty feet. To our left, waves rolled over and crashed into the jagged shore, churning up into swirls of bubbling vortices.

We dropped down to the bottom just thirty feet below, then rode the blistering three-knot current. I was taken aback by the abundance of sea life intermixed amongst the rocky bottom. There were schools of fish all around, and everything from parrotfish to hogfish dancing around the turbulent coastal waters. Sporadically the jagged bottom would give way, opening up to reef formations as pristine and untouched as I've seen anywhere on Earth.

We had a ways to go, so we leveled our bodies and sat tight, enjoying the ride and being careful not to get sucked into a violent undertow. Mick's plan was for us to drop down, drift for an unspecified amount of time, briefly explore the wreck, then drift along farther until surfacing and being picked up by Rico.

It wasn't exactly an airtight method of keeping the wreck's location a secret. If I were so inclined, I could rediscover the site doing simple math and with sweeps of a magnetometer. But that would require a lot of time, effort, and resources, so it was good enough for Mick.

"It's just a precaution," Mick had said with a smile.

We hovered over a stretch of brilliant white sand, spotting a nurse shark partly tucked under a tangle of staghorn coral, then rounded a massive jutting rockface. Finning around the sharp corner, it was like we'd entered a different body of water entirely. The change was sudden, unlike anything I'd experienced before. In a matter of seconds, the visibility went from fifty feet to forty. Then thirty. Then maybe twenty as a swirling cloud overtook us.

The three of us remained close and switched on

our lights. Just when I thought Mick might cancel the dive, the water cleared up again, the dark cloud receding and fading. I sighed a trail of bubbles in relief.

As we pressed on, the water cleared once more, offering a near-perfect glimpse into the breathtaking undersea world. It was an amazing dive, even if we weren't drifting toward a wreck. In addition to the abundance of marvels to take in, it filled me with excitement and a primal sense of adventure knowing that the waters were rarely dived—that only the most daring aquanauts had seen what we were seeing.

Mick kicked ahead of us, then turned back and held up an open hand, indicating that we were five minutes out.

I kept my eyes focused ahead, wanting to spot the remnants before they were pointed out, or perhaps catch a glimpse of a scattered artifact not yet discovered. But as we rounded another edge, a cloud of swirling, murky water returned, making it difficult to see once again.

We switched our lights back on and shone the beams forward as Mick led us down along a jagged shelf—the coral and edges of limestone difficult to avoid in the ever-shifting current. The landscape shifted again, this time to a distinct seafloor made up of brick-sized rocks scattered amongst the limestone and sand.

Mick slowed and descended to just a few feet above the bottom. He closed in on a curved rock covered in marine life. I shined my light through the cloudy water, scanning the beam as Mick grabbed hold of the rockface.

As I closed in, I gasped a trail of bubbles as I realized what it was. It was half-buried in sediment, corroded, and crusted over with so much multicolored aquatic growth that it nearly blended in perfectly with the seafloor. But as I ran a gloved hand over the surface, there was no doubt in my mind what it was. A massive anchor.

THIRTEEN

Keeping myself steady, I pulled out my regulator and shot the others a big smile. Then I surveyed the area around me with new eyes, and realized that the distinct rock formation wasn't natural seafloor at all. It was a scattered pile of ballast stones.

I blinked and stared, excitement coursing through me as I was taken aback by the scene. The hazy water dispersed a moment, and Mick aimed his light ahead, the glowing pillar illuminating a row of cannons. The heavy bronze pieces of artillery were mostly buried and layered in grime, the old instruments of warfare frozen in time.

We let go of the bottom and continued on another ten yards, gazing over what remained of the ship's wreckage. Most of the vessel itself was long gone, broken apart and rotted away and carried by the Caribbean's whims hundreds of years earlier. But I managed to spot pockets in the seafloor securing chunks of timber, along with clusters of pottery that were now little more than shards.

As expected, there wasn't much left. And I knew that much of the vessel and its cargo was likely spread far out over the bottom. But the spread of artifacts and remnants before me still took my breath away.

Diving a shipwreck always filled me with a wave of emotion, especially one that had gone down in a storm, as this one most certainly had. I thought of the passengers and crew. The lives lost. Hurled into the sea and smashed against the rocks, or trapped in the bowels of the vessel as it broke apart and sank. Their final moments chaotic and dark and terrifying. I closed my eyes and took a quick moment of silence, giving the dead their time.

I returned to the present and Mick led us along the bottom, then kicked hard to buck the current. I grabbed hold of the seafloor as he stopped. Then I froze, my brain barely able to process what my eyes were seeing.

Ahead, Mick shined his light on a long, tightly packed spread of chests and bricks that were mostly covered with sand. I gasped again, feeling the excitement fully taking over. Blinking, I realized that there were easily hundreds of the mostly corroded chests. Perhaps even thousands. And these bricks weren't ballast stones. They were gold bars.

It was an incredible sight, the kind of thing you imagine seeing when you're a kid reading about pirates and daring voyages and lost treasures. And it was all right off the coast of one of the most popular island destinations in the Caribbean.

I flattened myself to the bottom and held on while grazing a gloved hand over the most exposed chest in sight, hoping to see words or a symbol branded in what remained of the metal frames and hasps. Most of the chests had only skeletons remaining, the wood having decayed away long ago.

Sifting along the sand, I gripped one of the many loose coins littered among the bars, then wedged myself against a narrow ledge and held it up. Based on the markings, which I recognized from the coins at the Mel Fisher Museum in Key West, it was a Spanish doubloon. And judging by its weight alone, I estimated that that one coin alone was worth well over twenty thousand dollars.

I couldn't help but flash back to many years earlier when I'd been freediving for lobster with friends in the Florida Keys and had discovered a gold medallion lodged in the rock. Holding that doubloon took me right back there, to the overpowering romantic thrill of plucking a lost treasure from the bottom of the sea.

I set the coin back down, then observed Mick as he swept over the treasure beside me. Running his hands over the bars and coins, he plucked a doubloon as well. He took a brief moment to inspect the coin, then pocketed it and beckoned Dorothy and me to follow him.

We spent another minute fighting the current and gazing over the remnants of the galleon, fully soaking in the moment. Then Mick signaled that it was time to go.

I gazed over the scattered wreck and spread of treasures a final time, then let go of the bottom. The current swiftly grabbed hold of us, and the site vanished behind a veil of haze, flashing away like it'd never been there. Like it had all been a remarkable and fleeting dream.

We drifted back along, and soon the water cleared up again, allowing us to see the shoreline as well as the deep drop-off to our right. For the entire back leg of the trip, I couldn't get the site out of my mind. I'd gone out to run errands because I was antsy and looking for a little adventure the previous day. I'd never imagined it would lead to something like this.

I checked my new dive watch, and thirty-six minutes after leaving the wreck, Mick motioned for us to surface. The hull of *Craic of Dawn* was just ahead, blotting out the early-morning sun.

We performed our safety stop, then finned skyward. Even after being beneath the waves and unable to communicate verbally for well over an hour and a half, I was speechless when I broke out of the water. I inflated my BCD and bobbed lazily while sliding down my mask and brushing aside my hair.

"Incredible, isn't it?" Mick said with a laugh.

I smiled back at him and nodded, not sure if there was a word in the English language capable of doing the site justice. I find it difficult to rank dives, each one being special in its own way. But given the unexpected nature, the secrecy of it all, and the perfectly untouched wreck site, it was definitely in the top five.

Rico motored the boat over, pointing the bow into the current as we climbed one by one up the ladder. I sat and unclipped my gear, still mesmerized by what I'd seen.

"What do you think?" Mick said.

Dorothy smirked while brushing back her damp hair. "I think he liked it, Dad."

I gave a broad smile as I shouldered off my BCD and removed my fins. "I did. You've got one hell of a find on your hands."

It was a massive understatement.

"Worth the trip out?" Dorothy said.

"Worth a trip around the world. The viz usually that bad down there?"

Mick nodded. "Every time I've been down there that hazy patch is swirling. Must be part of the reason why no one's ever found it. It's like the ship's ghosts are trying to keep it hidden." He turned to the young mate. "Anyone near the shore?"

"Just a couple of fishermen about a mile back," he said. "They barely gave me a second glance."

Mick nodded, swept his gaze over the shore, then told Rico to take them back to the marina.

"Sounds like it was a success?" the young man said as he accelerated us north.

"Oh yeah," Mick said. He dug into his BCD pocket and pulled out the gold coin he'd grabbed. Held it out to his first mate. "I'd say so."

Rico's eyes lit up, and Mick added, "That's for you, as promised."

He grabbed it reverently while keeping one hand tight on the helm. "I... I don't know what to say."

Mick waved him off. "Given all the work you put in to keep my operation afloat, it's the least I can do." He patted the young man on the back. "Just remember, anyone asks, you bought it at a pawn shop in Cancun."

Rico stared at the doubloon, mesmerized by the sight. Then he and Dorothy exchanged a quick, friendly glance, and he pocketed the coin and was back to piloting us back to town.

We peeled off our wetsuits, then Dorothy handed me a bottled water, which I downed in one long pull. Then we snacked on cheese and crackers and chips. While eating, I sat on the deck with my back against the port gunwale and my right elbow resting on the transom. I gazed out over the water, then at the swirling wake behind us. The lonely, quiet, empty coastline. And I thought about the extraordinary secret the waves concealed.

Mick settled in across from me. The forty-something Irishman was shirtless, his feet crossed, and his head tilted back, looking like there wasn't anywhere else he'd rather be in the whole world than right there, lounging at the stern of his boat.

"I gotta ask," I said after downing a mouthful of Sun Chips. "How did you manage to find that?"

"He nearly drowned, that's how," Dorothy said.

"I didn't nearly drown," Mick said, giving her shoulder a playful jab. "But I did almost get swept out to sea."

Dorothy chuckled and held up her hands. "Oh, sorry. 'Cause that's so much better."

I eyed Mick curiously, then he continued. "You know, it's an ironic thing. I've been looking for shipwrecks for much of my life, and the last twenty years on Cozumel. Much of my free time over the years has been spent dragging a tow fish through the water or diving popular fishing sites, hoping to find a wreck." He shook his head and brushed back his long, messy hair. "But fate has a sense of humor, I guess. Because I stumbled upon this wonder completely by accident."

He took a swig of soda, then continued. "I was spearfishing along the shore. Been doing it for years and I usually hit the same spots, but for a couple days in a row I just wasn't finding anything, so I moved progressively south. One day I spear this beauty of a grouper. Just a monster, but it put up a good fight, dragged me far into murky water. The relentless creature managed to get away, but as I was coiling up the line, the spear slid across the seafloor and tinged against something that sure as heck wasn't a rock. So I dove down and the rest, as they say, is history."

"Then you barely made it back," Dorothy chimed in with a giggle.

"Right. By the time I was done exploring and marveling at the find, and trying to burn its location into my memory, the current had picked up and shifted. And the winds began to howl." He shook his head. "I was already exhausted when I left the wreck. Then it took nearly half an hour of kicking with everything I had to traverse the short ways back to shore. The thought of finding a shipwreck but never being able to tell anyone was a powerful motivator. Land had never felt so good, and I climbed up and kissed the beach."

We continued along past the Mayan ruins, then closed in on the lighthouse, making our way back around the northern tip.

"Well, I'm glad you were able to make it back," I

said. "That wreck and all its history would've remained lost. I only hope that you can win the salvage rights soon."

Mick nodded, then fell silent a long moment, clearly in deep contemplation.

"You know," he said, "I've dedicated my professional life to the underwater world. It's not a pursuit that tends to lead to much financial security. As you've seen by my humble shop. I've won and I've lost over the years. But this is a loss I will not accept. I've been searching for a wreck most of my adult life. I've nearly gone bankrupt half a dozen times. And now, after finding it, big governments don't want to reward my hard work. They want me to tell them where it is. And you know what they offered me, Logan? The equivalent of five thousand dollars. Can you believe that?"

It was astonishing, but I could believe it, having experienced my share of government logic at work. Still, the sum was laughably low.

"Do you have any idea what a galleon like that is worth?" He waited for me to spit out an answer. I did have an idea. A pretty good idea, in fact, but I let him tell me anyway. "We're talking upwards of half a billion dollars in gold, silver, and jewels. And they offered me five thousand."

"Well, I admire you're sticking it out and fighting," I said. "I imagine most people would've already hauled up what they could and sold it in secret."

Mick nodded and grabbed two more bottled waters from the cooler, handing me one. I cracked it open and took a refreshing series of sips.

"How was that feeling, though?" Mick said, leaning back into the gunwale. "Pulling up that gold coin from the depths? Snatching it from the jaws of history and being the first to hold it in hundreds of years? I bet you've never felt anything like that before."

I agreed. The feeling was indescribable, but I decided to tell him that it wasn't completely unfamiliar.

Upon their inquiring, I went on to tell them about the medallion I'd found on a ledge at Neptune's Table in the Florida Keys years earlier—a find that had led to the eventual discovery of the *Intrepid* years after.

"Wait a second," Mick said, leaning forward and brushing aside his hair. "You discovered the *Intrepid*?"

I nodded casually. "Me and my friends, yeah."

"I knew I recognized your name from someplace," Mick said, his jaw reaching for the deck.

Dorothy laughed. "You're just full of surprises."

"Why didn't you say anything?" Mick said. "A find like that, most people would be bragging about it everywhere they went for the rest of their lives."

"I don't know about that," I said with a chuckle. "And I like to keep a low profile. Arian Nazari, the Arab oil baron who helped us salvage the wreck, was nice enough to redirect most of the media attention away from me and my friends."

The three of them stared at me for a moment, then looked at each other. Following a series of rapid-fire questions, I regaled them with a brief version of the story, then redirected the conversation back to the wreck at hand.

"Any idea what ship it is?" I asked Mick.

He shook his head. "The Spanish ministry of culture completed an inventory of shipwrecks in the Americas a few years back. They identified over six hundred vessels that went down between the late fourteen hundreds and late eighteen hundreds. And less than a quarter of those have been accounted for."

I nodded, having read about the project. "But that list includes *all* vessels that went down. You just need the ones that sank on their way back from the Americas. Or, given its location, from the major nearby ports of the time between here and Havana."

Mick smiled. "You know your stuff. I've compiled my own list based on old maritime logs, but it's still extensive, with over two dozen unaccounted-for galleons that fit the potential bill."

I thought for a moment, then said, "If you could find a remnant that proved what ship it is, you'd have a better chance of filing your claim and getting a nice slice of the pie. You could go to Spain. Dig up old ship manifests and logs. Then, once you know what ship you're dealing with and how much precious cargo she was laden with, see the government's eyes light up. Seeing specific figures might jog them into some commonsense thinking."

Mick chuckled. "If only there was someone I knew who had experience salvaging Spanish galleons."

I matched his smile, leaned back, and peered out over the water. "How's the weather look tomorrow?"

FOURTEEN

Warren Beauchamp Jr. woke to his buzzing phone. He shifted his tired, aching body, reached into his pocket, and pulled out the device just enough to see who was calling. A long sigh escaped his lips. Then he grunted and shook his head when he noticed the time.

Silencing the phone, he blinked, taking a moment to brush away the mental cobwebs. Then he pushed himself off the bed of his truck. There was a tangle of blankets and a young naked woman in the mix. She stirred just barely, raven-black strands of hair covering most of her face. Junior crawled backward, then turned and slid his feet to dangle off the lowered tailgate.

The morning breeze was stiff, but weakened by the

surrounding bushes and palm trees. The sky was lit, but the sun's rays had yet to rise over the surrounding jungle. Silence enveloped the empty landscape for a mile in all directions. Aside from the swaying, creaking branches, all he could hear was the surf to his right, the low, sonorous rumbling of the sea meeting a jagged shore.

Then another sound penetrated the stillness. The return of the rhythmic buzz in his hand.

He sighed again uncontrollably, slid off the tailgate, and landed barefoot in the dirt. Stepping over a minefield of empty glass bottles and beer cans, he found his underwear and pants. He put them on slowly, letting the call drag on and die off. Then he ambled around the base of a coconut tree.

The buzzing returned. This time he answered.

"Where the fuck are you?" a voice spat.

Junior checked the time again. Sighed. Then remembered what day it was.

"I'm on my way," he said unconvincingly.

"Like hell you are. It's too late. I've sent someone else."

"No, I—"

"It's done." There was a short pause, and Junior could feel it coming. A pent-up storm about to be released. "That's twice, Warren. Twice in a week's time that you've failed me. Don't think for a second that you're immune just because of your last name. We're in a damn crisis and you're off screwing around. Pull yourself together. And be at the dock at two, you got that? Two o'clock. You mess up again and you're done. Don't think I won't do it."

The call ended abruptly. Junior held the phone in

place a moment longer, letting the words sink in. Then he lowered it, sneered, and spat into the nearby brush.

Pocketing his phone, he turned and strode back to his pickup. Made his way to the cab. The driver's-side door was open, and a man was sprawled out in his boxers, a petite woman curled up beside him and a blanket half-covering their bodies.

"Roman?" Junior practically yelled.

There was no movement, so he flicked the guy's forehead. Still nothing, he grabbed a nearby bottle of water, took a long pull, sloshed it around in his mouth and spat it out. Then he splashed the remaining liquid over the guy's face, causing him to spring awake. The guy looked around in confusion, then stared at Junior.

"Clean up," Junior ordered. "We're out of here in ten."

The guy scrambled up, causing the woman to stir as well. Without bothering to wait for a reply, Junior turned back and stomped away, threading through the thick trees that soon opened up to a wide stretch of blue. Wind whipped at his face as he stopped along the ridge of a steep cliff. Below, the surf raged and swirled and foamed against the steep shoreline.

He peered out, anger boiling inside him as he unzipped his pants and relieved himself. He finished, zipped back up, then eyed the broken fingers of his right hand. With his left, he instinctively felt the pistol lodged into the back of his waistband. Then he flexed his injured hand as well as he could, wincing from the sharp, tingling pain.

"If I run into that asshole again, I'm gonna pick another fight," he said. "Then I'm gonna put one right between his eyes. No. First I'll make him cower in fear. Then I'll finish him."

He gave a sinister smile. Then his eyes trailed up, and he froze, his gaze fixed out to sea just as a boat motored along the shore to his right. He squinted, then the color drained from his face and a chill crawled up his spine.

He stepped backward, concealing himself in the cover of branches as the boat cruised closer.

Turning on his heel, he raced back to his truck. Roman was out and picking up the trash. The women had both awoken as well and were searching for their scattered clothes. Junior went straight to the metal toolbox in the bed. He squeaked it open, found what he was looking for, and headed back to the shoreline.

"What's going on?" Roman said.

Junior didn't answer. He just picked up his pace and was breathing fast by the time he returned to the cliff and raised the binoculars to his eyes.

Keeping himself hidden in the thick brush, he focused on the boat just as it was on the same line, eyeing the hull and its logo first, then scanning the passengers one by one. His jaw clenched, then he lowered the binos.

Footsteps pounded at his back. Roman arrived.

"What's going on?" the hefty guy said again, stumbling in untied shoes and sliding a T-shirt on. "I thought we were leaving?"

The man stopped beside Junior, then followed his gaze to the passing boat. In lieu of an answer, Junior just handed him the binoculars.

He grabbed them and peered through, focusing on the passing boat.

"That's Mick Flanagan's boat," Roman said. "That crappy charter no one ever uses. And that's... wait." He adjusted the knob to focus, gasped, then lowered the binos. "That's the American who keeps causing trouble." He grunted. "What the hell is he doing diving with Flanagan?"

Junior kept his eyes locked on the boat, which was nearing another point. Soon it would be out of their sight.

"And what are they doing diving on the eastern side of the island?" Junior said. "No one ever dives here, right?"

Roman shook his head. "Rarely ever. It's stupid to dive here. Pointless. Crappy viz. Currents. Not a lot to see anyway."

"Then why are they doing it?" Junior said again.

The man shrugged, and Junior thought harder. He was dehydrated and hungover, and tired. But eventually it clicked.

"Didn't Mick claim to discover a wreck on this side?"

Roman laughed. "He's the madman who's claimed a lot of things. But the guy's a hack. A chump. Just trying to get attention any way he can. Not that it's worked. He rarely gets any business at that dump of a dive shop."

Junior's gaze narrowed as he snatched the binos and took a final look at the vessel before it vanished from view.

"If it's a lie and he's a hack, then why in the hell are they diving over here?"

The man didn't answer.

"There's a way we can find out," Junior said,

tightening his gaze.

"No," Roman said, his face turning ghastly. "Your dad said we've got to leave the tourist alone."

Junior knew that Logan Dodge wasn't an ordinary tourist, but Roman was right. His father had made it clear that if they messed with the American again, they'd be toast.

As Junior focused a final time on the boat, eyeing each occupant in turn, he fixated on one in particular yet again. This time it wasn't Dodge.

"We don't need to mess with the tourist for answers," he said in a slow, sly tone. "No, perhaps there's a far easier way to figure out what these suckers are up to."

FIFTEEN

We returned to the marina at half past ten, having spent most of the hour-and-a-half-long voyage back discussing the dive and getting to know each other better. Mick told me that he'd moved to Cozumel nearly twenty years earlier, following a beautiful woman and the sun away from his rainy abode in Ireland. Though he'd been diving his entire life, his father having worked as a commercial diver on ships in Belfast, the Mexican island was his favorite place in the world.

"I had it all for a little while," Mick said philosophically. "Not money. No, never that. But all of the important stuff."

The boat fell silent, then Dorothy said, "My mom died ten years ago."

"I'm so sorry to hear that," I said. "I've lost both of my parents, and it's devastating." A rush of memories tried to fight their way into my present mind, but I brushed them back for another time. "And losing your wife... I can't even imagine."

Mick nodded, then shook it off. "But our life isn't so bad." He gazed out over the paradise. "And the good luck hasn't completely run dry."

"How did you guys meet?" I said, asking Rico, who was manning the helm and listening intently.

"I grew up on the island," the young man said. "Never met my parents. Lived at the orphanage. It's actually pretty nice here. Lots of generous foreigners help keep it well funded. As for diving, let's just say the water has called me for as long as I can remember."

I smiled. "I know the feeling."

"The kid's a prodigy beneath the waves," Mick said. "One of the best divers I've ever met. And he's only nineteen. How many have you logged?"

"Nearing two thousand. I was certified at ten years old, as young as PADI will allow."

The number blew me away. I knew instructors who'd been diving a good chunk of their lives who hadn't hit that many.

Mick leaned over and patted Rico on the shoulder proudly. "I'm telling you, he could be running PADI, or a major dive operation, or whatever he wants someday. Not sure why you stick around with me and my shop."

"I like your shop, Mick," he said. "And I get to dive the most beautiful place on Earth every day." He shrugged, then looked out over the perfect blue water that was tinged turquoise along the white shore. "What more could I want? If I were a zillionaire, you know how I'd spend my time? Diving off Cozumel. So I feel like the richest man in the world."

I couldn't get the smile off my face if I wanted to. The young man was wise far beyond his years. A seafaring poet and spiritual trailblazer. Like the Dalai Lama in boardshorts.

"Besides," Rico added, "it's not all about the pay." He stuck his hand into his pocket and fished out the gold coin Mick had picked up during the dive. "It's about the benefits."

I turned to face Mick's daughter, who was sitting on the cockpit bench, facing backward with her bare feet on the gunwale beside her father.

"What about you, Dorothy?" I said. "You content living here your whole life?"

"I'd like to go to school," she said. "Medical school. But it's expensive, so I don't know. And not to mention hard to get into."

"You'll get in," Mick said. "You get perfect grades. And your test scores are off the charts."

She grinned with pride. "I'd like to become a doctor and then I'll probably come back here. This island has a way of luring people back. Like a spell."

I nodded. A spell was a good way to put it. Or a drug. I felt the same way about my home in Key West. A beautiful, sun-soaked drug. An addiction. And I felt myself missing my home yet again, even though we'd only been gone a little over a week. Despite all that had happened, despite those living in the Keys who still didn't like me, it was my home.

Rico eased us up along the same stretch of dock

we'd left from, and I helped tie us off before we lugged the gear off.

"Let's rinse it down, Rico," Mick said. "Remember, we've got a group going out at noon."

I helped with cleanup, rinsing down the BCDs and wetsuits, helping any way I could. Once everything was tidy and the tanks were refilled for their next dives, I thanked Mick for everything.

"No, thank you for saving Dorothy," he said. "The two things are far from equal, but I'm glad you enjoyed the dive."

"You still up for another go tomorrow?" I said. "You still don't have a name for her yet."

Mick looked toward the skies. "If the weather and currents abide, yes. Same time work?"

"I'll see you then."

Dorothy gave me another hug, and I shook Mick's hand.

I swung by Lobster Shack and picked up lobster and shrimp rolls, along with a bag of freshly made tortilla chips, for lunch. When I returned to our place on the southwest shore of the island, it was empty. It was nearly noon, and after setting the bags of food on the counter, I headed toward the balcony, assuming that Ange and Scarlett were at their usual spots on the beach. A note on the dining table stopped me.

"Viva Punta Sur," it said with a smiley face and a heart.

I smiled, stowed the food in the fridge, and grabbed my beach towel and snorkel gear before heading back out to the Jeep. Heading south, I cruised five minutes before turning off on a dirt road with a gate and a wide arch that read "Punta Sur Eco Beach

Park." Paying the entrance fee, I drove along the water on one of the most picturesque stretches of road I've ever seen. Calm waters splashing less than ten feet from the tires at times. Tall, proud palm trees flapping healthily in the wind. Smooth sandy routes.

The place was paradise, and one of the more popular spots on the island. I'd only been there once before for a quick stop but concluded that if I could only spend a single day on Cozumel, Punta Sur was where I'd go.

I parked in the dirt-and-rock driveway at the end of the line. Grabbing my stuff, I headed toward a trio of beach clubs, each with their own restaurant and spread of beach chairs along the pristine coast.

"You must be Mr. Dodge," a friendly voice said just as I stepped off the gravel and onto a wooden path.

"That's me," I said. "I'm glad they chose yours. Your beach chairs are the most comfortable."

The man led me past a big palapa with a bar, through a sea of dining tables and hammocks, and to the beach where padded chairs were laid out in rows with intermixed umbrellas. I spotted my wife and daughter two lanes up from the surf, in a shaded spot with a nice view of the water through two other groups.

"There's the treasure hunter now," Ange said as I approached. "Success?"

She was sporting her white bikini and looked amazing, lying on her stomach, her bronzed skin sparkling.

I set my stuff down on an end table beside her, and Scarlett came up to an elbow, eager to hear an answer to Ange's question.

"Success," I said with a nod.

"Can I get you anything?" the waiter said, holding out a menu.

"Three coconut waters, a shrimp cocktail, and a plate of grilled grouper," I said, without looking at the menu.

The man smiled. "Coming right up, sir. You ladies doing good?"

"We're perfect," Ange said.

The moment I spread my towel and plopped down, Scarlett migrated to the other side of me and leaned over.

"Well?" she said, her eyes big. "You gonna tell us about the wreck or what?"

I told them all about the trip, from beginning, to spotting the anchor through the cloudy, churning waters. Animated and passionate, trying my best to express just how incredible it'd been. I only stopped when the drinks and cocktail arrived, which I swiftly downed, the early morning and dive making me far hungrier than I'd thought.

"Unbelievable," Scarlett said, leaning back into her chair. "How much do you think all that gold's worth?"

I glanced around, just to make sure no one was listening. "Half a billion, more or less."

Scarlett's only reaction was to laugh at first.

Then she said, "Oh, is that all?"

"It's clearly a Spanish galleon," I said. "Massive vessels with one purpose in mind: transporting as many riches as possible from the New World back to Europe. We're talking as much as five hundred tons of cargo. Incredible feats of marine engineering."

We talked more as I finished my lunch, savoring the fresh grouper along with the Spanish rice and vegetables.

"What's he going to do next?" Scarlett asked.

I wiped my lips with a napkin. "We're gonna dive it again tomorrow, weather permitting. Hopefully we can identify it before we leave."

"Then what?"

"Then it's politics. Money. Usually comes down to that."

I chugged the rest of a coconut water then inquired about their morning dives.

"The caves were amazing," Scarlett exclaimed, whipping out her phone and showing me a few shots she'd snapped with her GoPro.

I grinned as she thumbed through the images displaying her and Ange beaming as they explored a mystical underwater world of color and life.

"And the fish pedicure was actually pretty nice," she added. "Once I got past the initial ticklish phase."

I took a twenty-minute power nap, then hit the water. Punta Sur offers some of the best beaches and liveliest reefs on the planet. And there are no hotels or residences around. Just two hundred and fifty acres of pristine, untouched beach and lagoons.

We spent most of the remaining daylight hours in the water. Snorkeling up and down the coast. Snapping pictures and videos of each other while freediving down amongst the vast assortment of coral and tropical fish. Relishing our little slice of Heaven.

We stayed until they closed, cruising back to our unit just before sunset. After showering, relaxing, and eating the lobster rolls I'd picked up earlier for dinner, Scarlett talked us into heading into town to catch a movie at the local theater. The new *Mission Impossible* was playing, apparently. And one of the showings was in English.

Halfway through the film, just after nine o'clock, I received a phone call. It was from Mick.

I shuffled down the row and answered while exiting the dark room. The tone of his voice told me instantly that something was wrong.

SIXTEEN

Four hours earlier, Mick and Rico had returned to the dive shop after a long day out on the water. After cleaning and stowing the gear, servicing the tanks, and tidying up the place, the young man had nestled into a chair with an advanced scuba manual, a notebook, and a thick folder.

He went over their dives that day, making notes of various observations and lessons. The young man lived a mile inland from the shop, renting a room in a cheap neighborhood, but often stayed long into the night, learning and researching. He was so engrossed by the material that he didn't notice the dark-hooded figure stride by the store and peek in through the window bars. He also didn't notice when the figure returned, backtracking for a second pass minutes after the first.

"I still don't get it," Mick said, appearing through the curtain separating the room. He held a plate with a PB&J in one hand and a chilled cola in the other. He set them down on the table in front of Rico, then slouched onto one of the barstools. "I don't understand why you still stick around here."

Rico lowered his textbook. "Because it's all about the dive here," he said, like it was a question the young man had pondered many times before. One with a well-thought-out, ready answer. "Not the money. Not the attention. Not awards or prestige. Just the dive, and the love of it. The passion."

He marked his page, then set the book aside and leaned forward to eat the sandwich. "Thanks," he said, holding up one of the halves before taking a bite and washing it down with Coke.

The shop owner leaned back, his elbows resting on the weathered counter. "Well, if you can find a way to keep the love of the dive and make a little money, I'd highly encourage that." He scanned around the cramped, simple space as if scrutinizing his lot. Then shook his head. "You don't want to be me, kid. Pushing fifty with nothing but a leaky roof and sunspots to show for it."

"You have Dorothy," Rico said. "And you have this shop. And you have the galleon. Maybe the fates are rewarding your labors after all."

"Or just toying with me."

They both laughed and Rico finished the sandwich and downed the rest of the soda. Mick fell into deep thought, then leaned forward and pulled a folded piece of paper from his back pocket.

"Got another one for you," he said, holding it up and setting it on the counter. "This one's the best yet."

"Why do you try so hard to get me to leave?"

"It's a good one, really," Mick said, ignoring the question. "An offer from a dive shop in the Bahamas. I know the owner. He's a good guy and knowledgeable, both in business and diving. The pay's double what you make here, includes room and board, and there's a lot of room to move up. And the diving is incredible, and diverse."

Rico fell silent. "You think I should take it?"

"I think you should start living up to your potential. Go somewhere where you can really shine. This place will always be open to you, long as I'm alive. But you've got a bright future, kid."

Rico went quiet again, then rose and carried the empty soda can and plate back into the small kitchen. When he returned, his expression had changed. His furrowed brow had flattened. He'd already made up his mind. Padding across the room, he leaned over and grabbed the folded piece of paper. Opened it and read the heading.

"Exotic Divers Nassau."

"One of the best ops in the world," Mick said. "The big leagues, kid."

He read over the first few lines. A quick summation of the job and the offer and what to expect. Then he glanced up at the wall behind the counter, his eyes focusing on the picture of Mick and Dorothy.

"I'll think about it," he lied, sliding it into his pocket.

"Take tomorrow off to think it over."

"No way. We're going to the wreck again, remember?"

Mick chuckled. "Right. Have a good night. I'll see you tomorrow, bright and early, then."

The sun had been down for half an hour by the time Rico shouldered his bag and headed out the door. The night was calm. Barely a breath of wind rustling the palm fronds high overhead. The sky was mostly clear, and the stars appeared in thick clusters as he made his way farther inland, away from the lit, busier downtown streets and toward the local residential areas.

He thought about the offer in his pocket while making the same journey he'd walked a thousand times over the past five years.

Maybe it is time for a change, he thought. *Maybe it's time to check out a bigger pond and find out what I'm made of.*

He shook his head, tossing out the idea.

Maybe I would... if the island's beauty was the only thing keeping me here.

He passed by an unassuming restaurant, a dim light coming from within along with the faint sounds of mariachi music. Crossing a potholed street, he slipped into an abandoned lot. It was the same shortcut he always used. A mostly torn-down abandoned house, barely anything left beyond the foundation.

Halfway across the lot, he heard a slow, sharp whistle. It came from behind him. He stopped and glanced over his shoulder, expecting to see someone beckoning their dog, but he saw no one. Facing forward, he continued for two more paces, then again the whistle cut across the still air. This time slower and louder. Still at his back.

He stopped again. Turned. This time there was someone there. A hooded figure thirty yards back. Standing perfectly still and bathed in moonlight. The whistle sounded again, coming from the shadowy figure. Then the stranger's right hand came out from behind his back, holding something. Rico blinked and focused, then realized what it was. A baseball bat.

He turned and took off forward, his heart pounding as he pumped his arms and sprinted as fast as he could. He swiftly reached the end of the abandoned lot, slid through the break in the fence, then crossed between the back of a closed auto shop and a dark house.

Maintaining his speed into the short straightaway, he glanced back for the first time since making a break for it. The figure wasn't there. The abandoned lot behind him was dark and empty and still.

He turned back forward just as a second figure appeared from the darkness, wrapping big, powerful arms around Rico's midsection and stopping him so fast he lost his breath. The hulking stranger spun and threw him into the side of the brick wall.

Grunting and rolling with the impact, Rico looked back and spotted the first guy approaching, blocking off his escape at the other end of the alley.

The masked brute who'd stopped him chuckled as he stomped closer, lowering a metal chain from his right hand.

"We can do this the easy way or the hard way," the man grumbled.

Rico remained still, then made up his mind as the beast of a man bent down to grab him. Rotating his body in a blink, he snapped his right leg skyward, plowing his shin into the guy's groin. The stranger's eyes bulged through his mask and he cursed in extreme pain, his knees wobbling then giving way as he toppled forward, barely catching himself against the wall.

Rico used the moment to slither free and make a run for it. Two more men appeared as he dashed out from the other side of the alley, both standing beside a black truck. They froze as they saw him, then gave chase as he darted right. The road ahead terminated abruptly at a dead end. A ten-foot-tall chain-link fence with coiled barbed wire on top blocked his escape.

With no choice, Rico leapt onto the links and raced up as fast as he could. Reaching the top, he tried to squeeze through the sharp, jagged wire but got stuck, his backpack getting caught. Then the fastest attacker reached the base and jumped up, snagging Rico's left heel.

Adrenaline coursed through the young man, and he breathed frantically. The guy tried to heave him down and he slid back a foot. Keeping his grip tight on the metal, he gritted his teeth, shook his leg free, then smashed his foot into the guy's face. As the man stepped back, Rico removed his backpack, forced himself through, the sharp metal cutting all over his body, then landed on the other side. The second his shoes hit dirt, he took off down a neglected road flanked by thick encroaching jungle.

He ran fifty yards, then slid out his phone with a

shaky hand and placed a call while fighting to control his rapid breathing. Mick answered on the third ring. The moment his voice came through, the roar of a big engine and the squeal of tires tore across the air. Rico turned back as headlights blazed, and the truck accelerated into the fence, smashing the barrier free and flattening it before barreling down the bumpy path.

Rico veered off the road, disappearing into the dark forest and weaving his way through the tangles of thick branches. Seeing a spotlight at his back, he dove for cover behind the stump of an uprooted tree. The truck braked to a stop. More spotlights switched on and scanned over the forest all around him. Heavy footsteps drew closer.

Rico held up his phone. Mick's voice was coming through, the shop owner asking over and over what was going on.

"Mick, I'm in trouble," he whispered, cupping the speaker with his hand. "There's men after me. They're—"

He sprang wild as arms grabbed him from behind. He dropped his phone, made a fist, and threw a punch toward the apparition's gut. The man caught the blow, forced him to the earth, and shoved a knee into the kid's chest. Rico fought and struggled, then froze as the barrel of a pistol stared him down from six inches in front of his face.

SEVENTEEN

Paralyzed with fear, Rico breathed heavily, his heart pounding like mad. He shook as his eyes traced up from the weapon to the man's eyes, focused and evil in the bleeding moonlight.

More heavy footsteps approached, and the big man who'd grabbed him in the alley staggered over.

"You should've chosen the easy way, punk," he said, then struck Rico with a solid boot to the gut.

He curled up and wheezed, coughing up blood and struggling to breathe.

A third dark figure appeared from the shadows. The one with the baseball bat, his boots crunching the leaves right beside Rico's ears.

"On your stomach," the man grunted, shining the beam of his flashlight into the young man's terror-filled eyes.

Rico did as he was ordered but questioned it.

I should fight. I should thrash and buck and try and get away with all I have.

But he knew it was futile. There were four of them, at least. And they had him outnumbered and outgunned.

Lying in the dirt and leaves, he held still as his arms were forced behind his back, then restrained with a thick plastic zip tie. Then his ankles were secured as well, and they duct-taped his mouth. Not a single strip, but all the way around. Twice. The adhesive tight across his hair, tugging the strands.

The last thing he saw was the line of shadows from his attackers, then everything went pitch black as a sack was slid over his head and secured around his neck.

"Get him in the truck," a hard but young voice said. A voice Rico recognized.

Hands grabbed his ankles, and another pair hooked him under the armpits. They flipped him onto his back, then heaved him off the canopy. Rico weighed a hundred and fifty pounds soaking wet, so the men easily carried him back to the road and jostled him onto the hard bed of the truck. Then they dragged him all the way forward against the toolbox. Raised the lid, and heaved him up and into the tight space.

He'd just entered when the top slammed shut. He heard fumbling with a clasp and the clicking of a lock. The sounds of the men stuffing into the cab, and the doors closing behind them. Then the engine fired up with a rough growl that settled to a grumble. It backed out, rattling over the remnants of the battered-down fence before reaching the pavement and turning around.

Rico lay still, listening to the rhythmic sounds of the engine and frame. The big tires gnawing at the road. His heart was still rapid-firing, quaking with such intensity that he could hear it in the tight confines of the box.

He tried to keep calm—fought to with everything he had. Tried to visualize where they were driving, each turn and change of speed. They were heading farther inland, that much was certain. And ten minutes later they turned what he thought was south. He closed his eyes and pictured a map of his island home. Pinned their position onto it. There wasn't much there. Farms and rural houses.

After another ten minutes, the paved road turned to dirt. It shook and jostled him around as the truck weaved back and forth. Bounced up and down. Another five minutes passed. He tried to place them again. They'd be near the heart of the island. A whole lot of nothing for miles in all directions. Dense, flat tropical jungle as far as the eye could see.

The truck braked to a stop and he heard a big gate swing open with a creak. The truck accelerated again, cruising onto a flatter dirt road. It slowed, then stopped again. The engine shut off, the constant violent vibrations giving way to perfect calm.

Muffled voices filled the air, then the bed creaked as two men climbed into the truck. They unlocked and opened the lid, dousing the box with a wave of brilliant light. Rico could see the faint glow through the fabric of the sack but couldn't make anything out as he was grabbed again and lifted out of the container. It was perfectly quiet, warm, and there was no wind.

An overhead door rumbled down from the ceiling, and they carried him down a set of stairs, then plopped him into a metal chair. The strings around his neck were loosened, then the sack was thrown off, basking him in a wave of bright light. He closed his eyes and blinked. Slowly made out blurry figures standing over him.

"Hello, Rico," a voice said.

It was the same voice from back in the woods. The one he'd recognized.

The blurriness faded and Warren Beauchamp Jr. came into focus just inches in front of his face.

"Wha... what do you want with me?"

Junior laughed. "Don't play dumb with us, kid." He crossed his arms. "Like Roman said back in town, we can do this the easy way or the hard way. But in the end, you'll give us what we want. Everyone always gives us what we want. One way or another."

Before Rico could ask again why he was there, Junior planted his hands on his knees and bent down, staring daggers into the young man. "What were you and Logan Dodge doing on the eastern side of the island this morning?"

Rico tried to hide his surprise, but his eyes widened and his mouth slacked uncontrollably. "We were diving."

Junior laughed. "No shit. But why?" He leaned forward, just inches in front of Rico's face. "Why were you diving there? Could it have anything to do with your boss's claims that he discovered a shipwreck?"

Rico sighed. "We were diving the wreck. Logan wanted to see it."

"And... what did you see down there? At the wreck?"

Rico shrugged. "I didn't see anything. I stayed on the boat."

"What did the others see?"

"Piles of ballast stones. Cannons. An anchor."

"Nothing else?"

Rico shook his head.

Junior stepped back, frowning and eyeing the young man like a disappointed teacher. Then he motioned to Roman, who cracked his knuckles, then grabbed a hammer from a counter at Rico's back. He knelt down, pinned Rico's left foot to the floor, then smacked the steel head into the exposed flesh.

Rico threw his head back and cried out, intense pain shooting up his body. His screams turned to frantic gasps for air and his face turned red.

Junior smiled, enjoying the young man's pain. He lunged forward, grabbed hold of the metal chair, and spun it around so Rico could see the counter behind him.

"Look around you," Junior spat. "What do you see?"

There were knives. Bolt cutters. Saws. Ropes. And there were bloodstains on the sleek concrete at his feet.

"What's this, Rico?" Junior said, holding up the gold coin Mick had given him. "This was in your pocket. What's a poor orphan like you doing with a gold coin in his pocket?"

Rico fell silent as Junior stared at him, waiting for

an answer. When none came, Junior snarled softly, then nodded and strode over to the worktable.

"You know, kid, there are a lot of effective methods for getting people to talk and do what we want them to do down here." He opened a drawer and pulled out a cooking blowtorch. "But for me, the simplest method is often the most effective."

He clicked a spark, and the short jet flame flashed to life. Rico could feel the heat radiating off the spraying inferno from two paces away, and it slowly amped up as Junior sauntered closer.

"This is the part where you tell us everything," Junior said, smiling sinisterly while waving the torch in front of his captive's face. "Where the wreck is and what it contains. And if you don't, I'm going to personally run this flame over every inch of your worthless body."

EIGHTEEN

I rushed back to my seat in the theater and whispered to Ange what had happened. Naturally, her reaction was similar to mine. And she planted her hands on the armrests, preparing to rise and take action.

"You two stay here," I whispered.

Scarlett, intrigued, looked away from the screen and leaned over. "What's going on?"

I placed a hand on Ange. "I'll check it out. You two stay. I'll try and be back before it ends."

She bit her bottom lip. Turned to look at the screen, then shifted back and kissed my cheek. "Be careful."

I nodded, rose, and shuffled back out of the theater.

Hopping into the Jeep, I fired it up, threw it in

gear, and blasted across town. Just under ten minutes later, I came to a stop next to two police cars and a small cluster of people gathered beside a chain-link fence that had been battered down.

Mick had explained that the first thing he'd done after calling the police was to follow Rico's path to his rented room roughly a mile inland from his shop. It was along the rushed walk that he found the broken fence. The tire marks. And Rico's backpack tangled in the spiral wire.

I rushed over and met Mick beside the police, who were hunched over the torn-up backpack.

"Any sign of him?" I said, hoping there'd been a positive update in the time it'd taken me to drive across town.

"Nothing yet," Mick said.

I looked around. "Where's Dorothy?"

As if my words had summoned her, the young woman appeared, stepping out from a nearby alley. She was wearing her orange waitress shorts and a black sweater, having evidently left straight from work. Kneeling down, she was scrutinizing the ground while shining one of their dive flashlights.

"Looks like there was a scuffle here," she said. "This trash can is knocked over, and there are scuff marks on the ground."

I eyed the police who were searching the bag. One of them was Officer Ramirez. He did a double take when he noticed me, then rose.

"What time did he call you?" I said to Mick.

The man didn't check the time stamp on his phone. He'd clearly already been asked the question.

"Eight thirty," he said.

I glanced at my watch and ran the math. It'd been an hour since he'd been taken.

After scanning over the broken stretch of fence, I peered back down at the bag. "His phone in there?"

"No," Officer Ramirez said. "Just books and dive gear."

"You tried calling it?"

"Only about a hundred times," Mick said.

"Recently?"

Both men shook their heads.

"Try again," I said.

Ramirez raised his eyebrows at me. "Are you a detective, Mr. Dodge?"

"No," I replied, still trying to recreate the scene in my mind. "But I've aided law enforcement on a few investigations in the past."

"He can help," Mick said. "That's why I called him."

Closing my eyes, I stepped away from the group a moment. Then I opened them, my gaze trailing from the alley to the fence and backpack, then the dirt road beyond it.

Officer Ramirez followed my gaze, then turned on a flashlight, illuminating where the pavement met the dirt. There were two sets of partially overlapping fresh tire tracks leading between the thick trees.

"You checked there?" I said.

"Just a quick sweep," Ramirez said. "Enough to see that the vehicle just stopped and backed out. We just got here. Wanted to search the bag and area around it first."

I nodded, then strode along the side of the dirt road, careful not to disturb anything. Mick handed me his backup flashlight, which I powered on. Standing over the muddy tracks, I could feel my blood simmer and then boil.

If I hadn't been certain who was responsible when I'd heard the news, that assurance came the moment I laid eyes on the marks. They were wide and deep. Ample grooves. Hefty spaced-out treads. Big off-road tires supporting a substantial amount of mass.

I glanced back at Mick, then shone the beam around the thick trees. "Try calling again."

He fished out his phone and did so as I walked along the edge of the dirt road, careful not to disturb the marks or anything else as I stuck to the encroaching grass.

We were silent a long moment, then Mick lowered his phone and shook his head. "Nothing."

"Try again."

He looked at me confused, then pressed call a second time, holding the phone up to his ear. I continued along slowly, listening. Just as another long moment was about to come to a close, I heard something. A faint artificial humming noise. Then it vanished.

"Nothing, Logan," Mick said.

I crossed the road and stepped into the forest.

"One more time, Mick."

He sighed. "Logan, I—"

"One more time," I repeated.

He did so. Then the humming returned. Louder and clearer. I crunched across the leaves, brushed aside branches, and shone my light at a phone resting screen down in the dirt near the base of an uprooted tree.

"Over here," I said.

I kept my distance as Mick and Officer Ramirez approached. Using a stick, I flipped the phone over. It was an old-style Nokia, and the screen revealed nothing but a slew of missed calls.

"Could check it for prints," I said, though for me that was pointless.

I already knew who the perpetrators were. All I needed to figure out was where they'd taken him.

I scanned the light across the disturbed dirt and leaves. Bent down when something caught my eye. It was blood. A light splatter of it across a dead palm leaf.

I stared at the dark crimson liquid for a moment. Not because I thought it would help me find Rico, but for motivation. It was his blood. Of that I was certain. The innocent young man had been grabbed and struck before being taken away. And staring at the splatter sparked a roaring blaze within me.

I rose and trekked back to the road without a word. Mick caught up to me when I reached the fence, with Officer Ramirez right on his heels.

"Well?" Ramirez said.

"I don't know," I lied. "But you should check that phone for prints. And have all ferry, airport, and marina personnel be on the lookout for him, of course." He hustled to catch up to me, and I added, "Then I don't know, send out a search party? Broadcast an emergency radio alert? It's a small island, right? He's got to be here somewhere. And you could have Coast Guard and police boats search all outgoing vessels."

Ramirez nodded. "We're already on it."

I paused, folding my arms as I took in the scene one more time.

"Let me guess," I said, shooting a stern gaze at Officer Ramirez, "young Espinoza has a record of past involvement with the cartel as well, huh? Just explain it away with that. Just like the others. No use even looking for him, right?"

The lawman clenched his jaw. "We'll find him, Logan. We all know Rico. And we know he isn't involved with cartel." Then he sighed forcibly and looked away before meeting my gaze once more, his eyes intense. "Trust me, you're not the only one upset by this."

I turned to Mick. "Take me through his path."

Mick nodded and motioned me toward the alley. I redirected him to my Jeep.

"We'll start at the shop," I said. "Where he started. Dorothy can come too." I strode toward the driver's-side door, then turned back to Officer Ramirez as I grabbed the handle. "We'll call you if we find anything more."

He nodded and I could tell he was close to saying thanks but only managed, "Good luck."

Mick climbed into the passenger seat and Dorothy into the back. I backed out and headed west. When we'd put some distance between us and the scene, I turned to Mick.

"You both need to pack a bag. You're staying with us."

"What? Why?" Mick said.

I looked him sternly in the eyes. "You and I both know good and well why Rico was taken tonight. Or do you think it was just a coincidence that the kid was abducted on the same day you showed me the wreck?"

Mick fell silent. "Someone saw us."

"Yes."

He shifted in his seat uncomfortably, then turned and peered at the empty road behind us. "But why would that lead someone to take Rico? No one believes me about the wreck anyway."

"It's true," Dorothy chimed in, her voice cracking with emotion. I peeked at the rearview mirror and watched as she quickly swiped away a trailing tear. "No one believes it's real."

I braked to a stop at an intersection, then gunned us back up to speed.

"Think about what the kid left behind?" I said. "His bag. With nothing but books and dive gear. And his phone."

"Why is that important, though?" Mick said.

"It's important because it tells us something he didn't leave behind."

Mick threw his forehead into his palm. "The doubloon."

"Exactly. And what do you think is going to happen when these guys find that? Gold coins like that are rarely resting alone at the bottom of the sea. And never at the site of a wreck."

Dorothy leaned forward, still choking up with emotion. "But Rico doesn't know where the wreck is. Not exactly. Only Dad does."

"Which is why you're coming to stay with us," I said. "Just until I get to the bottom of this."

I turned south, cruised a couple more blocks, then eased off the gas. Keeping my eyes peeled for movement in the dark street, I surveyed the outside of Mick's dive shop and the nearby structures. After driving past to make sure the nearby alleys were clear, I threw the Jeep in reverse, then accelerated us back to the shop. Braking to a stop, I motioned for the door while keeping the engine idling.

Before Mick slid out, I grabbed him by the arm. "I'll be here. Five minutes."

They were back in three, both carrying backpacks. Mick switched off the lights and locked up the place behind him.

"Good thing our guests checked out this morning," he said as they climbed back in. "You still want to walk Rico's commute route? He heads that way first before turning—"

"No," I said, putting it back in drive and gassing out of there. He shot a question at me with his eyes, so I added, "'Cause we already know who did this."

NINETEEN

Warren Beauchamp Jr. was breathing heavily, his forehead filmed in sweat, when a door opened behind him. He stepped back, then turned to see one of his men holding up a cellphone.

"Your father called," was all the man said.

Junior turned rigid, stepped away from his victim and grabbed a rag from a counter. Washed his hands in the sink, the blood splashing away in the soap and pooling into the drain.

"Well?" Junior said.

The man sighed. "Boss wants to see you at the main house."

Junior nodded gravely. Toweled off his hands.

"Keep him locked up," he said, pointing toward Rico.

He sat with his hands still bound behind him, his battered body motionless and his head bowed.

Junior pocketed the gold coin, then straightened his shirt, climbed the stairs, and stepped out through a back door and into the night. The air was calm, the wall of trees surrounding the structure barely swaying. But there was a storm coming. Not winds and rains, thunder and lightning. Much worse than that. And with every step, Junior could feel it brewing. Growing stronger. More imminent.

He threaded through the trees and came out onto a path that wound west. Up ahead was a large Spanish Colonial single-story house surrounded by a wall. At the entrance, he stopped behind a wrought-iron gate and a sentry eyed him for a split second before creaking it open without a word.

Junior made for the interior, passing long-ago-abandoned flowerpots and a weathered, bone-dry fountain. He entered and crossed a simple living room into a big, dimly lit office with a solid mahogany desk stretching nearly across the room near the opposite wall. There was a lit fireplace in the corner, flames causing the dried logs to crackle and pop. Two worn leather couches faced each other in the middle of the space. Behind the desk were windows, but the curtains were drawn.

Junior closed the door behind him, then sat on one of the couches and waited. He knew the drill. It wasn't his first grilling.

By the time he heard approaching footsteps, it was nearly midnight. And he'd been waiting the better part of an hour.

The door swung open suddenly, and the leader of

their operation appeared, wearing his usual tailored Italian suit. He shot a rapid, irritated look toward Junior, then Diego appeared at his back, the massive bodyguard barely fitting through the doorway.

Diego shut the door at their backs, then took post behind Junior, his muscular arms folded in front of him. The leader sauntered behind the desk. He drummed his fingers on the hardwood and let out a long, disappointed breath.

"Which of my words were unclear this morning, Warren?" he said, his voice cold and calm. "I told you this was your last chance. I told you what would happen if you didn't show up today." He paused, rubbing his mouth. "And now I learn that... not only did you not do as you were told, but you also abducted someone without permission."

"I... I can explain," Junior stumbled. "There—"

His mouth clamped shut as the leader pointed a finger, the man's eyes hard and menacing. Junior swallowed. Then felt his pulse quicken even more.

"It must be made clear that no one is above this operation," the leader continued, ambling around the desk and closing in on Junior. "Not even you. We are in desperate times. Hanging on by a damn thread." The intimidating man closed in dramatically, his hands planted firmly on his hips. "Ever since those damn bankers in Mexico City figured out what we're up to, we've been forced to cut expenses to the bone with all our businesses. Forced to acquire funds by any means necessary. And you choose now to screw off and pull shit like this?" He stopped directly in front of the young man. Licked the inside of his cheek. Shook his head. "There are only so many chances that can be given. Only so much insubordination that can be tolerated."

In a sudden flash of movement, the leader tightened his left hand into a fist, stepped forward, and bashed his knuckles into Junior's cheek. His ring struck hard, gouging into the tender flesh. The young man's head spun, and he caught himself on the leather, nearly falling.

Recovering as best he could from the sudden, severe strike, Junior peered up and shot an evil glare toward the leader as blood trickled down from the wound.

"You think you're better than the rest, kid?" the suited criminal said. "You think you're untouchable? Well, let me just show you how gravely mistaken you are."

The man turned and strode across the office. Cracked open the door and motioned his head. Footsteps resounded. Then a moment later, Warren Beauchamp Sr. appeared in the doorway.

"Have a seat across from your son, Warren," the leader said.

The gray-haired man did as ordered, walking slowly. He wore a gray suit without the jacket. Slumped onto the couch across from Junior, but kept his gaze on the man in charge.

The boss retraced his steps and threw another sudden punch, this one striking Junior across the jaw, the ring slicing a second violent gash. Junior jolted and winced from the blow. More blood trickled down.

Then the leader slugged Junior in the gut, pounding the air from his lungs. The young man keeled forward, nearly falling from the chair again.

He heaved, his eyes big as he looked from the boss to his father.

The leader chuckled. "He won't do anything, kid." He reached out and grabbed Junior by the neck and squeezed. "I could wring the life out of you right here and now, and he won't do a damn thing. You know why? Fear. He knows what I'll do. He's witnessed what I'm capable of firsthand."

He released Junior's neck, letting the struggling man catch his breath. The leader flexed the reddened knuckles of his left hand as he stepped back around his desk, opened a cupboard in the back wall, and ceremoniously pulled out a well-crafted wooden club with serrated blades embedded along the sides. Gripping the old Mesoamerican sword by the handle, the man turned and held it up for the others to see.

"Are you familiar with the macahuitl, Junior?" he said, inspecting the weapon's craftsmanship. "Quite simply, it is viewed as one of the most barbaric and horrific melee weapons in the history of mankind. Over a meter of solid oak, weighing in at six pounds, with prismatic blades fixed along the sides."

He brought the club closer and tapped a finger to one of the cutting edges. "Did you know that obsidian can be honed to a blade far sharper and more durable than any other substance on Earth? In fact," the man said, sauntering around the desk toward the others, "the volcanic glass is so sharp, the blades are still used in surgery to this day."

He closed in on Junior and demonstrated the obsidian's effectiveness by cutting a slit into his left shoulder. Junior cried and covered the wound with his hand, looking up at the leader with equal parts terror and rage in his eyes.

"On the floor, now," the leader barked, pointing to the spot with the macahuitl.

Junior hesitated, so the man cut him again. This time across the other shoulder, and deeper.

The young man gritted his teeth and hunched forward as blood flowed from the deep wound.

"Now, you useless piece of crap," the leader hissed.

Junior quivered as he slid down. Looked to his father, the man just staring back blankly.

"On your knees!" the leader shouted menacingly. When Junior did as he was told, the leader nudged him with the weapon. "In the middle."

Junior shifted over, crawled, then reached the center of the office and looked up, his breathing panicky, his eyes big and wild.

"This thing will split your skull in half like a frail, dried log," the leader said as he raised the weapon high over his head.

He held it there a moment. Watching as Junior shook, cowering in fear. His head bowed slightly, his shoulders and cheek and jaw bleeding. His eyes struck with sheer terror.

The leader counted to five in his head, enjoying the suspense, then spoke slowly and calmly. "Now, you have ten seconds to convince me not to end your miserable, sorry excuse of a life right here and now." The stoic killer narrowed his gaze. "One... two..."

"There's a shipwreck," Junior gasped. He coughed, fought back the pain, and swiftly added. "Filled with gold. It's—"

"Bullshit," the leader snapped, then flexed his

arms back, raising the macahuitl even higher.

"It's true," Junior rasped. "I... I can prove it."

He shoved a shaky hand into his pocket and pulled out the gold coin. Held it up like an offering to spare his life.

The leader softened a moment, eyed the coin, then snatched and examined it. It was old and worn. A Spanish doubloon. He'd seen similar ones before.

"The guy we captured tonight?" Junior gasped. "He had it on him. Says it came from the wreck they found just off the coast. We saw their boat this morning and the divers aboard, including the guy from—"

"What good is it to us? Even thousands of these won't be enough."

Junior collected himself as best he could, his eyes still flashing toward the razor-sharp obsidian edges. "I've searched it. A lost galleon like that would be worth hundreds of millions. Don't you see? This could change everything. Save the whole operation. We could all live like kings."

The leader fell into deep thought while examining the coin. "And... this kid you abducted today. He told you where it is?"

Junior's head lowered slightly. "No. He doesn't know exactly. But the guy he works for, Mick Flanagan. He knows."

The leader stood still a moment, then rotated the macahuitl side to side, the shiny blades twinkling in the light from the fire. He turned on his heel suddenly, ambled around the desk, and set the weapon on the hardwood.

"This had better lead somewhere," he said. "If not,

the tortures you've witnessed these past weeks will be nothing compared to what I'll do to you, understand?" He stared at the coin once more, then added, "You'll go and get this diver the kid works for. Right away."

Junior smiled, then his eyes widened. "You want us to go now? Cops will be out in force after what—"

"You let me handle that." The leader motioned to Diego, and the massive bodyguard stepped out from the shadows. "You go with them. Make sure there are no mistakes."

TWENTY

"Where does the punk live?" I said, glancing over at Mick, then eyeing Dorothy through the rearview mirror as I drove west toward the waterfront.

It's a small island. I figured they should at least have an idea.

"He's got a place not far from here," Mick said.

I turned left, cruising south along the seawall. Less than five minutes later, I pulled into the parking garage beside the movie theater. The timing matched up nearly perfectly, with Ange and Scarlett stepping out through the sliding glass doors a minute after we stopped.

Mick climbed into the back, Scarlett sat beside Dorothy, and Ange took the passenger seat so I could bring her up to speed. I told her everything while cruising back onto the coastal road, continuing south.

She fired off a question before I finished.

"Does he know where the wreck is?" she said, her analytical mind in overdrive.

Mick shot me an impressed look, then said, "No. Just a broad area. Not close enough to pinpoint it without intensive searching with top-of-the-line equipment."

My wife had managed to identify the most important question. It was the most pivotal query for two reasons: one, it showed that we all knew the motive for Rico's capture, and two, it showed that the kid was likely still alive. If he had been abducted to help criminals locate the wreck, they'd likely beat him for answers. Since he didn't have the answers, they'd leave him alive. At least for the time being. In my experience, once criminals get what they want from someone, the victim is usually dealt with in the most discreet way possible.

"The police on it?" Ange said.

"Just like they're supposedly on the other missing people as well," I said sarcastically. "This one seems different, though. Local kid. Visibly upset officers at the crime scene. And no chance of reasoning it away with cartel involvement. But—"

"But you're going to get involved," Ange said.

I sighed. "Every time I speak to Officer Ramirez it's like the guy's got higher-ups breathing down his neck. I don't know who it is. Likely a bought-off politician or police chief. Whoever it is, somebody's got them on a leash. Big money and power behind the scenes. He even said so back at the boat launch."

We fell silent as I accelerated past the southern

cruise pier, the landscape gradually shifting from city to forest. I pushed the Jeep hard and soon pulled into our complex, the guard opening the gate. Crunching across the gravel, I parked in our reserved spot.

I left the engine running. Sat frozen with my hands on the vibrating wheel, then shot a look at Ange. It was a familiar one. One she knew well. We had a whole conversation with our eyes, then I looked at the dashboard clock. Every second that ticked on was increasing the chances of no one ever seeing Rico again.

"Come on," Ange said, pushing open her door. "Everyone inside."

Dorothy slid out, then Scarlett. Mick hesitated, then leaned forward.

"I'm going with you," he said flatly. Before I could interject, he held up a hand. "Logan, the kid's like a son to me. We're the only family he's got."

I nodded to him and he climbed back into the passenger seat.

Ange strode over, leaned in through my window. "You'll call if things get out of hand."

"Yes, ma'am," I said, planting a quick kiss on her cheek.

"And I'll be tracking your phone. Just in case."

She stepped back as the statement left her lips, her fiery blue eyes boring into mine. Then she turned toward the stairwell with Scarlett and Dorothy.

I sat quiet for a second, thinking over her words, then shoved my door open.

"I'll be right back."

Hustling up to our unit, I went straight to the master bedroom closet and grabbed my backpack.

Shouldering one of the straps, I retraced my steps, landing a second kiss on my wife's cheek for good luck before hitting the stairs and climbing back into the Jeep.

I set the bag on the back seat. In addition to other items I've deemed essential over the years, the pack contained a tiny magnetic tracking device I figured might come in handy.

I slid the shifter into reverse, backed out, then gassed out of the complex and back onto the main road, heading north.

"That's why you called me, huh?" I said after a minute of silence. "You knew I'd intervene."

He nodded. "You're the kind of man who gets stuff done. I knew it right off the bat. A man of action. Someone who can disrupt the status quo with the best of them."

I'd never heard myself described that way, but I liked it.

Mick tapped a fist against his chin. "I just don't get what Rico has to do with the three other victims. What connects them?"

I remembered what the taxi driver on our first day on the island had said. How one of the men who'd vanished had reappeared on a remote beach, his body rotted and decayed and eaten away by marine life. I remembered picturing a mangled corpse washing up while swimming at the beach a few days earlier. For a brief moment, I pictured it again. This time with Rico's face.

I snapped out of it. Thought over Mick's question.

"What do these guys engage in?" I said, trying to logic my way through it. "This Beauchamp and his son? Keep it simple."

Mick shrugged. "Business."

"And what is business all about?"

"Money."

"There you go. Money connects them."

"So they grabbed Rico for the prospect of finding treasure. But what about the other three?"

I shook my head. "We'll find out. But when we do, it'll be green. You can see it in these guys' eyes. The greed. It's there."

We cruised back past the southern cruise pier and the stretches of hotels that followed. Then I slowed as we cut through a short residential area and parked against the curb.

"That's the place?" I said, Mick having pointed out the house on our drive to the villa.

I pointed the crown of my head through the side of the windshield, toward a lot two driveways down and on the opposite side of the street.

Mick nodded, his gaze narrowing. "It was sold just after the Beauchamps arrived. I see his truck pull in and out of there from time to time."

I gazed at the shared wall running along the street, each property with its own separate barriers running perpendicular and partitioning off the lots. Gates blocked the driveways. Lots of tall trees all around. Dark for the most part.

The house was unassuming from the street, but most likely nice on the inside. Probably a pool out back. Not waterfront, but just across the road. Close enough to walk to both branches of downtown, but far away and quiet enough to avoid suspicious onlookers. A smart location. One above Warren Beauchamp Jr.'s mental paygrade. No doubt chosen by the guy running things. His rich father.

I pulled up just a half lot away from the driveway and shut off the Jeep. Mick and I both climbed out, but before I shut the door, I pulled out the floormat.

I looked up and down the street. Seeing we were relatively clear, I approached the wall, then unfurled the mat. Reaching high, I used it to cover a spread of cemented glass bottle shards.

I climbed over first, heaving myself up, taking a brief scan of the shadowy grounds, and sliding up and falling into the yard. My initial scan had been for just one thing: dogs. Thousands of years of technological advancements, and I'd yet to encounter a more effective and efficient home security system. Fortunately, there weren't any.

My second sweep was for cameras, and besides the one by the gate and one above the front door, there weren't any of those either.

Mick climbed up and dropped down beside me. Surprisingly agile for any man, let alone a guy in his late forties. The short driveway held only one vehicle, a silver sedan.

"I don't think Rico's here," Mick said.

"He isn't," I stated.

Before he could say more, I took off into a fast walk along the adjacent wall, sticking to the shadows. No dogs, weak security system, one car in the drive. I went for the fastest means of entry. I used a rock to crack loose a section of window around the right side of the residence, then reached in to unlatch the lock and hinged it open. I slid down into the dining room. The place was clean. Small but well appointed. And the furniture looked brand-new.

I went straight for a nearby closet. Opened it up and began rifling through raincoats and sliding out drawers.

"I don't get it," Mick whispered. "If you know Rico isn't here, why'd we break in?"

A sound caused us both to freeze. A muffled, synchronous ringing noise coming from upstairs. I hurried stealthily up the tile steps to the second floor. Managed to reach the top and trace the sound to a back door before it was silenced.

When I was halfway down the hall, the door opened and a shirtless guy stepped out. He instantly flicked on the lights and was blinking and rubbing his eyes. He held a phone in his right hand, but nothing else. It was a good two seconds after the lights turned on before he realized I was there.

When he did, he stared, dumbfounded, his mouth agape.

"What the hell—"

I lunged forward, grabbed him by the shoulders and bashed his head into the wall. He went down fast and hard. Knocked out at my feet. I knelt down and scooped up his phone. Stepping over his body, I entered the bedroom he'd exited and flicked on the light. Listened carefully for anyone inside to react to the words and the loud thump. When it was clear this guy was the only one home, I searched the room.

I turned over the closet, not finding what I was looking for. Then I checked the nightstands. No dice either. Then I threw open the dresser drawers one at a time and found a Taurus 9mm pistol in the third one I tried, and then a Bersa .45 in the fourth. Both were loaded with full magazines.

I handed the Taurus to Mick.

"These are why," I said, stowing the hand cannon in the back of my waistband while striding back into the hall.

Mick followed as I hustled down the stairs, climbed back through the window, skirted across the yard, and scaled the wall. Eight minutes after leaving, we were back in the Jeep. I unfolded and repositioned the floor mat, then fired up the engine right away and accelerated north.

"That was the only lead I have," Mick said, glancing back over his shoulder toward the house, which was growing smaller at our backs. "I don't know where to look now. I don't know how else to find these guys." He paused. "We should head back. Search for a clue or something, right? Maybe splash some cold water on that guy's face and force him to talk."

"We don't need to find them," I said, keeping my eyes on the road.

I slid the guy's phone out and showed Mick the home screen. There was a brief message.

Meet at Lucky Divers. 1300.

Mick's eyes lit up, and I said, "Your shop's gonna have visitors tonight."

TWENTY-ONE

Less than an hour later, at just past one in the morning, a black SUV with tinted windows braked to a stop right in front of Mick's dive shop.

"Next time make our presence more obvious," Diego growled, shaking his head as he eyed the dark shop. "And where's your other guy, Warren? He was supposed to meet us here, right?"

"He's not answering his phone," Junior replied. "And you're worried about some old washed-up charter captain?"

Diego snarled, then turned to the driver. "Keep it idling."

He opened the passenger door and climbed out. Three others followed suit and were led by the hulking bodyguard to the shop's front door.

Diego carried a metal battering ram and, upon reaching the entrance, heaved back the thirty-five pounds of steel and bashed it into the door. The single explosive strike did the trick, smashing the door free.

They flooded inside single file. Made a mess of things, pushing aside chairs and tables as they barged back through the curtain. They clicked on flashlights and shined the beams over lockers filled with various dive gear, the smell of neoprene and saltwater hanging thick in the air. They paused as they heard noises coming from upstairs. Voices.

Diego pointed toward a narrow staircase, and the three others followed him. Duct tape in hand. Ready to grab Mick, just like Junior and his boys had grabbed Rico earlier that very evening. The stairs cut ninety degrees at the halfway point, and at the top was a short hall with three closed doors. One down to the right, and two back to the left. The one at the end of the hall had light bleeding out through the cracks around the door. And the voices were coming from inside it. By then it was obvious that a television was on. Some guy talking about the wonders of diving and such.

Diego ordered one of the guys to search the other rooms, while the remaining two followed him down the hall. The brute reached for the knob. It was unlocked. He withdrew his pistol, then motioned for the other two to do the same. With three barrels aimed at the door, he rotated his grip and pushed, slow at first, then a thunderous shove.

He barged in, scanning his eyes and pistol over the space. It was a small bedroom, with clothes on the floor and a messed-up blanket on the bed. A single nightstand, a dresser, and a smudged-up mirror. The TV was loud and displayed images of divers exploring a colorful underwater world. But there was no sign of life.

As the three walked over the room, they clicked off the television, then heard shuffling in an adjoining bathroom. The soft patter of bare feet against tile, then a quick gasp.

Diego smiled, stepped to the door. When the others were ready at his back once more, he grabbed the knob. This one was locked. His smile broadened, knowing full well that few things jack up the heart rate of a victim faster than pounding a door free.

He took a half step back, planted his weight on his left foot, then spun and bashed his right heel into the slab just beside the knob. The thin old door splintered free with barely any resistance, one of the hinges tearing free as the wood swung and cracked and hung over to the right. The moment the doorway emptied, Diego focused in on a golf club swinging straight toward him. He shifted and inched back, letting the clubhead smack into the wooden frame.

Mick, who was wearing shorts and a tank top, yelled out and tried to swing the 2-iron again. But Diego caught the attack, then chuckled as he jerked the club free and punched Mick in the gut. The man crumpled and went down. Diego grabbed a fistful of his tank top and hauled him up.

"You're even dumber than we expected, you know that?" He laughed again, turned and tossed him to the bedroom floor.

"What do you want from me?" Mick gasped.

"Oh, don't worry," Diego said. "You'll find out

soon enough."

He motioned to Junior, who grabbed Mick by an arm and hauled him up with the other guy.

"Get this useless pile of trash downstairs," Diego said, then glanced at the time.

Four minutes, he thought. *Could be a new record.*

Diego took up the rear as they dragged Mick down to the living room. Halfway down the steps, Junior froze, then turned back.

"Where's Roman?" he said.

He and Diego exchanged glances. Then Junior called out his name but heard nothing in reply as they stared up into the darkness.

"Punk, you tape his wrists," Diego said, tossing Mick to the floor once they'd reached the bottom. "Brooks, check it out."

They both did as ordered. Diego held Mick in place while Junior ripped a length of duct tape free and wrapped it tight around Mick's lower wrists, his palms facing each other.

"Anyone else here with you tonight?" Diego said.

Mick shook his head.

"Your daughter's not here?"

"No."

"No guests in your crappy hostel?"

"No."

A loud thud shook the quiet shop. Diego withdrew his pistol and whipped around. The noise was followed by more silence.

"No one here, huh?" Diego said.

"Let's go," Junior said, holding on to Mick nervously. "We have what we came for."

Diego glared at the spoiled punk. "Pathetic

coward."

"We—"

"Stay here," the beast of a man snapped, shoving a finger in the guy's face. "You leave before I get back and I'm gonna break every bone in your useless body."

Junior swallowed hard, sheer terror gripping at him. It wasn't just the man's size or intensity. It was his eyes. His ghastly persona that sucked all the air out of the room. A killer through and through. And a damn good one. Hard and inhuman.

Junior nodded, and Diego turned and swaggered toward the stairs. He waited a moment, then heard a faint commotion coming from the top. Then a body tumbled into view, jarring down the steps and coming to a stop just after it tumbled around the corner. It was Brooks.

Diego's expression tightened.

A lesser man might have been scared off. But the monster of a man saw it as a challenge. A personal provocation. A throwing down of the gauntlet.

He knew who it was that was calling him out. It was a small island. He'd been informed of the connection with the dive operator and had been itching for an encounter since he'd heard what had happened at the boat launch.

Raising his weapon, Diego took on the steps slowly, ready for anything.

TWENTY-TWO

The first guy went down without so much as a whimper.

In my experience, when someone enters a room with their weapon drawn, alert and ready, their eyes tend to focus on the back wall first. Human instinct, I guess. And this guy was no different.

I was crouched in the shadows as he approached the door. My pulse elevated and my breathing fast, though quiet and controlled, having just climbed the side ladder of the adjoining building and entered through Dorothy's bedroom window.

I waited, ready as the guy reached the door. He shoved it open. Hinges squealing. The slab smacking against the wall. His pistol leveled. Aimed at the wall directly in front of him. Chest height. Head swiveling, but not fast enough. His first step inside came before he'd completed his survey, leaving me in his blind spot just beyond the outstretched fingers of his peripherals.

By the time he realized someone was there, it was too late. I already had him by the wrist, leveraging his lower arm with one hand while shouldering his bicep with the other.

The weapon fell free, landing softly on the pink rug as I forced the man to the floor and shoved a folded-up towel into his face to keep him quiet. I knocked him out with a short, powerful blow to the back of the head, then turned and kept perfectly still. Listening.

I heard a door splinter in the far bedroom. Then a scuffle broke out. Chaotic curses and attacks, followed by grunts of pain and submission.

With no one having heard the takedown, I dragged the guy to the middle of the bedroom, kicked his weapon aside, then checked the hall before swinging the door and leaving it open just a crack.

Then I turned and crept into what I thought was Dorothy's closet, shutting the door behind me. Turned out it was a small office and storage space. A tiny desk filled with papers and notes. An old desktop computer. Cabinets and shelves of densely packed folders. The heart of a small, family-run dive operation struggling to make it. Numbers adding up and canceling out others, hoping to stay alive for another year beneath the waves.

Scanning over the organized chaos, my eyes rested on a short metal bat. It was usually used to quickly put down a flopping fish, but Mick utilized it as a paperweight.

I grabbed the bat and listened carefully, just inches from the door as a line of heavy footsteps trudged down the hallway, men escorting Mick down the steps to the living room. As I'd hoped, the scuffle with Mick and his golf club had caused them to forget about the rest of the house, and their other man. That was, until the excitement wore off.

The conversing subsisted downstairs for a moment, then footsteps returned as one of them headed back up the stairs. His movements were slow. Cautious. And he called out a guy's name as he ascended.

Like a moth to the flame, he crept straight for the cracked-open door. I gripped the handle, trying to time my entrance carefully, picturing him in my mind as he entered the bedroom. I peeked through, catching a blurry glimpse as he moved across the room.

Just as he reached the other side of the bed and gazed down at his friend's motionless body, I threw the closet door open, lunged forward, and swung the bat toward his head. But this guy was more experienced than his buddy I'd just put to sleep. He managed to dodge left just as the makeshift weapon completed its arc, the dense metal object grazing his chin and driving into his shoulder. Painful and potent, but not a knockout blow.

As I reared for another go, he sprung loose with a rapid jab to my side that landed solid. Then he swung his pistol sideways, aiming for my head. I ducked, swooped, wrapped my arms around his midsection and heaved him off the ground. Then I muscled him back and dropped him, throwing him facefirst into the corner of the tile and sheetrock.

His neck cracked. Then the rest of his body collapsed with a loud thump. I withdrew my pistol, aiming toward the door and taking a moment to catch my breath.

Muffled conversation echoed from the ground floor, but no one came up the stairs.

I guess they're waiting for an invitation.

I stowed my weapon back in my waistband, then slid the dead guy's pistol under the bed and grabbed him by the ankles. Still enraged by the thought of Rico being taken, I dragged him out of the room and threw him down the stairs, picking a fight with whoever remained.

His lifeless body tumbled violently to the landing, then came to a stop halfway down the bottom set of steps. Then I was back in the shadows.

I paused, but didn't have to wait for long. A smile formed on my lips as I heard movement heading for the base of the stairs. When a heavy boot struck one of the lower steps, I headed down the hall into the master bedroom. I clicked off the lights, leaving only the moonlight spilling in through the window.

When the sounds of heavy movement reached the top, I knocked over a mug resting on Mick's chest of drawers, the sound of shattering pottery piercing the quiet.

My adversary spun and lurched down the hall. I crept behind the bed, lay down on my side, and propped my left foot against Mick's bedside lamp. Resting on my right elbow, my arm bent at a wide angle, I grabbed the corner of an empty suitcase under the bed with my left hand and waited.

Within seconds, the door swung open and a monstrous figure filled the frame. Tall. Wide shoulders. A towering specimen with his pistol raised straight ahead.

I narrowed my gaze and shoved the lamp with my foot, sliding it across the nightstand and into the wall. The guy sprung right and opened fire, sending two rounds into the shadowy corner. I slid back the suitcase, putting the guy's shoes and lower pant legs in view for a split second.

The man lunged forward and I pulled the trigger, his movements too sudden for the round to hit home. In a blink, he was off the floor and somersaulting over the bed. I redirected my aim, firing two more shots through the fabric and springs. But my athletic, colossal opponent just beat the lead projectiles and avalanched off the edge of the bed and into my sprawled-out body.

I felt every pound of his massive frame as he body-slammed me, his hands going straight for my right forearm. Driving a knee into my chest, he clobbered my weapon free, nearly splintering my wrist in the process.

I bit back by plowing a fist into the man's jaw, then redirected my hand back, hooking behind the top of his neck and slamming his head down while snatching the weapon held firmly in his grasp. We rolled left, and I shoved his gun hand skyward. He pulled the trigger in rapid, deafening succession, blasting a line of holes in the ceiling before I managed to force his weapon free as well.

The act of disarming him put my body in an awkward position. Left me open, my right arm overextended. The brute seized the moment, grabbing hold of my shirt and landing two powerful punches into my midsection before rocking back and hurling me across the room. I struck the wall beside the window, my spine battering a dent in the sheetrock, then spun and crashed into the dresser. Stumbling, I fought to regain my balance.

The man wasted no time. Didn't give me a moment to recover. The second I focused through the confusion of the impossibly strong blow, I saw him charging at me like a bull. I braced and he forced me into the corner, throwing a series of blistering punches. I blocked what I could and threw my own, exchanging blows and fending him off like a boxer tied up in the corner of a ring. He yelled out, grunted, then grabbed me by the neck and lifted me clear off the floor.

He was far bigger and stronger than I was. And he had me cornered, and I could feel my neck crunching under the force of his herculean grip. I landed a punch across his nose, which only made him grit his teeth and squeeze harder.

With just seconds until my mind went lights out, I remembered the layout of the bedroom. Remembered what was mounted up in the corner above my head. Unable to see it, I reached high, felt around a fraction of a second, then gripped the edges of the mirror.

Pulling with everything I had, I jerked the glass oval free and slammed it down. My adversary loosened his grasp and lowered me as he tried to raise his free hand in defense, but he wasn't fast enough. The mirror barreled down, bashing into the top of his head and shattering to pieces.

He lurched back and hunched over, giving me a brief opening. I kneed him in the chest to create separation, then slid to the floor, spun, and threw a roundhouse into his gut.

He tumbled backward into a controlled roll, then abruptly came back tall and strong with a knife in his right hand. He snarled, blood dripping down from the cuts to his head and face. Enraged, he eyed me like I was his worst enemy.

Battered myself, I fought to control my breathing as I reached behind me and came back with my dive knife. He yelled and charged again. Trying to catch him off guard, I reared back and hurled the blade, still dizzy from the blows to my head. My aim was off, and the knife whooshed through the air before finding a target in the man's right thigh, the razor tip burying itself deep.

His knee buckled, and he nearly faceplanted as he stopped and took the weight off his right leg. Rolling left, I grabbed hold of Mick's 2-iron resting halfway under the bed. Squeezing the handle tight, I whirled around and smashed the clubhead into the guy's skull. His head cracked, and his neck snapped. And he went lifeless, his body toppling like a falling tree and breaking the bed frame on his fall.

I eyed him for a moment as I caught my breath. Wiped the blood from my lip, then found my pistol and exchanged it for the golf club.

The brief lapse in the commotion ended abruptly as the sound of a gunshot echoed from downstairs. I gripped my weapon tight and made for the door, raising it chest height as I traversed the hall and took on the steps. The front door slammed, then two more shots followed. I reached the living room to find Mick lying beside the couch, his pistol raised toward the open entryway.

Through the barred windows, I saw Junior limping toward the idling SUV. I rushed for the door and exited just as the vehicle's engine thundered and its tires burned rubber, leaving plumes of thick, bitter smoke as they accelerated. I took careful aim and fired, shattering the rear window and pelting the license plate. The SUV blasted away in a noisy blur, then screeched right onto a major cross street, heading inland.

I lowered my weapon and reentered the house just as Mick came to his feet.

"Where'd you hit him?" I said as I grabbed one of the knives he had for sale and slashed the tape restraining his wrists.

"Lower leg," Mick said.

I nodded and motioned outside. "Come on. This night's far from over."

Following me out into the glow of a streetlight, Mick examined me for the first time.

"Holy crap, are you all right?"

I didn't bother inspecting myself, knowing that would only make it worse. I was well enough to move and see and wasn't bleeding to death. That was all I cared about at the moment.

"I'm fine," I said, then motioned to the Jeep.

It didn't take an extensive look at our surroundings to notice the lines of locals gazing out their windows or standing in the street, wondering what all the commotion was about. Sporadic gunshots drew attention just about anywhere in the world, but shootings were especially rare on Cozumel. It was statistically one of the safest places on the whole planet. A tourist town.

My ears caught distant sirens as I opened the door and slid into the driver's seat. I grumbled the engine to life, then performed a tight U-turn, cruising south.

"You get it planted?" Mick said.

I pulled out my phone and brought up a GPS application. Thumbing the screen, I got it to display a red dot moving steadily east across the island.

Prior to engaging the criminals, I'd climbed out Dorothy's window and vaulted onto the roof of the next-door laundromat. When the SUV had pulled up and the four men had headed inside, I'd immediately climbed down a side ladder and attached the tiny tracking device to the undercarriage before returning to the second floor of Mick's shop.

"Oh yeah," I said, observing the tracker's movement across the screen. "We got 'em."

TWENTY-THREE

Ange was sitting in the living room with our laptop open when we arrived back at the unit.

We hadn't notified the police yet. We'd left a mess back at the dive shop. Two dead and one on the brink of it. Gunshots and broken glass. Vehicles peeling out. And witnesses.

Fortunately we made it the nine miles back to the complex without being stopped. The last thing we wanted was to have to deal with the incident at the shop—to waste precious time dealing with red tape. Explaining what had happened and most likely being taken into custody and questioned.

No, it would be far easier to explain everything once we had Rico safe and sound, and the culprits either in handcuffs or dead. Then we could deal with the fallout of it all. But the priority was finding the teenager. And making sure that, when he was found, it wasn't after he washed up dead on a beach a week from now.

"Jeez, Logan, what happened?" Ange said, eyeing me up and down as we entered.

On the drive back, I'd called Ange to inform her that I'd placed a tracker on the criminals' getaway vehicle. What I hadn't mentioned were the little altercations I'd gotten into after planting the device.

"I'm fine," I said, doing my best to ignore the afflictions.

Dorothy and Scarlett rushed from the bedroom.

"Did you find him?" Dorothy said.

"Soon," I said sternly, moving over to Ange.

I winced as I dropped down beside her and eyed the monitor. The adrenaline from the scuffle was wearing off and I was beginning to really feel it. Every potent wound and bruise.

"What happened?" Ange said again.

"We had a run-in with the Beauchamp punk and his buddies," Mick said.

"You killed him?" Scarlett said.

I shook my head. "Not yet. Fortunately he made it out."

The girls looked at us, confused, then I pointed to the monitor. "But we have his position."

"Beauchamp's buddies did this to you?" Ange said, making no attempt to hide her bewilderment.

"Well, there was another guy," I said. "He proved more... problematic."

"When are you going to save Rico?" Dorothy said, intensity in her voice.

I took a breath and sighed, staring at the screen a moment before looking up at Scarlett sternly. "Scar, you two head back into the bedroom, all right?"

Her mouth dropped open and she was about to protest when she saw the look on my face turn more severe.

"Come on," she said, turning abruptly and nudging Dorothy.

Mick's daughter stood paralyzed for a moment. "Promise me you'll find him, okay?"

Her eyes turned watery, then she buried her face in her hands. Mick stepped over and wrapped his arms around her tight.

"We'll find him," I said as he walked with her back into the bedroom.

I blinked and turned back to the monitor. "What are we looking at, Ange?"

"They drove down a dirt road here," she said, pointing near the middle of the main road that cut across the center of the island. "They headed southwest for five miles, then turned east, eventually reaching an open terrain surrounded by hills and deep forest. I haven't searched yet, but I'm willing to bet it was all bought up roughly six months ago. Same time most everything else was." She zoomed in on the road. "They came to a stop here. A big, fenced property. There's an old Spanish Mission-style house and a few surrounding structures. But they pulled up to the main house. Tracker's still here, just outside the wall around the house."

After showing me their location, she shot me a familiar look. It was a look that said a lot of things. The biggest being "Are you sure you want to do this?"

Teaching a few punks a lesson was one thing. But this was going on the offensive against an unknown adversary. Declaring war. And despite the relative safety and distance from cartel violence in the Yucatan, we were still in Mexico. A foreign country. It was hard not to think about the last time I'd made enemies with a Mexican cartel leader. I didn't think that was what we were up against, but there was still a chance.

Regardless, the criminals we were up against were clearly powerful, relentless, and heartless. The kind of men who will do whatever it takes to keep their operation running smoothly. Kill whoever it takes.

"This is a foreign entity, Ange," I said. "An outside group that has infected this place like a virus."

"I hope you're right."

I thought hard. Closed my eyes.

"Okay," I said. "You ready?"

We needed to move right away. Sooner the better. At the moment, they'd be scrambling. Taken aback by the surprise loss. Rethinking. Rehashing. Formulating a new plan of attack. It was the best time to make a move, even if Rico's life wasn't hanging in the balance. But that fact made a quick response even more crucial.

Asking Ange if she was ready was a stupid question. The woman had taken on highly trained adversaries and overcome overwhelming odds time and time again over the course of her life. Fact is, a woman like Ange is always ready. Always prepared. She couldn't help it even if she wanted to.

"Let's get the bastards," she said, rising from the

couch.

Mick stepped back out as we were getting ready.

"We need you to stay here," I said, grabbing the Taurus 9mm and handing it to Ange. "Look after the girls. No one in or out until we get back."

He was reluctant to sit this one out but agreed when I assured him he'd done enough.

"We'll have the sat phone, but just in case we can't get ahold of them, call in to the police in thirty minutes. Give them this location." I pointed to the laptop screen, then added, "Tell them there's a shoot-out in progress."

I strode to Scarlett's room, then tapped my knuckles on the wood. She cracked the door open and poked her head out. It was dark and silent, and she blinked a couple times for her eyes to adjust.

After asking her to stay put and saying our quick goodbyes, she realized that she'd left her phone in the living room. After a short search, running her hands in the corners of the couch, she found it nestled in the cushions, then took a moment to check the screen before turning back toward us.

"I'll have it on the nightstand," she said.

"Don't worry, Scar," I said. "We'll be back before you know it."

She approached the bedroom slowly, then whispered goodnight and crept back inside, shutting the door behind her.

"Hopefully they're able to sleep," Mick said. "Dorothy and Rico are close, so this is hitting her hard."

"We'll find him," I said again. "Just stay alert. Don't let anyone in but us. And call if you see or hear anything suspicious."

Ange and I double-timed it to the Jeep. Flew out of the complex, heading south. Minutes after we left, the trees opened up, giving way to the coast. Long stretches of pounding waves and white surf to our right. Glistening in the moonlight. A clear sky full of densely packed stars. The air warm, but refreshing from the breeze. A beautiful evening.

"Turn's coming up," Ange said, eyeing her smartphone.

We'd brought a paper map as well, just in case the signal was bad in the middle of the island.

A quarter mile later we spotted the turn to our left. A lonely stretch of neglected path riddled with weeds and potholes. Judging by the GPS, there were two dirt roads that could be used to reach the compound. One from the northern side and this one branching off from the eastern shore. It was clearly rarely used but was closest to our unit.

I pulled off the road, into the rocks and dirt. The headlights streaked across a metal gate.

"Good thing we've got a four-by-four," I said. "Hold on."

I turned sharp, then gassed it up onto a steep rockface, testing the tires' grip. The engine had no trouble, and we jostled effortlessly around, then onto the dirt road.

"Easy to see why Jack loves these things," I said.

My beach bum friend had Wrangler in his blood. Wouldn't own anything else. Though he didn't exactly push the off-road vehicle's limits in South Florida.

I rumbled along at thirty miles per hour, avoiding

the bigger potholes and bushes and plowing right through the smaller ones. The landscape shifted from blankets of low-growing foliage to thick jungle. The sounds of the raging coastline died away at our backs. Soon we were in the thick of it. A few old houses, but mostly nothing but untamed wild. Like we'd been transported from the bustling tourist mecca and scuba diving Heaven that is Cozumel to middle-of-nowhere rural Mexico. We were maybe seven miles as the parrot flies from some of the busiest cruise ports in the Caribbean, but it might as well have been a hundred.

Ange checked the GPS, then looked up. "Another half mile."

"Jeez, this was all part of the purchased land?" I said, taking in the vast, empty landscape.

"Looks like it. Nearly a thousand acres."

For five more minutes there was no sign of life other than birds, armies of chirping crickets, and the occasional scurrying raccoon. The trees opened up slightly again near our turn. The road continued on, clearer and well-trodden, and we turned right onto a much smoother surface. Another quarter mile along, and the landscape opened up again, revealing sporadic trees surrounding the silhouettes of distant structures. There was a metal gate a couple hundred yards ahead.

"What's the play here?" Ange said.

"I'm tired of messing around with these assholes," I said, gripping the wheel tighter. "That's the play here."

Ange smiled. Brought back the slide of her Taurus to inspect the chamber, then checked the magazine.

I drove us right up to the gate. Braked beside the tiny makeshift guard shack. Noticed a security camera mounted to a post, its lens fixed right on us.

Good.

"Who the hell are you?" a guard said in broken English. He aimed his assault rifle at us. "Out of the car. Both of you."

I held up my hands, shoved open the door, and slithered out. Stood tall with my arms raised. Ange followed suit, opening her door and stepping out.

"Are you armed?" the guy said, keeping his weapon locked onto me.

He was alone on the perimeter. No other sentries in sight.

He closed the gap between us. Just a half step. Big mistake.

"Big-time," I said.

His eyes widened. Then they bulged out from his skull when I snatched the barrel of his weapon and threw a row of knuckles into his trachea. He wheezed, weakened enough for me to tear the rifle free, then fell lifeless to the dirt when I bashed the stock into his forehead.

His body stirred up a thin cloud of dust as I looked up and stared at the security camera. I performed a quick weapons check of the guy's rifle, then took aim, blasting a round into the device and blowing it to pieces.

A motor whined, and the gate rattled open. Ange exited the tiny shack, having found the controls. I handed her the rifle, then we climbed back into the Jeep and let ourselves in. I gunned it straight ahead, putting the Spanish-style house right in the middle of the windshield.

Up ahead, I spotted faint movement. Dark figures along the outside of the wall.

"Ange—"

"I see 'em."

She climbed over the center console to the back seat. Propped herself up with the barrel of her newly acquired long-range weapon resting on the top of the passenger seat. She opened fire, letting loose two three-round bursts. Just enough to spook the hive.

"It's shaky," she yelled.

I turned as the men returned fire, pelting rounds off the dirt. A couple managing to strike the frame. To our left was a cluster of flanking trees around a water tank. I aimed for the left side of it, wanting to use it as cover. The two men outside the wall were standing stoically, rifles raised.

"On my mark, Ange," I said.

Just when the trees shielded us from our enemies' view, I braked. I threw it in reverse and backed out. Braked again when the house came back into view. The two men had expected us to keep going and were thrown off.

"Now!"

Ange opened fire, putting both men down with well-placed shots.

I put the Jeep back in drive, accelerated along the back of the trees again, then popped out on the other side, gunning it straight toward the side of the house.

A third gunman emerged from the shadows and opened fire, managing to crack the windshield and pelt the grille. Ange retaliated, and he took cover behind a stack of pallets.

I grinned.

"Hold on, Ange!"

Seeing what I was about to do, she dropped down to the back seat and braced herself against my seat back.

When the silhouette of the gunman popped out a second time, he froze for a split second, then I plowed into the wooden platforms. We jolted as the Jeep sent the pallets flying, then bashed into the gunman, hurtling him into the wall. I braked and skidded to a stop. Withdrew my pistol and scanned the exterior.

"Clear," Ange said.

The wall was easily ten feet high, so I eased the Jeep up against it and left the engine running as we hauled ourselves up, using the roll bar as a launching point to leap and grab onto the top.

We expected to face more adversaries the moment we landed. Expected more men with guns to flood out and take aim. But the inside of the compound was unexpectedly quiet.

We moved in across the simple, neglected grounds. Mostly dirt and rocks and empty flowerpots. A hideout, not a sprawling criminal mansion to host parties.

We stuck to the shrubs and shadows, moving stealthily but with a purpose. The clock was ticking down. A young man's life hanging in the balance.

I brushed aside the fatigue and aches from my scuffle with the guy back at Mick's dive shop and kept myself focused and ready.

The front door was propped open. Ange covered me as I closed in, grabbed the edge, and swung it back, aiming my pistol one-handed. With no visible movement, we entered single file, then shifted side by side in the wide entryway and into a living room, running our eyes over every inch of the place. It was quiet and dark. Just like outside.

Then we heard scrambling. Shuffling of feet. Hushed tones and papers riffling. The sounds were all coming from an adjoining room. As Ange and I closed in, the footsteps turned to stomps, and the door flew open. A man I recognized from the marina rushed out, a shotgun in his hands.

He managed to raise his weapon barely an inch or two before Ange and I opened fire, loosing rounds into his chest from two different angles. His body shook, and he stumbled backward, striking the edge of the door frame before crashing to the floor.

A second attacker opened fire before he'd left the room, shooting sporadically in our direction through the walls. We took cover, me rolling left behind the corner of the kitchen counter, and Ange right behind a couch.

Yelling reverberated from inside the room, but I couldn't make out the words.

When I poked my head up, the second guy was in a full sprint, heading straight toward me. Ange managed to fire off a round, striking the guy in the leg and sending him tumbling forward. He clipped the edge of the counter, barreled over, and fell onto the tile floor right beside me.

He squirmed and aimed his weapon my way. Grabbing tight to the barrel, I held on as he pressed the trigger, firing off a barrage straight into the ceiling. Shoving my pistol into his gut, I blew two high-caliber bullets through his body, then turned and aimed back at the doorway.

Silence returned. Eerie, empty, silence.

I gravitated to the open door with Ange right at my side. Peeking through, I saw a long office with sofas. Heard a crackling fire. I drew closer, a big mahogany desk coming into view. Then I spotted Warren Beauchamp Sr sitting in a leather chair, the gray-haired man's hands resting on the desk. Holding nothing but a crystal rocks glass. I recognized him from a photo we'd found while doing an internet search on the drive over.

We entered the room, eyeing every inch of the space. It was empty aside from the criminal.

We closed in on the desk, our barrels aimed straight at the man. He was dressed in a gray suit. Looked neat and well-groomed. Calm and in control. He smoothly took a sip of his rust-colored drink, then set it down.

"It's over, Warren," I said. "On your feet. Hands above your head."

He smiled confidently. Took another drink.

"No," Warren said calmly. "It's not over."

"Let's put one in his kneecap," Ange said. "See if his numbskull gets the message then."

There was a short pause. Warren glared slightly at my wife, then took a third sip.

"Hands up and on your feet, Warren," I said. "I'm not gonna say it again."

He made a clicking sound with his lips. Tightened his gaze on me. Furrowed his brow.

"You should not have messed with me," he said. "We would have left you and your family alone if you'd just kept to yourselves. Even after what you did to my son. I overlooked your slight. Was lenient with you. Now—"

"On your damn feet!" I shouted.

My index flexed on the trigger, ready to put an end to the guy for good.

Ange closed in from the left. Me from the right. We were within ten feet of him when movements caught our attention from the sides of the desk. Two armed men appeared, springing from their crouched positions.

In a frantic blur, Warren flipped over his right hand, revealing a tiny silver pocket pistol.

I pulled the trigger, blasting a round into Warren's shoulder. As he spun back in his chair and toppled over, Ange opened fire on the gunman in front of her while taking cover.

Bullets whooshed all around in a frenzy as I hit the deck. I managed to put one of them down, then a dark figure appeared seemingly out of nowhere, sprinting through the open doorway. It was Junior.

The right side of his face was cut up and swollen. He held a sawed-off shotgun and opened fire a fraction of a second after I ducked behind the corner of a deep bookcase. A swarm of pellets tore across the space, splintering the wood beside me and blasting pages free like confetti before rattling against the desk and far wall. He stomped toward me, and I dropped down as he fired the second cartridge, blasting a three-foot hole through the upper part of the bookcase and nearly taking my head off.

Knowing he'd need to reload, I broke out and charged. He was just removing the empty shells, smoke wafting out, when he looked up and turned like he was going to try and hit me with the weapon's stock. He was too slow, and I bashed a fist into his hands, grabbed his forearms, then shoved a knee into his elbow. As his weapon fell to the floor, I pulled him forward then kicked him hard in the side, sending him crashing into what remained of the heavy-duty bookcase.

I lunged forward, not giving him even a moment to recover. Grabbing him by the shirt, I socked him in the jaw, then hurled him into the corner beside the desk.

As I closed in, his father appeared, gripping a macahuitl and swinging it like mad. I dodged two slashes, the sharp tips blurring right past me, then caught his wrists, jolted forward, and rammed my forehead into his nose, cracking the fragile bones. He lurched back and I tore the sword free.

I turned and swung it around as Junior came back at me, slicing the obsidian edges across his chest. Not a deep gash, but enough to make him squeal and keel over. I jumped toward the older Beauchamp, rotated swiftly, and bashed my heel into his stomach, sending his body into the back wall. The sixty-year-old man collapsed, motionless, and I focused across the room just as Ange finished off a fourth guy who'd surprised us, restraining him from behind and knocking him unconscious.

I grabbed Warren Senior by his shirt, heaved him up and slammed him onto the desk. "Like I said, it's over."

The man struggled to breathe, blood flowing down over his mouth and chin and dripping onto the mahogany.

"You all right?" I said as Ange collected herself.

She nodded. "You?"

"I'll be better once these two are behind bars and their little empire is dismantled. But that shouldn't take long now."

Ange strode over and scanned behind the desk. "Where's Junior?"

My head snapped left to where the punk had been moments earlier. Where he'd fallen after I'd cut him across the chest. He was gone, and I noticed a break in the curtain, and an open window.

TWENTY-FOUR

Forty-five minutes earlier, after Mick had walked back out into the living room, Scarlett nestled up close to Dorothy, placing a hand on the girl's shoulder.

"It's gonna be all right," Scarlett said. "My mom and dad are on it. And that's saying a lot. They've got pretty good track records for finding kidnapped people. Me being a good example."

Dorothy angled her head up and rested her chin in her hands. "You were kidnapped?"

"Twice, technically. And I was taken out of the country. Miles into rural Cuba."

Dorothy bit her lip. "I just… he's like family to us. Been working at the shop for years."

Scarlett tilted her head and squinted questioningly.

"I'm just worried," Dorothy continued. "Worried he's—"

"You like him, don't you?"

Dorothy paused, then nodded shyly. Then gave a barely noticeable smile.

Scarlett leaned forward. "You're dating?"

Dorothy rose to her feet and blushed. Then her eyes welled up with a layer of moisture, and she exhaled dramatically. "I have to find him."

Scarlett paused, thinking it over. "They're not gonna bring us along. I mean, we're teenagers."

"I have to, Scarlett," she said, her teary eyes peeking over her hands. "I mean, I know we don't know each other very well. But I need you to help me find him."

She thought again. "We don't even know where to look. We—"

She froze midsentence. Thought again. Looked up at the nightstand, then stood and looked at her phone. Thumbed a few buttons, then pocketed it.

"I have an idea." She turned to Dorothy, then stepped toward the door. "Crawl into bed."

"What? Why? I thought we were—"

"Just do it." She nodded toward the bed near the window. "Trust me."

When Dorothy was under the covers, Scarlett swiftly changed into her pajamas, then flicked off the light and gave her eyes a moment to adjust. Then she unlocked and cracked open the left window. She covered it with the curtains, then cut around and lay on her bed.

"I'm not sure how sleeping will help us find Rico," Dorothy said.

"It won't. But pretending to sleep will."

As Scarlett had expected, a knock came on the door just minutes later.

"Stay put," Scarlett whispered as she slid out from the bed. "Blanket over your face."

She stepped over and opened the door a foot.

"We're heading out, kiddo," Logan said. Ange kissed her forehead, and he added, "Mick's staying here."

The dive operator approached from behind them, then Scarlett nodded, having already expected that one.

"She asleep?" Mick said softly, peeking in at Dorothy's still, blanket-covered body.

Scarlett nodded. "Been out for a few minutes now. It's late." She looked to her parents. "Be careful, all right? And text me when you find…" She patted her pocket, then paused. She glanced back, then stepped out from the bedroom, shutting the door softly behind her. "Have you seen my phone?"

Logan and Ange prepared to leave and Mick stood idly as Scarlett pretended to search the living room. She closed in on the couch, blocking her actions as she stealthily slid her phone from her pocket and pretended to find it in the cracks of the cushions. She turned slowly, aiming the camera at the open laptop, then pocketing it.

"I'll have it on the nightstand," she said.

"Don't worry, Scar," Logan said. "We'll be back before you know it."

She tiptoed back to the bedroom, said good night, then shut the door softly behind her. She sat on the corner of the bed in the darkness. Listened as Logan said some final words to Mick, then he and Ange left, firing up the Jeep and driving out of the complex.

Scarlett waited another minute, listening as Mick settled in the living room.

"What now?" Dorothy whispered, her face still veiled behind the blanket.

Scarlett slid her phone out. Ended the recording, then played it back. Sifting through with the expertise and thumb dexterity of a teenaged millennial, she quickly found the frame she was looking for.

"Now we go and find Rico," she said, aiming the screen at Dorothy.

The smartphone's screen displayed a picture of a GPS image with a red dot indicating the position of the tracked vehicle. Using a different program, they were able to pinpoint the location on a map.

"That's over ten kilometers away," Dorothy said. "How are we supposed to get there?"

"Taxi?" Scarlett said, thinking they could ask the guard at the gate to call them one.

Dorothy shook her head. "They won't take you there. The roads are all bad. They'd maybe take us to the turnoff, if they weren't too suspicious about it, but we'd still have too much ground to cover."

They both thought a moment, then Dorothy said, "Wait a second. I got it. There are mopeds parked here?"

"I mean, this is Cozumel."

They quickly dressed, keeping quiet so Mick wouldn't hear. Then Scarlett shoved spare pillows under the blankets to make it look like they were sleeping, just in case Mick did peek in. And she also set a pair of shorts and a T-shirt on the floor near the foot of her bed and stowed her pajamas in a drawer. Just a few finishing touches.

Dorothy watched as Scarlett wrapped up staging the room, then said, "Why do I get the feeling this is far from your first time sneaking out at night?"

"Hey, I was an orphan most of my life. Foster and group homes. You learn a lot from those other kids. Tricks of the trade, you might say."

Carefully, Scarlett slid up the window. She'd chosen to leave the left one unlocked since it opened up to an eave and a nearby coconut tree, while the right one opened to nothing but twelve feet of open air and a concrete sidewalk. The two climbed out and Scarlett slid the window back down. Then she went first.

"Here goes nothing," she said.

Then she jumped, wrapped her arms and legs around the tree trunk, and inched her way down. She let go and her feet hit the grass. Gazing up at Dorothy, she threw her a thumbs-up.

The local followed, then looked up when she reached the ground, amazed at what they'd just done.

"Piece of cake," Scarlett said, patting her on the back. "Come on, let's go before your dad finds out."

"You think he will?"

"Most likely. But we'll be long gone by then."

They crept in the shadows until they were out of sight of the unit, then walked along the footpath, acting casual.

They had their pick of the litter in one of the lots, and Dorothy chose a Yamaha Zuma 150-cc parked under a shade structure in the darkness. She told Scarlett that the off-road tires and good-sized engine would be best for the dirt roads in their future.

"Now what?" Scarlett said, eyeing the moped.

Dorothy smiled, knelt down beside the front tire and pulled out her ring of keys. Attached to it was a small pair of Phillips and flathead screwdrivers. She used the Phillips to remove the front panel, revealing the starter. Then she stripped two wires and managed to jumpstart the engine. It purred while she reattached the panel, using just one of the screws to save time.

Scarlett laughed. "And you implied I was the delinquent."

"Sometimes it pays to have worked part-time at a moped shop," she replied with a smile.

Dorothy drove and Scarlett held on in back as she cruised them out of the lot. Knowing that confidence was the key to looking the part, they rolled past the guard shack and threw a wave to the security guy. He was young and smiled back at them as they motored out, heading south.

"All right, looks like the turn is a couple miles down," Scarlett said over the howling wind.

Dorothy nodded and hit the gas, pushing the little vehicle to its limits and keeping it at its top speed of sixty miles per hour. They had a lot of ground to cover if they were going to cut the distance between them and Scarlett's parents.

They flew along the coast, managing to reach the turn in under five minutes. Slowing, Dorothy weaved between a mound of rocks and the edge of a metal barrier, bouncing them onto the dirt road.

"Those tracks are fresh," Dorothy said, motioning toward the road ahead. "Looks like we're heading the right way."

They both held on tight as she pushed the little vehicle too fast for the road, bouncing and rattling their way along. Dorothy braked to a stop as the distant sound of gunfire echoed across the air. As the sporadic gunfire persisted, they both wondered at the same time what exactly they were going to do when they got there. Neither of them were armed. And neither of them were experts in the art of infiltration.

But neither said a word as Dorothy accelerated them back up to speed. The gunfire halted following a loud crash, and they eventually reached the turn toward the compound. Dorothy picked up their speed even more as the road evened out, and they soon approached a long running chain-link fence and an open gate. Dorothy braked to a stop and they eyed a guard lying on his back and a security camera lying in pieces near the base of the fence.

"My parents were definitely here," Scarlett said.

They scanned over the place, their gaze fixating on a dark house roughly three hundred yards away. The gunfire had stopped, and the place was eerily quiet.

Not wanting to bring attention to themselves with the engine, they left the moped there and continued on foot.

"This place is huge," Scarlett said, gazing around the compound. "And there are buildings spread out all over the place. Sheds and garages."

Dorothy gasped. "How are we supposed to find Rico here?"

Scarlett held up a hand. "Stop." They both came to an abrupt halt and dropped down to the tall grass. "Look," she added, pointing toward a dark figure appearing from the backside of the house.

They stared as the figure came into focus in the moonlight. It was a man, limping along and wheezing and snarling. Heading east toward an outbuilding a short hike from the main house.

"Holy crap," Scarlett said. "That's—"

"Let's go," Dorothy said, and they took off after him.

TWENTY-FIVE

Scarlett and Dorothy ran across the compound, keeping their eyes and ears alert to danger as they followed Warren Beauchamp Jr. The guy stumbled his way along, droplets of blood splashing in his wake. He passed right in front of them before vanishing behind a cluster of trees two hundred yards from the girls.

As they approached, they could see the metal roof of a garage sticking out through the palms. The main overhead door was facing the opposite direction as they crept in from the back less than a minute after Junior. Scarlett froze, then turned back to look at the main house off to the west. From that angle, they could see the rented Jeep parked beside the wall surrounding the structure.

"I'm sure they're fine," Dorothy said, placing a hand on Scarlett's shoulder. "Like you said, this isn't their first time doing this sort of thing."

Scarlett nodded, then turned back toward the garage. Eyed the side door.

"Come on," she said, nudging Dorothy.

The two broke from the tree line, slowing as they approached the side of the structure. Scarlett grabbed the knob. Slowly, she eased it open and they both peeked inside. It was dark and quiet. They slithered in, shutting the door silently behind them.

They were greeted by a tall shelf filled with tools. Creeping around it, they saw Junior's pickup truck, coated in dried mud and resting in the middle of the space. Then they heard talking and Dorothy pointed toward the top of a staircase. Her eyes grew big when Scarlett grabbed a hammer from the shelf beside her. But she nodded and grabbed a weapon of her own, going with a pair of pruning shears with a sharp point. The voice grew clearer when the two girls reached the top of the stairs.

"You've made some powerful friends," Junior spat, wincing as he fought back pain. "But it's not going to save you."

"I told you everything I know," Rico gasped. "I can't help you anymore."

"Exactly. You can't. You're useless. Nothing but a witness now."

Scarlett crept down the steps with Dorothy right on her heels. The two froze as they saw Junior with a baton in his hands, hovering over Rico, who sat tied to a metal chair.

"And we have a strict rule when it comes to

dealing with witnesses," Junior said, tapping the baton against his hand.

The criminal froze as the faint, distant sound of sirens filled the air. They were muffled but getting louder with each second.

"It doesn't matter," Rico said. "You'll be arrested and fry no matter what, you bastard."

Junior froze, pretending not to be affected by the verbal assault. He stumbled closer, his blood dripping across the sleek floor, and bashed the baton into Rico's gut. The young man shook and fought for air.

"I was going to be merciful, but because of that, I've changed my mind. You always have to make things hard on yourself, don't you, kid?"

Junior turned away. Stepped to an old wooden counter. The girls used the opening to reach the bottom of the stairs. They crawled under the table just as Junior returned, holding a blowtorch in his hands.

He clicked and sparked a jet flame to life. Held it up menacingly, then aimed it at Rico. "Any last words before I melt your windpipe shut?"

He stepped closer to the young man, putting himself within two strides of the table.

Scarlett crawled out silently, then stood tall right behind the criminal, a dangerous blend of courage and anger taking hold. "How about go to hell, you asshole!" she shouted as she wound back the hammer, then swung it in a short arc and bashed the heavy metal head into Junior's upper back.

Vertebrae cracked, and Junior squealed and went down like a flailing fish, sprawling onto the floor. He let go of the torch, the device rattling to the concrete and the flame screaming out into nothing but air.

Scarlett reared back for another attack, but Junior caught her arm. Forcing himself up, he geared up for a strike of his own when Dorothy emerged, screaming as she stabbed the tip of the shears into Junior's side. He yelled out again, cursed, then punched Scarlett and grabbed Dorothy by her hair. Yanking hard, he twisted her back. She threw elbows into his face and chest, but he fought through them, driven by his anger and rage.

Yelling like a madman, he hurled Dorothy into the edge of the table, then caught Scarlett by the throat.

"Looks like I just got myself three for one," Junior spat, his voice laced with hatred.

In a flash, Scarlett remembered an important lesson her parents had taught her. One about doing everything it took to defend yourself. Fighting dirty, if need be.

With Junior squeezing tight, she let out a primal cry of her own, then gouged a thumb into the criminal's left eye. Junior wailed and loosened his grip enough for Scarlett to jerk herself free. Then she landed a punch square into his solar plexus. He heaved and relaxed, punched her again.

Wheezing, going berserk, and barely able to see, he turned back just as Dorothy squared up behind him. She stood just a few feet away, holding the flaming torch in her hands.

His eyes lit up with terror, and he barely managed to let out a yelp before Dorothy stuck the torch out, the flame scorching Junior's face. His skin melting and burning, he gurgled and squirmed, writhing on the floor.

Scarlett grabbed her hammer, and when he rose

again like a demented, disfigured demon, she finished him with another swing of the hammer, this time striking the back of his skull. The blow punched a brutal crater through the bone, and Junior dropped, faceplanting onto the floor.

Dorothy stared in shock at what she'd just done and seen. Her mouth was open. Her body quivering. She blinked and focused on the torch still clutched in her hands—the flame still screaming out in a tight pillar of extreme heat.

Scarlett dropped the hammer and stepped over, helping Dorothy find the kill switch. The flame died and she dropped the torch. Scarlett wrapped her arms around her. Held her tight a moment as Dorothy shook, tears streaking down her cheeks.

Then the two turned to look at Rico. The young man was barely recognizable. His body was beaten, his face red and swollen.

Dorothy stumbled over and collapsed over him, tearing up more as she ran her hands through his sweat-soaked hair. Rico coughed and swallowed, and stared into her eyes.

"You came for me," he gasped.

She dropped into him. Scarlett cut the tape securing his wrists together, and his arms fell free with a grateful sigh, coming to rest around Dorothy. He leaned forward off the chair back, pressing into her.

Scarlett smiled faintly as she watched them, then blinked back to reality as her ears tuned in to the ringing sirens. She reasoned that they were coming from the main house just a couple hundred yards away.

The piercing sounds died off, then moments later, the creak of an opening door caught their attention. Footsteps approached the top of the stairs, then Scarlett's parents appeared, both wielding and aiming pistols.

TWENTY-SIX

Ange and I lowered our weapons, waves of surprise and relief washing over us as we scanned over the room. In a blink, we were down the stairs and hugging Scarlett tight. She was visibly shaken. Understandably so, given the gruesome scene. Our adventurous daughter had involved herself in our adventures before, but one glance at Junior's mangled body made it clear that this time was different.

A big part of me was angry with her—was irate that she'd disobeyed us and put her and Dorothy's lives in danger. But this wasn't the time to let it show and chastise her. Not after everything they'd just experienced.

"Are you all right?" Ange said, loosening her grip just enough to inspect our daughter.

"You're hurt," I added, focusing on a cut across the side of her face.

Scarlett shook her head, buried her face back into us, and squeezed tight.

"I'm fine," she gasped, on the brink of trembling. "We're both fine."

When the initial storm of emotion abated, I turned my attention to Rico, who was hunched over in a chair, Dorothy draped over him. Seeing that the young man was in rough shape, I strode over to examine his injuries.

"Holy crap," I whispered, taken aback by the cruel nature of the wounds.

There was nothing life-threatening, but the dark bruises, cuts, and the burn marks along his arms made me want to vomit. I've seen some horrific things in my life. Things I'd rather forget. And the young man's tortured body immediately jumped high up on the list.

We freed his legs, hauled him upstairs and whistled over the paramedics, who were near the main house beside the ambulances and squad cars. The medical professionals rushed over, carefully strapping Rico into a stretcher and carting him to the back of the nearest ambulance. Dorothy followed, the emotionally rattled teenager keeping a hand clasped in Rico's.

"He's going to be all right," the paramedic said as they heaved him into the back and gave first aid.

Dorothy had to stay behind, the young woman crying as the vehicle's sirens blared and it rushed out of the compound.

Mick arrived less than a minute later, hopping out

of Officer Ramirez's police car and sprinting toward Dorothy. He was worried sick at first, then angry, then proud when he found out what had happened. What our daughters had done.

Just as they finished explaining their side of things, Warren Beauchamp Sr. was escorted out of the house in handcuffs. The bullet wound to his shoulder was bandaged enough to stop the bleeding. He was groaning in pain. Infuriated. Spitting curses to the officers, and then worse ones to Ange and me when his sinister eyes locked onto us.

"This isn't over!" he shouted like a raging lunatic. The shift in behavior from the calm, collected, corrupt man to a fuming maniac was drastic. "You hear me? This isn't over!"

Officers packed him into the back of one of the squad cars. Officer Ramirez, who'd been standing with his hands in his pockets, strode over to the group.

"It's over," he declared. "With the evidence we have here alone, he's gonna be sent to a maximum-security prison. Mexico abolished capital punishment years ago, so he'll spend the rest of his life behind bars after it's all officialized."

He joined the other officers in taking control of the scene, and the five of us stood silent a moment.

"I don't know how they did it," Mick said to Ange and me. "They were asleep one minute. Then I checked on them and they were gone."

I shot Scarlett a look, knowing her handiwork when I saw it.

"Well, it's a good thing we did," Scarlett said. "Junior was about to kill Rico when we found them."

Mick turned serious. "How is he?"

"Hurt bad," Dorothy said, her voice still laced with worry. "But they assured me he'll live." She paused, tilted her head down and wiped at her face. Mick held her tight again and she added, "It was Junior. He... he—"

"He won't be hurting anyone ever again," Scarlett stated.

The next hour was a blur of activity. Statements and questions. Crime scene cleanup and protocols. It wasn't until nearly four in the morning that we made it back to the unit. Mick thanked us for everything, then Dorothy and Scarlett hugged, teary-eyed and emotional.

"Keep me updated on how he's doing, all right?" Scarlett said.

Then my daughter winked at her and she and her father headed for the door.

"Do you have a place to stay?" I said, knowing that their house was a wreck and the scene of another brutal fight that had taken place earlier that morning.

I would have offered to have them stay with us, but I got a better idea.

"We rented two rooms at Barracuda when we first got here. Technically they're still ours. Or yours if you want them."

The two smiled, then Mick nodded. "You know, you're a very easy family to like."

"I was about to say the same thing," Ange said.

Mick tucked in his lips, speechless, then he and Dorothy said goodnight before I walked them out to give them a ride back to town.

We drove north in silence, then Dorothy climbed

out first when I braked to a stop in front of the familiar, orange-colored waterfront hotel.

I placed an arm around Mick, then spoke softly so only he could hear. "Keep an eye on Dorothy and make sure she gets whatever comfort and help she needs. Traumatic experience like that. She's probably gonna need a lot. And we can help. Whatever we can do."

He nodded his thanks, then I handed him the keys to the rooms with a smile and patted him on the shoulder as he slid out of the Jeep.

"Keep me updated on the wreck," I added, leaning across the center console and handing him the keys to the hotel rooms. "We're still here a few more days. And you still need a name for her."

The two of them waved, then disappeared inside. I sat there in silence. Took a moment to wrap my head around the evening's events, then drove back to the unit.

I returned to find Ange and Scarlett on the couch, holding each other. I wrapped my arms around them both uncontrollably.

We told Scarlett we were proud of her. Told her how much we loved and cared about her. I don't know how long the Dodge trio remained intertwined. But eventually, we loosened our holds on each other and I kissed Scarlett on the forehead as Ange and I ushered her to bed.

Once she was in bed with the lights out, I downed two Extra Strength Tylenol, then washed up in the bathroom, examining my new assortment of cuts and bruises. A couple new scars to add to the collection. Then I collapsed on our bed, the weight of the day forcing me down.

The moment the adrenaline and excitement passed, it was like a wave of reality slammed into me. That reality being that I'd just had one of the longest, most dangerously eventful twenty-four-hour periods of my life. And that was saying something.

The past day had been grueling, and my body ached all over, but all I could think about was Scarlett and how close she'd been to being taken from us. Part of me wished I could go back—that I'd given Beauchamp and the murders more of my energy from the beginning. Maybe I could've solved the whole thing sooner and prevented her being involved at all.

Ange, insightful as always and somehow reading my mind, sat down beside me, and explained that it wasn't my fault.

"You wanted a break," she said. "You needed one after all that has happened over the past few months. We all did. There's nothing wrong with that. But you stepped up when the troubles came, just like you always do."

"We both did," I said, clasping a hand in hers.

"All three of us did. We need to accept the fact that Scarlett isn't an ordinary teenager in any sense of the word. She's going to want to be involved in whatever we're doing, she's proven that again and again. And aside from shipping her off to a military school, I don't think there's anything we can really do to stop it. So it's not your fault she was in danger."

A combination of Ange's words and the pain relievers helped me relax. She was right, and managed to so often say exactly what I needed to hear.

She switched off the lights and cozied up beside me under the covers, her warmth and the smell of her hair lulling me to sleep along with the distant sounds of rumbling waves upon a sandy beach.

TWENTY-SEVEN

We spent the next day recovering from all that had happened, and dealing with the aftermath of taking down Beauchamp's operation. After sleeping in and having a late breakfast, Ange and I met with detectives in the lobby of the complex and told them our side of all that had happened. Remembering what Officer Ramirez had told us about corruption dipping into law enforcement, we also informed them that we'd emailed our written statements to three major Mexican news networks anonymously.

Catching us off guard, the two detectives nodded their approval of the precaution.

"I'd have done the same thing," one of them said. "Fortunately, we don't believe Beauchamp was connected with major Mexican organized crime. Just a rich foreigner who'd been riding the line of legality here. That was until he decided to go on a killing spree."

"He cracked yet?" I said when we were wrapping up.

Both men smiled. "Less than an hour after he was brought in. Began trying to make deals. Then he spilled everything. The whole operation from the ground up. Even told us about his past in the States, where he previously tried to swindle his way into taking over a waterfront community in Southern California."

Part of me wished that we'd finished him—that we'd ended the man's life when we had the chance. But after his son had snuck out the window, he'd surrendered. Thrown his hands up and begged, and complied with our tying him up before chasing after his coward of a son.

"So what now?" Ange said.

"Now he'll try and make more deals. Maybe go to trial. Either way, he's going away for a long time. Life if we get our way. His illegal business dealings are reason enough for a long time behind bars, but he has the blood of too many people on his hands not to spend the rest of his life in a cell."

"Our country offers you thanks for all that you've done," the other said. "Do you have any more questions for us?"

"Only a request that you keep our names out of this," I said. "As we told Officer Ramirez early this morning, we prefer to remain anonymous. Not to have our names mentioned in the official reports."

It was a request we generally made, both of us

having learned from experience that it was best to fly under the radar in such circumstances.

"I think we can manage that."

The two men rose, then headed out through a set of double doors, leaving Ange and me by the couches.

"You think everything will really work out as it should from here?" Ange said.

I thought it over, then shrugged. "I think we've done all we can." I glanced through one of the windows to the distant beach, then rose and offered her a hand. "Come on. Last I checked, we're supposed to be on vacation."

We spent the day under our favorite palapa, its dried palm leaves shading a perfect stretch of white sand just steps from the surf, only venturing from our padded lounge chairs to splash into the water or pick up food and drinks from a nearby beach club.

We filled up on grilled grouper and shrimp and downed pitchers of mango juice and ice water. It was a perfect afternoon of nap, sun, swim, eat, repeat until the bright blue sky began to fade.

Mick and Dorothy showed up just before sunset, carrying takeaway dinners of enchiladas, steak tacos, and tamales from their favorite Mexican restaurant in town. We ate and listened to music and downed margaritas while watching the sunset.

They gave us an update on Rico, letting us know that he was still at the hospital, but that he was improving and in good spirits.

"We're heading to the hospital after this to bring him food and to watch his favorite movie, *Raiders of the Lost Ark*," Dorothy said. "Then tomorrow we're taking him home."

"That's great news," Scarlett said. "I'm sure he'll like this better than hospital food."

"Do you three have plans for tomorrow?" Mick said.

Ange and I exchanged glances, then I leaned forward. "We were actually thinking of heading to the mainland," I said.

"We've heard that there are some amazing ruins," Ange added. "And that there are some cenotes worth stopping by for a dip."

Mick and Dorothy chuckled. Though I'd never seen them myself, I knew it was as big of an understatement as there could be. It didn't take more than a quick search through online images to see that some of the most impressive ruins and beautiful natural underground pools existed in the Yucatan.

"I'll offer a few suggestions if you'd like," Mick said. "Some of our favorite, more secretive spots."

They ran through their top picks and said they'd message us directions.

"When you get back, you can join us for a late dinner at Casa Mission," Dorothy said. "Then we could watch the fireworks."

Given everything that had happened, I'd completely forgotten that the following day was New Year's Eve.

"We'll be there," Ange said, answering for the three of us.

They left just after the distant, vibrant colors sank into the horizon. Downing my margarita, I migrated to the softly lapping surf and sat in the sand, the water splashing and receding over my lower body. I sat in silence, ruminating over all that had happened. Clearing and relaxing my mind. Then I rose, took one more look at the purple western sky, and returned to the girls.

The next morning we woke just after the sun, ate strawberry banana French toast, then loaded up the Jeep. Fortunately, Officer Ramirez had taken care of everything with the rental company, managing to switch out our old shot-up vehicle with a different Wrangler. And fortunately the local government was footing the bill. Once ready, we cruised downtown.

Most of the ferries that run back and forth between Cozumel and Playa del Carmen are walk-on only, but one offers rides for vehicles, and we caught the seven a.m. boat.

Half an hour later, we were driving onto the mainland and cruising south out of Playa through the beachfront town of Akumal and into Tulum. Less popular than the tourist mecca of Cancun to the north, the place looked ready to explode. Construction at every corner. Massive resorts and condos sprouting up all around.

We headed to one of the most popular archaeological sites first, an impressive array of Mayan ruins right along the coast. Catching the place less than an hour after they opened, we had the sites mostly to ourselves.

We climbed up the clifftop castillo, a beautiful watchtower built in the thirteenth century and set up on a rocky bluff right along the crashing waves. To say it was picturesque and awe-inspiring just didn't do it justice. And we spent nearly an hour there, snapping pictures, climbing whatever we were allowed to, and walking barefoot in the surf before climbing back into the Jeep and heading inland.

Next we traveled to a spot Mick and Dorothy had recommended, an impressive assemblage of ruins called Coba. In addition to boasting the largest network of stone causeways in the ancient Mayan world, it isn't nearly as excavated as other sites in Mexico. The whole place is still mostly intermixed with the thick jungle, and more structures are still being uncovered every year by archaeologists, adding an extra layer of excitement to the visit.

We rented bicycles at the entrance and pedaled our way from site to site, engrossed by the impressive feats of architecture and the compelling history of the clever people who'd lived there. We finished the ride with a stop at Nohoch Mul Pyramid. At over a hundred and thirty feet tall, it's the tallest temple pyramid in the Yucatan. Though it pales in comparison to Egyptian pyramids, or even ones in other parts of Mexico's mainland, the awe-inspiring structure is a sight to behold, piercing up through thick tree coverage and towering over the flat landscape.

The trip up was harder than it appeared, the stones smoothed slippery from all the climbers. We utilized the rope and reached the top coated in sweat. The view was incredible, carpets of thick green stretching out in all directions.

After riding back, we ate lunch near the entrance to the site at a place called El Faisán, which served up some authentic Mayan cuisine. The poc chuc and subanik were delicious, and the place had a nice veranda view of the small Lake Coba. By the time we finished, it was just after two o'clock and eighty-five degrees. We were all hot and layered in sweat and ready to find somewhere to cool off.

We followed Mick's directions again, driving for half an hour along remote roads before turning onto a rocky path with a barely legible sign that said "Cenote."

"He did say it was secretive," Scarlett said, not deterred in the slightest.

A quarter mile down the rough road, we came to a stop in a tiny lot with just two vehicles parked. Both old and beat-up. Locals. Just beyond was an information placard and a railing following a path.

"This must be the spot," I said.

We climbed out, followed the path, read a sign giving warnings and a couple of rules, then followed a narrow, steep staircase built into the limestone. It spun around once, then opened up on the top edge of a huge, cavernous space. Far below was a pool of crystal-clear water with a jutting rock cutting into the middle and a flat area near the base of the stairs.

There were five college-aged locals jumping and swimming as we trekked down the stairs toward the base. Twice on the way down, we reached platforms that extended out over the widest part of the pool below.

A man smiled, then welcomed us and did a backflip off the highest one, his splash resounding across the space like we were inside a drum. The friendly locals gave us a quick overview of the cenote, then had to leave, allowing us to have the place completely to ourselves.

Scarlett jumped in first, radiating enthusiasm as

she splashed into the pool, then rose up with eyes filled with excitement and wonder.

"Why's it so hard to swim here?" she said, fighting hard to stay afloat.

"Freshwater," Ange said.

She eyed her quizzically, and I explained, "It's not nearly as dense as saltwater, so you're less buoyant than you're used to being."

I jumped in as well, with Ange right on my heels. The water felt amazing after the long, hot day out in the sun exploring ruins.

After splashing around a few minutes, I climbed out and grabbed my fins.

"But a benefit to that is you'll be able to freedive down much easier," I said, tossing Scarlett her mask.

We geared up and free dove along the underwater walls, spotting fish below and pretending we were flying as we weaved along the cave's unique formations. I took it easy, not going too deep or fast, the past couple days' encounters having taken a toll on my body. Fortunately, a steady dose of Tylenol had kept most of the pains at bay.

Heaving ourselves out, we took turns diving off the platforms. The rush of free-falling forty feet was amplified by the thrill of being in an underground cavern and splashing into still, pristine water.

After nearly an hour of splashing from high up and freediving into the natural wonder, we relaxed on the rock's edge.

After a minute or two of silence, I brought up something that needed to be said. I didn't want to. Not then. But it was important that we had the talk.

"I'm proud of you for your courage and

selflessness, Scar," I said, trying to sound both serious and fatherly. "Putting yourself in harm's way to help a complete stranger. But I'm... I'm just glad you're all right."

"Things could've turned out very differently," Ange added. "Maybe next time listen to us when we ask you to stay out of it?"

Scarlett thought a moment. "No one has ever learned to swim by having the strokes explained. At some point, they all dove in."

I couldn't help but chuckle slightly, then turned serious again. It was an expression often used by a friend of ours in Key West, Pete Jameson. Her saying it made me suddenly miss our island home and friends. But the wise metaphor wasn't going to get her out of this.

"You're sixteen, Scar," I said. "Trust me, someday very soon, you'll be able to dive in all you want."

I could tell if given the chance, she'd do the same thing again in a heartbeat. And it was a facet of her character that stirred up both admiration and worry inside me.

TWENTY-EIGHT

After Scarlett appeared to have gotten at least some of the message, I climbed back up the stairs and lightened the mood again with a cannonball. We spent two hours there in all, swimming, diving, and finning into the bowels of the cenote. Then we packed up and headed home, catching the eight o'clock ferry and making it back to the unit just in time for a nap before heading out to dinner.

It had been one of the best days of my life, and the perfect recipe to help us forget the recent incidents and slip right back into vacation mode.

Casa Mission is a beautiful Colonial-style restaurant surrounded by lush gardens and tranquil fountains, situated ten blocks from the downtown waterfront. We were told that the hacienda was known for its relaxed but lively atmosphere, well-kept grounds, and delicious food.

Scarlett had a quick chat with a caged parrot on the walk across the grounds, then we met Mick, Dorothy, and Rico at a big table stretching along an artistic stone railing and overlooking the courtyard and biggest fountain.

"Great to see you on your feet," Scarlett said, greeting Rico first.

The young man smiled as best he could. "Thanks to you and Dorothy," he said, grinning at Mick's daughter. "And your mom and dad, of course."

"And Mick," I said. "We never would've figured out where they were hiding you without his help."

We were introduced to the rest of the large group as they arrived, though a few of them we already knew. Including Benny and Uno from our dive trip, and Armando, the taxi driver who'd picked us up our first day on the island.

Given how friendly everyone was, we felt at home right away. The owner and staff were all kind and welcoming, and a mariachi band serenaded us while our waiter whipped up fresh guacamole right at our table and passed out baskets of homemade corn chips.

We ordered plates of delicious appetizers, including their famous coconut shrimp. And for dinner I got the surf and turf, the lobster clearly hauled in earlier that day.

While eating, another familiar face appeared, threading through the tables to come and say hello—Officer Ramirez, who was out of uniform and sporting a casual blue shirt with half the buttons undone and a pair of jeans. He looked relaxed, with his shoulders loose and his hands in his pockets. After greeting everyone, he asked if he could have a word with me in private.

"I meant to tell you," he said as we peeled away from the group and sauntered beside the fountain and a line of ancient-looking trees. "The mayor wants to meet you. Says he has a gift for you to thank you for all that you and your family have done."

I smiled, thought it over about half a second, then shook my head. "Tell him I appreciate the gesture, but no, thanks."

I hadn't had the greatest track record with mayors as of late. The new Key West mayor, a guy named Nix, hadn't liked me from day one. And I'd yet to sway his opinion of me.

"You sure?" Ramirez said, surprised.

"I'm sure."

Then I gazed back toward our table and focused on Rico enjoying his meal, surrounded by friends.

"I kinda figured you'd turn it down," he said. "But at least allow me to express my thanks," he added, sliding his right hand from his pocket and shaking mine. "If you're ever back in Cozumel, you should reach out."

"I'll do that. In the meantime, the best way to thank me is to ensure Beauchamp pays for all he's done."

Ramirez nodded. "That man will get what's coming to him. I can assure you of that."

"Good," I said.

"That's why I moved back here to Cozumel. To keep this island clean of filth like Beauchamp and his gang."

I eyed him quizzically, then said, "That explains the hint of American accent. Let me guess, you lived in Texas for a spell?"

"Most of my adult life," Ramirez said. "My dad moved us to the States when I was a teenager. He managed to obtain citizenship then became a cop. Spent a whole career serving others. He's the one who inspired me to swear in, and after years serving in the States, I decided it was time to rediscover my roots. So I moved back here. Back home."

He fell silent, then looked away, choking up a little.

I rested a hand on his shoulder. "I'm sure your dad's proud."

"He would be, yeah."

I gave him a moment, then gestured back toward the group. "Come on, you look like you could use a drink."

He chuckled. "After the past few days? I think I'm gonna need a lot more than one. But not tonight. I switched shifts with another officer so he could spend the evening with his family. I'm on my way to the station now, just wanted to stop by and offer my thanks. In case I don't see you again." He patted me on the back again, then added, "Have a safe trip home, Logan. And keep up the good fight."

"You too," I said with a smile, then he turned and headed for the street.

We all enjoyed the company, food, and ambience for two hours, then the owner and his wife handed out party poppers, horns, plastic hats, and glasses of champagne. When the time came, we counted down from diez to uno before belting out "Happy New

Year!"

Confetti popped into the air. Horns blew. People clapped and cheered and hollered. And distant fireworks screeched and thundered in the night sky.

The group huddled up, thanked the hosts for everything, then migrated to the waterfront plaza near the ferry terminal, catching the crescendo of the fireworks display. The finale was surprisingly impressive, especially given how small the island is. And many locals joined in, lighting off fireworks of their own.

Some locals closed off their streets using their vehicles and had barbeques and bonfires and lit off rockets right there in the road as the entire town brought in the New Year.

We sang and danced and soaked up the wild night with newly made friends, and it was half past one by the time we made it back to the villa.

Scarlett, exhausted from the long day, hugged us both, then dragged her feet to bed. I fell silent a moment, staring out through the sliding glass door.

"I'm just gonna wash up," Ange said, kissing me on the cheek before heading into the bedroom and running the shower.

I migrated out to the balcony with a bottle of Casa Verde tequila and a shot glass. I got comfortable on the padded chair, propped my bare feet up on the railing, and clasped my hands behind the head. My gaze drifted up from the grass and pool, past the beach and surf, and trailing up the silhouetted palm leaves to the inky black sky soaked with stars.

I stared off into the infinite, then weighed anchor on my mind, letting it roam freely. The past year came back to me in flashes. It was difficult to fathom all that had happened during those twelve short months. All the changes that had occurred. I thought mostly of Scarlett, the kidnapped orphan who we'd eventually rescued, grown to love, and adopted.

I like to spend time looking back. To give the past its due, smiling at the happy moments and learning from the mistakes. Reminiscing and ruminating. Then I try and picture what lies ahead.

I chuckled at the thought. Took a sip of the smooth spirit, then relaxed even deeper into my chair.

After what the past year had held, and all the things that had happened since I'd moved back to Key West, there was no way of knowing. The horizon was a mystery. Complete and utter, and unbounded.

The door slid open and Ange stepped out. Her blond hair was damp and she'd changed into soft white shorts and a wide-necked tank top. I caught a captivating whisper of citrus and eucalyptus as she slid onto my lap and wrapped her arms around me, her head resting on my chest and her smooth thighs pressing against my upper legs.

"Thanks, Ange," I said, kissing her forehead.

"For what?"

"For everything. But at the moment, for giving me some time to think."

"I know you well enough to recognize when you need it. I hope I didn't interrupt too soon."

"Perfect timing."

She grinned. "Plus you always do this on New Year's. Any resolutions?"

I thought a moment, then slid a hand over her lotioned legs. "To end every night just like this. With the most beautiful woman in the world on my lap."

She kissed me, then ran her fingers over my lips and playfully pried my mouth open and gazed in like a dentist.

"What is it?" I tried my best to ask.

"Not every day you see a silver tongue."

We laughed and I brought her in even tighter, completely and utterly intoxicated by her.

"What about you?" I said. "Any resolutions?"

She thought it over while biting her lip. "I'd like to travel more. Maybe a couple big trips this year. I love exploring new places, especially with you two, and pretty soon Scarlett's gonna be off on her own. Taking on the world."

"I like it. We could take a big trip this summer. Get out of the islands for the rainy season."

Ange and I had always loved to travel. It was one of the many things we'd enjoyed about our previous employment, the work taking us all over the world. And for our honeymoon, we'd fed the wanderlust by spending two months traveling around Europe. Then we'd ended the trip with a relaxing stay at an overwater bungalow in Fiji.

Ange helped me polish off more shots of tequila as we talked for another hour, chatting about anything and everything. Then the kissing grew more passionate and I rose from the chair with Ange in my arms. We reached the bedroom in a blur of heat and passion, our hearts pounding against each other as we crashed onto the bed, worked off each other's clothes, and lost ourselves in the intense embrace.

TWENTY-NINE

I awoke just after sunrise for a run and a swim, and during breakfast, Scarlett had a surprise for us.

"If you're both up for catching some waves, I called and reserved board rentals for this afternoon at Playa Chen Rio," she exclaimed.

Excited, Ange and I both agreed. One thing the Keys doesn't offer is good surfing. I'd spent most of my high school years living in San Diego and spent many afternoons and weekends riding the breaks, so I jumped at the opportunity any chance I got.

We pulled up to El Pescador, a beachfront restaurant and bar on the other side of the island, around noon. We'd driven by the place a few times but had yet to stop by.

We entered a massive palapa that was surrounded

by a bunch of smaller ones, all facing a beautiful cove with crashing waves. There was a big bar, scattered tables, and lines of beach chairs cutting across the sand. Massage tables, volleyball courts, hammocks, and in the corner, a surf shop and school.

We picked up our gear from the energetic owner and headed out. Losing track of time, we spent over four hours riding and crashing into the swells, only stepping out of the water to drink or get a quick bite to eat.

The final leg of our trip played on with a similarly enjoyable tune. We relaxed by the pool and beach, snorkeled to our hearts' content, and even took another dive to explore the Spanish galleon shipwreck. This time Ange and Scarlett came along, after our daughter begged Mick's ear off for hours one evening.

Seeing my wife and daughter's reaction to the wreck appearing from the hazy water and watching them fin over the various remnants and the rows of mostly buried chests was nearly as special as seeing them for the first time myself. Their eyes lit up with wonder as they took in the incredible sight, running their hands over preserved history.

Scarlett was especially taken aback. Stunned speechless when we drifted along and eventually surfaced. Yet again, I saw that twinkling look in her eye. The lure of adventure. And again I wondered what sort of life lay in store for her, what adventures she was going to embark on someday.

We spent our last full day on Cozumel at Punta Sur, soaking up as much as we could of the lively, colorful reefs and mouthwatering Mexican food.

Relaxing to the fullest.

On the morning of our flight, we swung by Mick's dive shop to say goodbye to our new friends.

"I can't thank you enough for all that you've done," Mick said. "And I know this is far from even compensation, but I'd like you to each have one of these."

He held out three gold doubloons, just like the one he'd given Rico after our first dive.

We looked them over, beaming, and pocketed them. Then everyone went in for a hug.

"Thanks again, Scarlett," Dorothy whispered, and I barely noticed my daughter shoot her a wink.

"Let me know when you secure the rights to the wreck," I said. "We'll be back down in a heartbeat to help you haul it up. Anything you need."

Mick smiled, then shook his head. "I'm afraid it might be a while. I just hope I haven't died of old age by the time a decision is made in our favor. I'd like to fix up this place while I'm still on my feet."

"Well, for what it's worth," I said, "this might just be my favorite dive shop in the world."

We said our final goodbyes, then drove over to the rental place. After hauling our stuff out, I met with the attendant.

"Glad this one made out better," the man joked, our previous Jeep having been returned in less-than-ideal condition.

I handed him the keys just as a taxi pulled into the lot, a familiar face hopping out.

"Leaving so soon?" Armando said, wearing his trademark enormous grin as he grabbed and carried our luggage into the back, then opened the doors for us.

"Time flies when you're in paradise," I said.

He laughed and blasted the AC while cruising us across town.

"You were here at an interesting time," he said. "I'm sure you heard about all the excitement. The shoot-outs."

I shot a look back at Ange and Scarlett.

"We heard something about that," Ange said. "Just street talk."

"We heard they caught the ones responsible for the missing people," I said.

"Yes, it's true. Thank goodness for that. Now things can finally get back to normal." He eyed me and then the girls through the rearview mirror. "You look like you had a good vacation. All of you relaxed. Cozumel has that power."

"It was very relaxing," I said. "For the most part."

"Well, come back soon. And call me when you do. I'll pick you up."

He drove up to Cozumel International Airport, helped us with the bags, then smiled at us.

"Why do I get the feeling that smile never leaves your face?" Ange said.

He laughed. "When you live here," he said, holding out his hands, "there's always a reason to smile."

He threw a wave as he cut back around to the driver's door. "*Adios*, Dodge family. Safe travels and visit again soon."

~ ~ ~

Half an hour later and a quarter mile away, a man leaned against the trunk of his car. He held a pair of binoculars up to his eyes as three distant figures strode onto the tarmac toward a Boeing 737. He'd been standing there since before his targets had rolled up in their taxi—had observed their movements closely as they'd entered through the airport's sliding doors.

Then, he'd waited.

He focused the lenses, watching intently as the figures climbed up the stairs and vanished into the fuselage.

He lowered the binos and waited some more. Patiently.

That was the key to the whole thing: patience. Their leader had hammered that point home again and again.

The rest of the passengers embarked. The stairs rolled away. All doors were shut, and then the engines fired and warmed up to a steady drone.

He remained against his car as the plane backed away, then taxied along the apron. There was no other traffic on the tarmac, so the jet was given an instant green light. The steady hum of the engines amplified, then the plane shot forward, lifting up over the tropical landscape.

The man smiled as it gained altitude, then banked north, soaring into the distance.

He fished out his phone. Sent a quick, simple message. Just two words.

"Mark's airborne."

THIRTY

Scarlett had the window seat, Ange the middle, and me and my long legs had the aisle. But I still leaned over to gaze out the tiny porthole as we made our descent. I've always loved watching the approach. Running my eyes over the slow-moving, ant-like world below. The view is especially interesting on a clear day, and on that January afternoon, the Lower Keys didn't have a cloud in sight.

We flew over the outstretched fingers of the archipelago, the islands comprising the Dry Tortugas tiny specks on the horizon. Then we flew over the Marquesas Keys and Key West National Wildlife Refuge—clusters of flat dark spots fringed in turquoise and surrounded by dark blue.

Then we soared over Key West, the capital of the Conch Republic, resembling a concrete jungle in comparison to the surrounding islands.

I didn't know what to expect returning home after just two weeks, given the circumstances that had led to us taking the trip in the first place. But as I peered down at my island home, I felt nothing but happiness. Not a trace of trepidation or worry. It was our home, and the islands appeared to be welcoming us back with open arms.

The plane passed over the island, then slowed and banked back around, putting the rest of the archipelago momentarily in view, the long, broken-up arm of land reaching down from the mainland like a foreign tropical country just hanging on to the continental United States by the thread of two-lane US-1.

After a smooth landing down the stretch of pavement running just four hundred yards from the coast, we breezed through immigration and customs, then gathered our bags and headed out through automatic doors.

The smell of the South Florida tropical air put a smile on my face as we donned sunglasses and were greeted by the afternoon sun. We weren't three steps out when a familiar voice filled the air.

"Welcome back," Jack Rubio said in his patented laid-back tone.

He was standing just off our right beside a classic baby-blue Ford Bronco convertible. He was leaning into the back seat, trying his best to restrain a frantic, excited animal. Atticus, our rambunctious yellow Lab, managed to break free of his grasp, squirming over the back seat and vaulting onto the pavement.

He bolted toward us, his tongue hanging free. The

three of us knelt and braced as he jumped into us, unleashing a frenzy of slobbery licks and wagging his tail like mad. We took a moment to give him some love, scratching his favorite places. He was well fed, recently bathed, and happy as ever.

"He's been excited all day," Jack said, flip-flopping over to us. "I think he knew you were coming home."

"Thanks for looking after him, Jack," I said, rising and hugging one of my oldest friends.

"Say nothing of it, amigo. Everyone loves having Atty around." The wiry, tanned conch brushed aside his dirty blond hair and helped us with the bags. "How was the trip? You sounded blissful last time you called. Just what the doctor ordered?"

"For the most part," I said, then Ange and Scarlett both shot me a look.

"Uh-oh," Jack said, catching on while we heaved the bags into the back of Scarlett's Bronco. "Trouble in paradise?"

"Mom and Dad took down a corrupt criminal organization," Scarlett said, spilling the whole can of beans.

Jack laughed. Shook his head. "I swear, you two could take a trip to the middle of the Arctic Circle and find evildoers up to no good."

We closed up the back, and he waved at us to climb aboard. "Tell me all about it."

We gave him the rundown as he drove us out of the airport, then west toward the middle of the island. Just the high points. We'd give him a more extensive story over a meal and a couple of drinks sometime.

"Crazy," he said once we'd wrapped it up, each

chiming in at times. "Good thing your rebel yell's loud, Scar."

Ange chuckled. "I think if it were any louder you'd be deaf."

Scarlett gave Ange a playful nudge.

"How's everything here?" I said, soaking in the scenery.

The familiar palm tree and house lined streets. The historic island vibes lingering in the air.

"Cayo Hueso's as wild as ever," he said, fluttering back his curly hair. "A record number of tourists migrated to our southern point oasis for the holiday season. Duval looked like Times Square on New Year's when they dropped the conch shell over at Sloppy Joe's."

"How's the marina?" I asked.

"Busy. I don't know how Gus made running it look so easy. Seemed like the guy was always loafing about, lounging on his beanbag chair and watching television. But it's a grind, that's for sure. Seems like something's always breaking. We're completely redoing the planks at the end of dock bravo. So we've had to shift things around and it's a little cramped at the moment."

"I'll be there tomorrow to help out, if you'd like," I said, a big part of me excited by the prospect of some good manual labor.

Jack chuckled. "Don't feel obligated. I think you've got your hands full with your own building project."

As the words rolled off his tongue, he cruised onto Palmetto Street, then turned into our seashell driveway. Parked in the drive were two beat-up trucks and a trailer full of scraps. Beyond them was the skeleton of our new house, surrounded by power tool stations.

"They're really making progress," I said, then climbed out of the Bronco.

Atticus sprang free and took off, all excitement as he pranced around and sniffed every inch of the property.

The lead builder strode over and greeted us. The team was comprised of all locals, and many of them had been living and building in the islands for generations.

Just two months earlier, our old house had burned down in an act of arson. After dealing with the ones responsible, Ange had only borderline-sulked for a minute at most. There are a lot of things my wife does well, but playing a victim isn't one of them. She'd quickly flipped the mood, getting excited about the prospect of building something new. Something of our own design and liking. I'd loved the old house, but this was ours. From the ground up, we were choosing it all.

Even Scarlett stepped out for a look around. Though she'd only lived in our old place for less than a year, she'd been hit the hardest. After spending her entire life in the foster system, she'd finally had a place to call home. A refuge of her own and surrounded by people who loved her. And then it had been taken from her.

The new design was similar to the old place. Resting on stilts that were anchored to buried concrete footings to weather the frequent storms. Plans for a big wraparound porch. And a similar, simple interior. But it was wider, and we'd added another room to be used as an office and library off the left side. The kitchen would also be bigger, along with the bathrooms. But the living room would be slightly smaller, the three of us usually dining or entertaining out on the covered porch or in the backyard anyway.

She was still a shell, but the contractors anticipated it would be just seven more months before we could move in. She was coming along.

We spent half an hour on our property, checking over things and getting updates on the progress. Then we climbed back into the Bronco and Jack drove us to our temporary abode downtown.

The streets were packed and lively. The high season in the Keys. Jack parked just up from the waterfront and the Conch Harbor Marina, where I'd moored my boat ever since moving back to Key West.

We carried our stuff along the promenade, passing a bronze statue of Gus Henderson, the former owner, before heading down the dock. Atticus bounded ahead, leading the way to our boat at slip twenty-four. I couldn't help but smile as I gazed upon *Dodging Bullets II*, our 48 Baia Flash. A sight for sore eyes if there ever was one. We stowed our stuff below deck, then met back up with Jack topside beside the sunbed.

He was just opening his mouth when he was cut off.

"Jack, there you are," Lauren Sweetin said in her Southern accent, fast-walking from the marina office.

She froze when she saw us, then ran over and hugged all three of us at once.

"We're so glad to have you back," she said. "I wish we had time right now to catch up, but—"

"What's going on, sweetie?" Jack said, planting a kiss on her cheek.

"The internet's still acting up, even after the technician was here yesterday. And the fuel truck will be here any minute to top off our tanks. And we still haven't installed the new sails for the cat and there's a sunset charter setting off in"—she checked her watch—"three hours."

"You weren't kidding about being busy," I said.

Then I thanked Jack again. For everything.

"The workload never ends." He waved and stepped away before quickly turning back. "Hey, I forgot to mention, there's a familiar band playing at Pete's this evening. Should be a fun night. Though this weather's about to shift for the worst, so it won't be out on the balcony."

I peered up at the clear sky, perfectly blue in all directions. Not a cloud in sight. But none of us dared question him. Jack had a way of reading the weather in the Keys that was unlike any phenomenon I'd ever witnessed. He was in tune with the place. Born and bred. A fourth-generation conch. It was a part of him, and he knew it well. Knew its moods and tendencies. He probably hadn't checked a weather report in years, but if he said the weather was about to turn, it was as sure of a prediction to bet on as anything.

"See you guys there?" he said.

I looked to Ange and Scarlett, who both nodded eagerly.

"Mic gets hot at nine," Jack said, then rushed to the office.

THIRTY-ONE

We unpacked and tidied, then I plopped into the half-moon cushioned seat around the topside dinette, taking in the sights and sounds of the marina. Realigning my bearings. After walking Atticus to the nearby dog park and tiring him out with twenty minutes of tennis ball throws, the three of us took a quick nap, knowing that if we were going to Salty Pete's, we were in for a long night.

Just after sunset, we helped Jack and Lauren tie off the catamaran *Sweet Dreams*. Greeted the smiling tourists with smiles as they climbed off, raving about their experience. A Key West sunset is a bucket list item, or at least it should be. A sight so spectacular that it's a cause for celebration every evening at Mallory Square.

A chorus of whistles, conch horns, cheers, and

claps fill the air. Then darkness falls over the island, and it transforms into a completely different animal. The spirits of old take over. Years of pirates, smugglers, gypsies, and treasure hunters. Movie stars, authors, presidents, and sports heroes. A haven for the outcasts and elite alike that once rivaled the old buccaneer port of Tortuga. All part of the island's unique charm that combines to make it unlike any place I've ever visited on Earth.

We helped clean up and spray the deck, then hauled the trash and recyclables to nearby dumpsters. Once the work was done, I threw a hand over Jack's shoulders and massaged his tight muscles.

"Come on, old friend," I said. "Let's get you a drink and some good food."

"And great music," Lauren said. "The Wayward Sons are in town. I saw them once back up in Nashville."

Just as Jack had predicted, the clouds rolled in seemingly out of nowhere and the rain began to splatter on the windshield just as we pulled into Pete's. I parked my truck, and by the time we were at the front steps, it was pouring. Heavy, thick drops. From zero to sixty in a blink. In true Florida Keys fashion.

Usually, Atticus nestled into his favorite spot beside the entrance. Under the cover of a gumbo-limbo tree, and close enough to greet people as they entered and exited. But with the rain coming down so hard, we brought him in with us. Mia, the head waitress and a good friend, had no problem with it, given how well behaved and popular Atticus was.

"With this rain, we're gonna set up the band down

here," she said as we entered. "We're busy, but I've got just the place for you guys over here."

Mia led us to a booth along the left side of the dining room. The old restaurant's walls were covered in various maritime memorabilia, including stuffed fish, nets, a faded helm, and dozens of grainy photos.

Since the place was already packed, the five of us cozied into the single booth. With Atticus nestled at my feet, she fanned out the menus, and they were on the table for all of five seconds before a familiar pirate-like voice filled the air.

"Are my old seafaring eyes going bad, or has the Dodge family returned at last?" Pete Jameson said, seemingly out of nowhere, greeting each of us in turn.

The short, round-bellied, mid-seventy-year-old was nearly bald, with a little salty hair scattered about. He waved his hook of a right hand and wore a satisfied grin that rarely left his face.

"We were only gone two weeks," Scarlett said.

"That's far longer than I've ever been able to stay away," Pete said. "And it felt like longer. You three missed so much."

Ange laughed. "You'll have to bring us up to speed."

Pete began to, then saw that the makeshift stage was ready.

"First, I have to introduce our honored guests," he said, turning and threading through the sea of people and tables and chairs to where a trio of familiar faces stood with microphones in a cleared-out corner of the dining room.

After a quick thanks and welcome from the proprietor, the Wayward Sons lit up the night. Their unique cross between reggae and country gelled beautifully with the island culture, and people cheered and clapped along as they sang of distant ports, warm wind in the sails, and untamed beaches.

Their melodies were catchy and their lyrics memorable, making it easy to see why the band had gained so much popularity over the past few years. The band also held sentimental value for me personally, given that they were the first band I'd ever listened to at Salty Pete's.

We savored delicious seafood conjured up by Pete's incredible Scandinavian chef, Osmond, who we sometimes referred to as the Wizard of Oz for his supernatural cooking ability, or just Oz for short. Halfway through their set, the Sons took a break to get some food and drinks to fuel up for the second half of the evening. The musicians greeted Pete, then I watched as the conch business owner drifted into a corner, leaning against the wall and smiling as he took in the scene.

"I'll be right back," I said to the group, then slid out and sauntered over, leaning against the wall right beside him.

We were both silent for a good minute, then Pete whispered, "Camelot."

I chuckled softly. Leaned forward and eyed him curiously.

He cleared his throat. "Don't let it be forgot, that once there was a spot, for one brief shining moment, that was known as Camelot." He smiled, then added, "The famous theatrical lines speak of life as it was, and how it would eventually change and never be the same. That Camelot couldn't last. That all things, no matter how perfect or beautiful, will end. In times like this, I think about that." He placed an arm on me, a fatherly gesture. "It helps me to soak up every moment, my boy. Know that the fleeting nature of things makes it all the better."

I smiled at that, then looked around, taking it all in. My family and friends. The atmosphere. The smells and sounds and sights of our little sun-kissed Camelot.

We stood in silence another minute, then I shifted the subject. "I hear you're a good man to ask for advice when it comes to underwater ventures."

Pete smiled. "The last time you spoke like this, you were a stranger walking into this dingy, run-down place and inquiring about shipwrecks off these islands. What is Logan Dodge up to now?"

I grinned, looked away, then motioned toward the stairs. "You mind if we chat in your office for a bit?"

Pete looked me in the eyes, saw I was serious, then nodded. "Can't be too long, though. They're back on in ten. Camelot."

"The kingdom's holding strong for at least another night. And we'll be back to see it."

I followed him up the wide wooden staircase, weaving past the people seated to enjoy the packed show. Upstairs was well lit but quiet. A wide-open space with rows of glass cases containing artifacts from all over the islands. There were exhibits complete with lines of history. Everything from cannons to jewelry.

A couple people had ventured for a look around during the break in the music, and Pete greeted them as we made our way to a door nestled into the back corner. Pete's office was small but cozy and filled with shelves of books, both nautical resources and fiction. There were more pictures and maps and model ships. A worn oak desk with a faded nautical lamp, coins, and a stack of papers.

Pete fell into his leather chair, and I stood with my arms folded for a moment, looking out the lone window with rain streaking down the panes.

"Have you ever read anything about a Spanish galleon sinking near Cozumel?" I said.

Pete leaned back slowly, then his eyes lit up.

"Is this a... rumor, or...?"

I buried my hand in my front pocket, stepped to the desk, then rested it on the old hardwood, palm up and open, revealing the gold coin Mick had given me. Pete bent forward, clicked on his desk lamp. I held it closer and he grabbed the doubloon. Put on a pair of glasses, angled the light, and inspected it.

His mouth hung open. "You found this where?"

I smiled broadly. "At the bottom of the sea, Pete."

He hunched forward, staring into his desk. Laughing like a young, adventurous boy.

"You're gonna give this old sea dog a heart attack, you know that? I'm guessing this little guy wasn't lonely on the seafloor?"

"I said a galleon, didn't I?"

He laughed again. "Heaven almighty. This is... unbelievable. How did you manage to find this? Do you know how rare it is for lifelong explorers to find one old wreck? Let along a laden galleon? Let alone two of them?"

"Well, I didn't find this one. That honor belongs to one Mick Flanagan."

Pete's head snapped up. "You met Mickey?"

"You know him?"

"Friend of a friend. From many years back."

I wasn't entirely surprised. I imagined that Pete's friends of friends numbered in the thousands, especially within the diving and underwater exploration community.

"My knowledge is mostly restricted to the Keys," Pete said.

"Know anyone who might be able to help? We're trying to identify it."

"That's the tricky part, isn't it? What's the site's status?"

"Perfectly untouched. Aside from this and a couple other coins removed."

Pete nodded. "Easiest would be to find some distinct artifact. Or perhaps line up finds with the manifest. But—"

"But he can't salvage it without the rights."

"And he'll be hard-pressed to get the rights without a name. Catch 22." He thought a moment, still examining and running his fingers over the coin. "I know a few guys who could help. I'll start calling around. See what I can dig up. Lost Spanish galleon is a big deal, right? Lots of money the crown never saw. Gotta be some report somewhere. But if it's in Cozumel, it was severely off course. I'll see what I can learn." He handed the coin back to me. "This mean you're heading back to Mexico soon?"

I shook my head. "Doubt it. Mick first found the site nearly a year ago. Progress makes a turtle look fast when it comes to dealing with governments and money. You know that as well as anyone."

"That I do."

We fell quiet, then the singing and music returned, reverberating through the floorboards.

"It's one hell of a find. I'll let you know as soon as I discover anything," he said, and we rose. Before stepping out he rubbed the back of his neck, then chuckled when he looked at me. "Another Spanish galleon. You're either the luckiest man alive or a closet genius."

"I'm definitely not a genius. I can promise you that."

"Either way, I had no idea when we first met that I was talking to a real-life Dirk Pitt." He threw an arm around me, then pointed to the watch Ange had gotten me for Christmas as we made for the door. "And I see you've even got the timepiece now to round out the character."

THIRTY-TWO

Earlier that day, Mick Flanagan stood at the bow of *Craic of Dawn* as it motored into Puerto de Abrigo Marina. Rico was at the helm, and their two patrons sat in half-peeled-off wetsuits on the cockpit bench seat.

After tying off, helping the tourists with their stuff, and then seeing them off, Mick and Rico cleaned up the boat. The teenager tried not to wince as he knelt down to grab a piece of trash, but was quickly stopped by the shop owner.

"I can't believe you're back out here already," Mick said, snagging the empty bottle and tossing it into a plastic bag. "You were just kidnapped and beaten up for goodness' sake."

The young man smiled, resting a hand against the

cockpit roof. "Doctor said to relax and take it easy. And there's no better way for me to do that than to be out on the water." He gazed out over the opening into the harbor and took a deep, grateful breath. "Besides, this fresh ocean air tastes too sweet to miss."

Mick just chuckled as he twisted on a hose and sprayed down the deck. After lugging the BCDs and tanks into Mick's Volkswagen, they did a final sweep of the boat before disembarking for the evening.

"When are we gonna dive the wreck again?" Rico said. "Like Logan was saying, we need to figure out what ship it is."

"You're crazy, you know that?" Mick shook his head. Then he placed an arm over Rico's shoulder as they strode down the dock. "Let's give your body another week to heal before we drop down on the east side, all right?"

They climbed into Mick's old car. The AC didn't work, so they manually cranked the windows down to let the breeze in while zipping across town.

"You think any more about that offer I told you about in the Bahamas?" Mick said.

The young man rested his elbow on the sill and stuck his head out a little. "It's still a maybe."

"Like I said, my shop will always be an option for you." Mick paused, studying the kid. "Unless there's something else keeping you from going?" Rico stayed silent, and Mick added, "Or, someone, perhaps?"

Rico's head snapped left and their eyes met. For a moment, the young man looked worried. Like maybe he should throw open the door and make a run for it. Then Mick just chuckled and patted his knee.

"It's all right," Mick said. "I've known for some

time now."

Rico's face flushed, and he swallowed hard. "You're not mad?"

Mick shrugged. "I'm a little disappointed neither of you told me. But I understand. And no, I'm not mad. Like I always say, you're a good kid. And well… just know that I'm not exactly a guy who has a lot to lose. So if you hurt her—"

"That's not gonna happen."

Mick smiled. "Good. You two talked about what you're gonna do when she goes off to school next year?"

He nodded. "We'll just have to take things as they come."

Mick grinned and turned inland. "The wise-beyond-his-years seafaring poet. I'm actually glad you're dating, believe it or not."

"Really?"

"Yeah. Better you than any of these idiots her age running around."

They both laughed at that, and Mick braked along the backside of the dive shop soon after. Grabbing armfuls of gear, they strode through the back door, both of them freezing in place the moment they stepped inside.

"Hello, Mick," Warren Beauchamp Sr. said, the gray-haired man standing stoically in the center of the room with his hands resting casually behind his back.

Before either diver could respond, two men appeared from behind the curtain, both wielding handguns and aiming them forward as they forced Mick and Rico forward, then shut and locked the door behind them.

"What the hell," Mick gasped. "How did you—"

He stopped midsentence as one of the men struck him from behind, pounding a boot into the back of his leg and causing him to grunt and lurch forward. Mick fell to his knees, then a similar move put Rico on the floor right beside him.

"It doesn't matter," Beauchamp said, striding over to the two kneeling men. "But suffice it to say that I've got friends in higher places than you think."

The man stopped right in front of Mick, then eyed the diver sinisterly as he grabbed a pair of brass knuckles from his pocket and positioned it in his right hand.

Without another word, Beauchamp struck Mick in the shoulder, the solid brass nearly cracking bone as it radiated pain up Mick's body. Beauchamp struck the diver again, this time on the other side, then he slugged him in the gut, causing Mick to fall onto his hands, heaving to catch his breath.

"My son is dead now because of you," Beauchamp snarled. Then he grabbed a fistful of Mick's shirt and yanked hard. "You pathetic, useless pile of shit." He jerked Mick down, throwing him to the floor.

"I know you helped that tourist find us," Beauchamp continued, fuming with rage. He shook his head condescendingly. "That was a bad move, Mick. A stupid move. One that will cost you... and potentially cost the life of your kin as well."

Mick's eyes bulged and he gasped. Forcing his battered body up, he stared Beauchamp in the eyes. "Where is she? What have you done to her?"

The criminal smiled, enjoying the moment, then raised a hand and flicked his fingers. Shuffling of feet resounded from the other side of the room. Then a large man entered, holding Dorothy tight in his grasp, the young girl tied up at the wrists and ankles and her mouth gagged.

She gazed at her father through tear-coated eyes, her hair a mess and her body quivering.

Rico yelled and cursed and sprang forward. He made it half a step before the two guys pounced on him from behind, grabbing hold of his arms, throwing the young man onto his back, and pinning a knee into his chest.

Silence filled the air. Beauchamp let it linger a moment, then turned to Mick.

"Now, you're going to take us out on the water and you're going to show us what we want to find." He turned, grabbed Dorothy by the hair and jerked her forward, the young woman letting out a muffled squeal. "And if you don't… well, then I'll just have to find a way to motivate you. Won't I?"

THIRTY-THREE

The next morning, I kissed Ange on the cheek, then tiptoed out of the main cabin. After chugging a bottled water, I grabbed my running gear I'd left at the base of the steps the night before and crept topside. It was a calm morning. The harbor smooth as glass. The waterfront mostly quiet and still, aside from a handful of early risers.

It was just before six, an hour still until sunrise. I usually liked to rise earlier, around five-ish, but it would take some time to get back into the swing of my normal island routine. Rising early was a trait my dad had instilled in me at a young age and then the military had hammered into habit. And I always liked to start off the day with a bang, running, or swimming, or doing some form of exercise to work up a sweat.

I also liked running in the early morning because it gives you a chance to see the world without people in it. Like the world is there and on display just for you.

I pulled on my shorts, slid into a tank top, and laced up my shoes. Walking to shore, I sped up into an easy jog, heading downtown, then cutting onto Whitehead. After half a mile, I picked it up, brisking past the Hemingway House and the old lighthouse before wrapping around the southernmost marker and heading toward Fort Taylor. It felt good to be back in Key West, and also to be back in the States.

I took the waterfront route back north and spotted a familiar face sitting on a bench in front of the Margaritaville Resort. Cameron Tyson, a senior at Key West High, stood when he saw me, then ran over and matched my pace.

"I was hoping you'd pass by this morning," he said. "Scarlett said you guys got back yesterday."

Nearly as tall as me, and with short dirty-blond hair, Cameron was a good athlete and the heavily recruited star quarterback of the football team. He'd first started training with me a couple mornings a week after he'd picked a fight with a local troublemaker, then watched me end it. He also happened to be Scarlett's boyfriend.

I finished with my fastest mile of five and a half minutes, then we looped back to a stop at a patch of grass overlooking the basin and Sunset Key.

"How far did you run before joining me?" I asked.

"'Bout a mile."

I nodded. "On the grass. Hold plank."

He did as I said right away, bridging onto his

forearms and toes and straightening his body.

"How long?" he said, breathing hard from the run.

I glanced at my watch. "I don't know. Your season's over, right?"

He chuckled. "Yeah, but the All-American Bowl's next week."

"Don't laugh," I said. "That turns planks into torture real fast."

When his shaking became nearly unbearable based on his facial expression, I put him into a side plank. Then the other side. Then back to middle. I pushed him to near fatigue, then let him out of it.

"On your feet," I said, not giving him a moment's rest. "Air chairs."

Air chairs were one of my favorite exercises, one I'd first learned to both love and hate during Navy basic training.

"Air chairs, get there!" recruit division commanders would often shout at will. And the eighty guys in my division would drop into a low squat, holding still until we were told to do otherwise. If you do it right, with your weight on heels, knees back, back straight, it's about as bang for your buck of an exercise as there is.

Cameron did as he was told. And when he was nearly dead, I had him perform two more exercises before giving him a quick break, then getting into the lesson. Cameron wanted to learn how to fight, so I was teaching him a few moves. Mainly self-defense and avoidance techniques. Diplomacy is often the key. Most situations you can get out of without laying a finger on anyone, by swallowing your pride. Turning the other cheek. Backing off simply because it's not worth it. That kind of thing.

But sometimes it's unavoidable. Sometimes people throw punches first or cross the line. Sometimes you stumble upon innocent people being harassed with no law enforcement in sight. In those moments, striking quick and hard is the most effective approach. Take down your opponent as efficiently as possible. If the odds are against you, tip the scales quickly back in your favor. Any way you can.

It was a quick lesson. Just thirty minutes, but once over, we were both soaked in sweat. After he caught his breath, I helped him up off the grass and bought a fruit platter, mango banana smoothie, and two bottles of water from Bistro 245, which had tables right on the esplanade.

I liked the kid. He'd been cocky at first. But he was teachable, and he wanted to improve, and he had a good head on his shoulders.

We talked a few minutes, just surface stuff. How school was, how our trip had gone, the like. Then he went silent and finally said, "You're not gonna ask me if I've made a decision yet? About college."

I knew that Cameron had received a number of scholarship offers and that the deadline to make a decision was rapidly approaching.

"I wasn't planning on it," I said.

"Why? That's the first thing I always get asked."

I leaned back, popping a slice of watermelon into my mouth, then downed more of my water. I stretched and looked out over the sea, thought about it. I felt too young for the task, but here I was, trying to cook up some good father figure advice.

"It may seem like a lifetime ago at times," I said.

"But then it doesn't feel like that long ago that *I* was a senior in high school. I remember it clearly. Remember the confusion. The changes. And everyone always asking what you're going to do next. 'What are you going to do with your life?' And feeling like you need a good answer to that question or they'll assume you're going to be a deadbeat or something. It's kind of a funny thing, right? You live your whole life up until that point pretty much just going with the flow of things. Your life is mostly set up for you. Plans put into place by parents or whoever. Then high school graduation looms and suddenly you're expected to have all the answers. Like you're able to make some kind of wise informed decision to direct the course of your entire life at eighteen."

Cameron rubbed his mouth, leaned forward. "How did you handle it?"

I shrugged. "I had it easier than most, in that regard. I was joining the Navy, so I just answered with that." Then I examined his expression closer and added, "I take it from the conflict in your eyes you haven't decided yet?"

He shook his head. Took a moment to gather his thoughts.

"Can I ask for your advice? I'd be interested to hear your take on it."

I fought back a smile. He was seeking out advice. Another reason to like the kid.

"I'll do my best," I said.

"Well, I've pretty much narrowed it down to three. With my uncle's and coach's help." He cleared his throat. "University of Florida is my dream school. I first went there as a kid. Fell in love with the stadium.

The campus. Everything. I used to wear a Gator T-shirt nearly every day when I was little."

"But?" I said, figuring there had to be one in there somewhere or he'd have already committed.

"But it's a top ten program. One of the most competitive teams in the country. They already have a high-profile quarterback who's coming back for at least another season. Guy nearly won the Heisman this year. And there are three other five-star recruits waiting in line right behind him. I'd be the bottom of the totem pole there. Have to climb my way up. Fight for each and every step. Whereas with the other two I've narrowed it down to, I'd be more likely to see playing time. In fact, one of the coaches has already told me that he's confident I could be QB-1 by my second year there. Maybe even as a freshman. They're not as competitive as the Gators, but I could have a better chance of standing out there."

"What's your gut telling you?"

"My gut's telling me I want to play football. Not watch it on the sidelines."

I leaned back, downed the rest of my water, then ate a bite of pineapple. "I see your predicament."

"What should I do?"

"I'm not sure I'm really the best person to give advice on this topic. I don't know much about football, really. Beyond being a casual fan."

"You know about life, though. You know about success and what it takes."

"Okay. Well, then, what does success look like to you?"

"Being one of the best to ever play."

"All right. So NFL?"

He nodded. "I know it's crazy. But if you're going to aim, aim high, right?"

I laughed. "I think in order to have the drive and determination and outright guts to push until you reach the NFL, you gotta be a little crazy." I paused, then said, "Is playing for the Gators still your dream? 'Cause dreams change, right? Sometimes you have a dream when you're young, then you grow up and out of it. It's not that you're giving up on it, you're just making a better-informed decision about your future. You know yourself better. Your likes and dislikes. Wants and passions."

"It's still my dream," he said, not giving it a moment's thought.

"But you're afraid that maybe you can't play there. That the competition's too fierce."

He nodded.

I leaned back and rubbed my chin. Peered out over the water. Then I tilted forward, and eyed the young man again. "You know, I have this friend who I served with in the Navy. He's a public speaker. Travels around and gives talks in front of large audiences. Motivating people. He told me every time he speaks, he'll get a handful of teenagers who ask him the same question."

"What question?"

"'Do I have what it takes to be a SEAL?'"

Cameron shook his head. "And? How does he answer it? How could he know who does and doesn't have what it takes just by looking at them?"

I smiled. "Because the truth is, if someone has to ask whether or not they have what it takes to be a SEAL, then they don't. The ones who succeed, the guys that make it through? They go in with a very fixed mindset. They don't care what anyone thinks or says. They're going to be SEALs. And nothing can convince them otherwise. It's drastic, but it drives the point."

Cameron fell silent a moment, thinking over everything I'd said. "So you think I should go to the U."

"No. I just think whatever decision you make should be for the right reasons." I patted him on the shoulder. "But really, I don't think there is a wrong decision here. They're all great. You're gonna get a free college education. And from what I hear that's worth an awful lot these days. Cliché, but I'd advise you to focus on school. Let football be your release from it. Work hard, yes. Strive for greatness, always. Dream big, without a doubt. But make football a fun challenge, not the foundation on which your future happiness depends. That's putting a lot of pressure on something you're passionate about."

I let out a long breath and finished off the fruit. I'm not particularly chatty by nature, so I couldn't remember the last time I'd spoken so much.

"But at the end of the day, what do I know?" I said as we got ready to leave. "I'm just a simple guy. I love my family and friends. I love boats and diving and fishing and guns. So take my advice with a grain of salt."

Cameron jogged alongside me back to the marina, both of us taking it easy. We slowed to a walk and I patted him on the back before he veered inland.

"You're sitting on a winning lottery ticket either way," I said. "So don't stress about it too much.

Enjoy your final months in high school."

Scarlett was just heading down the dock when I returned to the marina, slinging her backpack over her shoulder and heading off for her first day back at school. She was all excitement, eager to catch up with her friends. It was her first year experiencing a normal public school setting, and her enthusiastic, lively, eager-to-learn personality had fit right in.

"I'll see you this afternoon, Dad," she said, giving me a quick, no contact hug to avoid touching my sweaty clothes, then climbed into her Bronco and pulled out of the lot.

I showered on the Baia, changed, and had breakfast with Ange at the topside dinette.

Jack, a late riser by nature, arrived earlier than usual to get a start on the dock restoration. Ange and I spent the day helping him and Lauren, all of us heaving the planks into position and screwing them down.

"Sorry for all the work, bro," Jack said for the second time that morning. "I was hoping to motor out and catch some bugs in honor of your return."

"This isn't so bad," I said, adjusting a plank before pinning it down and drilling a screw snug. "I was due for an honest day's work anyway."

An hour into our work, my phone buzzed. It was Pete.

"I'm surprised you're awake already," I said after answering. "Thought you'd be dozing till the crack of noon at least after the late night."

He laughed. "I caught barely a Z or two. Though I've never been a good sleeper when I've got treasure on the brain."

He paused dramatically, and I said, "All right, you've got all my attention, Pete. I'm guessing you found something?"

"Oh yeah. In fact, I think I might have the name of your ship."

I glanced at my watch. "It hasn't been twelve hours, and you already have a potential winner?"

"Impressed?"

"Very. Though not entirely surprised."

He paused again, enjoying it, then continued, "I called a guy who works at the Spanish culture ministry and he did a little digging. Turns out, there were only about half a dozen potential laden galleons that could've sunk anywhere near that part of the Caribbean. So then I called up a climatologist who specializes in Caribbean weather history and patterns, and he managed to quickly dig up historical weather reports and simulations which we compared to the dates and routes of the lost galleons."

I smiled as I wiped a layer of sweat from my brow. Pete was the right man for the job.

"That really narrows it down to one potential vessel in my book," he added, then cleared his throat. "Maybe two. But I'd bet my left hand it's the *Nuestra Señora del Juncal.*"

Pete went on to explain how in the early 1600s, the galleon had hit a storm en route to Havana. A storm that could have very likely redirected it to the area near the eastern edge of Cozumel.

We spoke animatedly for another five minutes, then ended the call. After telling the others what Pete had discovered, I made a mental note to call Mick that evening and give him the exciting news, then went back to work.

We ate lobster rolls for lunch, Ange swinging by Old Town Bakery and picking up the small, freshly baked loaves. They were delicious, the recently caught lobster bursting with flavor. For me, it was the taste of Key West. A taste I'd missed.

Then we cleaned up and went right back at it. It was hard work, especially with the twenty-fourth-degree north parallel sun beating down on us. But we broke up the exertion and monotony with intermittent breaks and managed to still make good progress.

Just after three, I surfaced wearing scuba gear, having just replaced one of the cross braces. I removed my regulator just as my phone began to buzz on the dock. Ange scampered over and scooped it up.

"I don't recognize the number," she said. "Send to voicemail?"

I nodded, then unclipped my BCD and handed it up to Lauren. Less than a minute later, my phone buzzed again. I grabbed it this time. Same number. I patted my hair with a towel and answered with a hello.

"Logan," a faintly familiar voice said. "It's Benny from Dive Paradise in Cozumel."

I would have smiled and asked to what I owed the pleasure, were it not for the undertone of seriousness in his usually relaxed voice.

"Good to hear from you, Benny," I said. "What's going on?"

"I apologize for calling you like this. I'm sure you're back home in the States. I just didn't know who else to call."

"Benny, what's going—"

"It's Mick," he said. He sighed, having trouble getting the words out. "I was fishing off the eastern shore this afternoon. No cruise ships today. Day off. I was out near the Punta Molas Lighthouse at the northern tip, hoping to reel in some dinner. Just before three, I saw a boat round the coastline. It was a Boston Whaler. One I recognized right away as Mick's dive boat. Then another followed closely behind it. A big workboat. Maybe twenty meters, with a deck crane."

"He secured the rights already?" I said.

"No. He didn't. I moved back into the brush and watched closely as the two boats chugged past. I didn't recognize any of the crew members. Then I spotted Mick standing on the other side of the dive boat's helm, his hands tied behind his back."

"Shit," I whispered, the word just spewing out.

Ange, seeing that something was clearly wrong, stepped over and eyed me quizzically.

"Yeah," Benny said. "And that's not the worst of it, Logan. As the workboat passed, I caught a glimpse of a familiar face aboard it as well. Standing at the stern, less than a couple hundred meters from me, was Warren Beauchamp Sr."

THIRTY-FOUR

It was well north of seventy degrees, but a cold, unnerving feeling washed over me. Ange and Jack were both at my side. Watching me in silence and tense anticipation.

"You're sure it was him?" I said, hoping for some kind of a mistake.

"Sure as anything," Benny replied, temerity in his voice. "He wasn't far off. And he's got a distinct look. It was him, Logan. I'm sure of it."

"But you never saw the others? Dorothy or Rico?"

Ange's face turned to stone. She felt the chill as well, a harrowing cold front that had blown in just for us.

"No," Benny replied. "I didn't see them on the boat. Then I tried the shop... they weren't there. Then

I tried the marina. Boat and dive gear gone. Mick's Volkswagen parked in the lot."

"You call the police yet?"

"Just got off the phone with them and I'm on my way to the station now."

"What did they say about Beauchamp?"

Again, Ange hardened, then drew close enough for me to hear her breathing.

"They said he was in custody. Last they saw him was in Playa during his transfer off the island."

I remembered yet again back to what Officer Ramirez had said after I'd had a little educational fun with Junior and his buddies—how even the local law enforcement were susceptible to bribery and corruption. Regardless of who or what had caused it, Beauchamp had somehow escaped. I ran everything over in my mind. Turned enraged and resolute.

"Logan, you there?" Benny said.

I shot Ange a questioning look, and she gave a slight nod, her eyes boring into mine.

"Keep me updated, Benny," I said. "We're coming back."

And we're going to end this, I wanted to add, but kept that part to myself.

We hung up and I swiftly brought Ange and Jack up to speed.

There was no point asking how or why at that moment. The important question then and there was what we were going to do about it.

Ange checked the time. "It's half past three. Benny saw them when?"

"Thirty minutes ago."

Jack rubbed his chin. "Hauling up chests is far

from easy. Even with a good-sized crane and an experienced salvage team. It's a slow, tedious operation. This guy say how big the workboat was?"

"Guessed around sixty feet."

Jack went silent, running numbers in his head. "Probably at least a thirty-ton carrying capacity in open ocean, so they should be able to theoretically haul up a lot of it. But then what? Just crawl to the mainland and sell it?"

"If Beauchamp's able to get out of police custody, then they've got serious connections," I said. "Safe to say they have a solid plan in place once they've got the haul on hand, so we need to stop them while they're raising it."

Jack paused again. "Job like that'll take days. And that's rushing. I guess it could be faster if there's no regard for preserving historical value."

"Sounds right up these guys' alley," I said.

"Let's call it twelve hours, playing it safe," Jack said. "So we know where these criminals are going to be for at least that long."

I thought a moment, then exchanged knowing glances with Ange, who said, "We can make the jump in the Cessna in just under four hours."

Less than an hour after Benny had called, Ange breezed through her preflight checks, got the all clear from ATCs, and fired up her Cessna 182 Skylane.

I sat beside her, donning the headset, and Jack sat in the back beside our bags of gear.

While downing mugs of coffee back at the marina, Ange and I had conjured up a loose plan. Though we needed a third pilot to make it work, we'd been hesitant to ask Jack given how busy the marina was keeping him.

Jack, who'd been listening in, looked at us, confused. "You're both pilots."

"We'll need someone to drop us off, then fly to a marina and check in with immigration and customs," I said. "If we do this, we're going to bring items they won't let us enter the country with."

I was just about to tell our conch friend that we'd find someone else when he beat me to it.

"Holiday season craziness is dying off," he'd said. "And the weekend's over. And after all the work we got done today, I think Lauren can manage without me for a short while."

Lauren confirmed she could handle it. Just for a day, two max. And Scarlett and Isaac agreed to help out after school.

With everything settled and a plan in place, Ange and I saddled up, raiding our safe in the Baia's master closet for necessary weapons. We also brought along two sets of rebreather gear, cans of Spare Air, a brick of prewired C-4 explosives, a grappling hook and length of nylon rope, two small spearguns, and various other items.

Manning the Cessna's controls, Ange swiftly brought us up to speed, splashing across the empty cove before piercing into the afternoon sky. We were soon at the amphibious aircraft's cruising altitude with the floats attached of just over a hundred feet and on a southwesterly course heading for Cozumel.

Though anxious to make the jump and get to our new friends as quickly as possible, part of me was glad to have the intermission. I needed time. Time and quiet to think deep about all that had happened.

Thinking long and hard was the best remedy I'd ever found to solving life's biggest puzzles. And I sat in silence and did just that for the better part of two hours, Ange and Jack giving me space. Ange doing a lot of deep thinking of her own.

How had Beauchamp gotten away?

It was the big, all-encompassing question swirling around in my mind. The question that would clear up everything else. I ran myself in circles. Hitting dead ends. Trying again. Then hitting more.

We needed to know—needed to put a face to our mysterious enemy.

I ran through everything we'd done and heard while on Cozumel. Everyone we'd associated with. Particularly every interaction with Beauchamp and his operation, from the altercation on the dive boat to the raid of their compound.

Then a memory flashed into my mind. A brief, but clear image.

Something I'd seen following the engagement at the compound. Something that, in the heat of the moment, hadn't caught me off guard. But now, given the time to properly think everything over, and given Beauchamp's escape, that seemingly inconsequential glimpse became the integral piece that put the puzzle together.

And then it hit me.

Dubious and far-fetched at first, then clear and obvious. And if it weren't for the instrument panel in front of me, I might've fallen out of my seat.

THIRTY-FIVE

I placed a hand to my mouth and my heart rate ticked up. I ran through it again, just to be sure, and got the same result. I tried with everything I could to refute the conclusion, but couldn't. And after calling a contact of mine at the CIA to cross-reference past events, the truth was solidified. Irrefutable.

It took four hours to make the four-hundred-mile jump, and I used the remaining time to give Ange and Jack my theory. Ange had been adamant I was wrong at first, but after I ran through all of the facts, she nearly toppled out of her seat as well.

Once she was over the shock and convinced of who the real culprit behind the scenes was, we utilized the remaining time to iron out the details of our plan. And to make a few adjustments.

Wanting to stack as many chips as we could in our favor, I called an old friend of mine who'd had my back time and time again over the years.

"Hey, Scottie," I said when he answered.

"Good to hear your voice, Logan," Scott Cooper said. "You calling to schedule our itinerary for next time I'm in the Keys?"

It was an inside joke between me and the former senator and Naval Special Forces commander. It had become a long trend that often when one of us reached out to the other, we were seeking help with a not so recreational matter.

"You guys aren't still in the Gulf by any chance, are you?" I asked, Scott and his covert team having offered their help in finding a lost weapons arsenal just two months earlier.

"Nowhere near it," he said. "Why? What's going on?"

I explained the situation as briefly as I could, focusing on the high points and the kind of help we were looking for.

"I thought you and the family were just heading to Cozumel for a vacation?"

"Things… escalated, Scottie."

"I'll say." He paused, then added, "Now I'm kicking myself for not being able to get involved. You know how much I love going after lost treasures."

"What kid at heart doesn't?"

He paused, then said, "Give me a moment. I'll see what I can figure out."

"Want me to call back?"

"Nah, thirty seconds. I'm in the control room on

the *Valiant* now."

I waited, and right at half a minute, his voice came back through, a tinge of excitement lacing his words.

"We may not be able to cruise over and offer our help," he said, "but you might be able to get the next best thing. Looks like there're some old friends of ours in that corner of the Caribbean. Passing through on their vessel."

I smiled when he told me who it was, then we dialed into a three-way call and planned out the whole thing. Once set, we ended it and I leaned back into the seat.

I remembered the words of a wise instructor I'd had back in BUD/S, a guy who'd said that a man is only as good as the people he surrounds himself with. As true a statement as I've ever heard.

With a beyond-competent team offering their support, Ange, Jack, and I went back to running through our plan. Based on experience, adaptability is essential. The ability to change on the fly. Completely scrap the playbook and jot up a new course. We didn't know what or who exactly we were up against. Benny had been certain that he'd spotted Beauchamp Sr., but we didn't know how many of the criminal posse remained. Benny had estimated half a dozen armed men on two different boats—Mick's dive boat and a larger work vessel for hauling up the chests of gold. But we knew that was very likely a gross underestimate.

Ange and I had surprise on our side. And we had our own weapons and gear. But we still needed to whip up something to even the odds. An ace in the hole. And additional backup plans.

We felt ready by the time we'd hopped over the Gulf, Cozumel's northern coast coming into view.

Jack hailed ATCs on the island and gave the guy on the other end our flight info, and he informed us where to land and that a government official would meet us there.

Not us, I corrected. *Just Jack.*

Sticking to the western side, Ange descended and splashed down in a cove between Isla Pasión and Cozumel's shore off the empty northwestern part of the island. It was a tough landing, with strong winds stirring up whitecaps even in the secluded body of water. Dark clouds were swooping in toward the island and distant thunder rumbled on the horizon.

She kept us steady, the Cessna rocking in the waves as she brought us closer to land.

Fifty yards from shore, we went for it. Ange and I slid into our drysuits, then Jack handed us our drybags, and we hauled them out onto the floats. Donning our fins, masks, and snorkels, Ange and I ran through the plan once more with Jack, then gave him a thumbs-up after he'd nestled into the pilot's seat.

"Good luck," he said through the window.

Ange and I took a big step out over the water, clearing the float as the plane continued on. We splashed into the sloshing cove, then bobbed right to the surface, the buoyancy of our drybags keeping us afloat. Putting our heads down, we kicked for the shore, navigating around the jutting rocks and finding a nice stretch of sand.

We planted our feet and rose out of the water. Removed our fins and clipped them in place while sloshing from the surf. Hauling our bags, we trekked over a rim of sharp limestone, then strode into the sandy interior littered with trees and bushes.

"That's one way to enter Mexico," Ange said as we removed our masks and snorkels, stowing them with the rest of our gear.

We slid off our drysuits, bunched them up and left them at the base of a coconut tree.

While prepping our gear and tightening it on our backs, I thought about the last time I'd entered a country illegally. It had been nearly a year earlier, when Ange and I had used sea scooters and rebreathers to travel underwater into Cuba from far offshore, entering Havana harbor.

By the time we were ready to get moving, Jack was already back in the air, soaring the bird south to the landing zone a short jump away. He already had a plan for what to say in case he was questioned about his unexpected stop. Simple engine trouble.

Ange and I trekked along the shore, threading through thick trees and foliage. There were no houses, hotels, or people in sight. Not on that part of the island.

While we moved, I thought about Mick, his daughter, and the young diver, Rico. Thought about Warren Sr. and the man who'd helped him get out of custody. And I thought about the treasure Mick had spent so much of his life searching for, and how a bunch of criminals were trying to steal it right out from under him. The thoughts caused me to pick up my pace, knowing that every second counted.

Soon, the beach opened up to a cul-de-sac and an old dock. Across the street were a couple of old trucks and men fishing along the shore.

I smiled as I saw a white taxi parked in the shade, its windows open, and a young Mexican man leaning against it. Ange and I popped out of the jungle coated in sweat and damp from the swim. Big drybags on our backs. Sunglasses on and our attentions focused.

Armando lowered his own sunglasses, then his mouth opened in surprise. Then he smiled. "I didn't expect to see you two back so soon," he said. "I knew there was more to you both than met the eye. That you weren't just normal vacationers."

He popped open the trunk and we stashed our gear.

"Thanks for picking us up, Armando," I said, shaking his hand. "I know it's—"

"Don't mention it, my friend. I just wish I would've known who you were before, and what you've done. I would've thanked you."

"You're thanking us now," Ange said.

He nodded, and we climbed into the back.

"Where to?" he said, eyeing us through the rearview. "I'm guessing you're not going to Barracuda?"

We told him and he fired up the engine and cruised us south for ten minutes before reaching town and turning inland. Less than half an hour after sliding into the taxi, he pulled off onto a dirt road on the eastern side of the island and drove slowly for another three miles before pulling off beside the coast on my signal.

"This looks like the spot," I said, pointing out my open window.

Ange leaned over and nodded. "This is it. That beach is unmistakable."

"Ixpalbarco Beach," Armando said. "Mostly only locals come here. There's good fishing nearby. But even better a few miles farther north."

"We've heard that," I said.

Since there was a small group of locals enjoying the surf, Armando drove us farther up to the corner of the beach, where the sand met a rocky shore. Then we climbed out and he helped us with our gear. Once it was out, I handed him a five-hundred-peso note.

"I can't accept that," he said, holding his hands up. "After all that you two have done, and are still doing for this community."

I thanked him, then he asked if there was anything else he could do.

"Just drive back and continue with your normal day," I said. "We were never here."

He nodded, slid back into his seat, and did a U-turn, bouncing back along the dirt road.

Ange and I heaved our gear down to the shore. We recognized the landscape from where Mick had us drop into the water, then drift to the wreck. Not only would it allow us to keep our distance from the site and sneak up on our enemies, but it was also the only landmark we knew of in relation to the wreck's location.

Climbing down into a sandy break in the jagged walls of rock, we slid into wetsuits and then strapped on our rebreathers. They were Draeger, similar to the ones I'd used in the Navy. Unlike scuba, the closed-circuit breathing systems resulted in no bubbles, which even on a choppy day would be noticeable from a boat.

Once our dive gear was on and tight and we'd each

performed buddy checks, we waded into the water. At waist depth, we donned our fins and full facemasks and did a quick mic check, the built-in internal communication device allowing Ange and me to talk to each other while underwater. I strapped on my waterproof gear bag, which contained my Sig and various other items, and attached a small drybag containing the C-4 to my waist. Then we clutched our spearguns and trudged deeper.

"Time to go hunting," I said.

"I'll try to save some for you," my warrior wife added as we dropped down into the surf.

THIRTY-SIX

Kicking with big, smooth cycles, we broke out through the opening of a narrow cove, out under the rough point break, then turned and moved steadily north, parallel with the shore. The current was even stronger, pulling us along at a blistering three knots at least. And with the added speed of our kicks, it felt like we were flying across the seafloor.

We took in the familiar scene, the same rocky coastline I'd glided over twice before, waves crashing wildly to our left, the bottom deepening, then vanishing altogether in the deep blue off our right.

The whole trip, I hoped we weren't too late. That Jack's salvaging calculations were correct, and that we weren't going to arrive at the wreck site to find nothing but remnants—only what the criminals decided to leave behind.

"We're close," Ange said through the radio.

She was right. The familiar jutting formation was just ahead. And as we cut around it, the water turned hazy, just like it usually did, the currents churning up sediment and swirling around like some kind of supernatural phenomenon, keeping the galleon hidden.

I relaxed a little as we caught our first glimpse of a boat floating overhead, a dark hull bobbing in the waves. We stopped kicking, letting our bodies flow with the current. Then a second, much larger hull came into view, along with a cable extending down from its bow.

Then figures appeared near the bottom less than twenty yards ahead of us. We grabbed at the rocky seafloor, keeping ourselves as flat as possible and stopping against the current. It wasn't easy. The Caribbean was relentless, and the rocks were smooth and slippery, making finding a good grip difficult, even with gloved hands.

"There's another," Ange said, pointing a finger toward the surface thirty feet above.

Counting the guy floating at the top of the cable, there were three divers in all.

The two others were down at the seafloor, fighting to break free, or rather break apart, old chests, and stacking gold bars onto a metal platform at the end of the cable. The two below were using surface-supplied air, wearing heavy dive helmets, diving suits, and weighted shoes—their gear pinning them down and making it far easier to perform the work than if they'd had scuba gear.

The gear was advanced, but the divers themselves were clearly amateurs. Their movements clumsy and awkward. No doubt they'd stolen the equipment from some nearby salvager for their own temporary purposes.

We waited, our muscles aching as we fought to stay put in the current, then made our move as the lift ascended, hoisting stacks of gold bars toward the surface.

"Here we go," I said, shooting my wife a look.

We pushed off in opposite directions, me finning toward the surf and her heading into deeper water. Then we both wrapped back, closing in on the two divers from the blind spots in their dive helmets.

I reached my target a few seconds ahead of Ange, the current swooping me around and launching me toward him. The guy noticed me at the last second. Jerked around and reached for the knife attached to his weighted belt. He managed to grab the handle, but I already had mine out and ready.

I grabbed the top of his helmet and buried the blade into his neck, the blade stabbing through right under the rim of the metal. His body shook and blood blossomed from the wound.

Seeing the unexpected attack, the other diver turned around to engage me. He managed to pull his knife free and take a labored step my way before Ange pounced on him from behind.

Wrapping an arm around the guy, she took him down with a similar stab of her knife.

With two divers down and the third one preoccupied with the surfaced platform, we eyed the bottom of the larger boat, then sheathed our knives and each removed two suction cup handles from our sides. They were the same ones I used to keep myself steady underwater while cleaning the hull of the Baia back home.

The next part was tricky.

We took a moment to gauge the current, along with our distance from the bow of the larger vessel. Ange and I exchanged glances. Counted to three, then jumped off the seabed, eyeing our target and kicking with everything we had. We tore up through the water at an angle and in a hurry, reaching the sea-crusted hull halfway down its keel. Twisting our bodies, we faced the bottom head-on and stabbed the suction cups into the sleek old iron one at a time.

The suction cups grabbed hold and we held tight, the strong little tools keeping us steady against the current. Water gushed past us, fighting to pry us free and take us with it.

Ange kept a steady eye around the underside of the vessel, gazing toward the cable and the highest sections visible from our angle.

While she kept watch, I went to work. Gripping the left suction cup handle firmly, I patted my right hand down my side until I felt the drybag secured to my hip. Clipping it free, I brought it up, wrapped its lanyard around both suction cups' handles multiple times, then secured it in place using a carabiner. Inside was the C-4 we'd brought, and the effectively positioned explosive would act as a backup plan just in case our primary one fell through.

Seeing that it wasn't going anywhere, I glanced through the flowing water at Ange. My eyes bulged as they focused on her. Still holding tight to the left handle, she had her speargun in her right hand, the razor tip of a loaded projectile aimed toward the bow of the vessel.

I angled my head to see what she was aiming at and spotted the scuba diver, descending hand over hand down the cable. The guy stopped, then bubbles burst from his regulator as he noticed the two other divers on the seafloor, both pinned to the bottom by their heavy suits, but their bodies lifeless and flapping in the current, blood trickling out and clouding around them momentarily before dissipating as it was carried away.

The scuba diver spun, looking around, then paused as he spotted us under the boat. Ange pulled the trigger. The tubing snapped free, and the metal spear torpedoed through the water, shattering through the right lens of the diver's mask before crashing into his eye. He thrashed momentarily. Let go of the cable. And the current ripped him away, his body spinning as he vanished into the haze.

With the three divers dealt with, we knew we had only a matter of seconds before the rest of the criminals figured out what was happening. Ange let go of her speargun, then we sucked in deep breaths and removed our dive gear.

Once free of the rebreather, I grabbed the grappling hook and tight coil of nylon rope from my side. After springing the metal device's arms out, I shot Ange a look, then let go, the wall of water tumbling me along the bottom of the vessel.

I kicked sideways with the current and reached the aft section of port side. Just as my body cleared the shadows, I turned skyward, kicking and breaking free into the bright afternoon air.

With only a moment to make a move, and knowing there were no second chances, I reared back the metal hook, eyed my target, and lobbed it with all my strength. The device soared high, its rubber-coated body colliding into the side of the pilothouse before it bounced to the deck and looped around the bottom rung of the railing. The arms caught the crossbars and the line went taut. The sound of a winch's groaning engine and a thumping air compressor, combined with the loud chatter of men at the bow, seemed to have masked the act. And no one appeared to notice.

I grabbed and heaved, pulling my way through the water as hard and fast as I could. Ange caught the line and broke the surface behind me just as I reached the stern of the vessel. Heaving myself up with all my strength, I grabbed the rail, snagged my right foot on the edge, and rolled up onto the deck.

A guy hustled around the corner just as I came to a knee and unclipped my speargun. He froze as he saw the rope, and Ange holding on to it in the water, then aimed his weapon when he saw me on the deck. I raised my speargun and beat him by a fraction of a second, pulling the trigger and skewering him in the chest. He stumbled back, flipped over the side and splashed into the water.

Releasing my speargun, I helped Ange aboard, then unstrapped my waterproof gear bag. Unzipping the main compartment, I retrieved my Sig, then left the pack and its remaining contents on the deck. Once Ange had her pistol out and ready as well, we performed a quick scan along the stern of the vessel before making our way around to the starboard side. A sound pierced the air that stopped us dead in our tracks—a young woman's scream.

"That's Dorothy," I said.

Her shrieking persisted, then she cried as if from being struck, then went silent.

We pressed on, resolve fueling our steps. Just as we reached the corner, a watertight door opened. A man took a step out, shotgun at the ready. I lunged forward, bashing my shoulder into the outside of the door as he appeared. He let loose, blasting a wave of pellets into nothing but open air as the heavy door swung, the thick iron bashing into him and sandwiching his body against the bulkhead. He relinquished his weapon to a chorus of cries and broken bones. I let go, and as he fell, I knocked him out with a kick to the forehead.

Ange and I rushed forward with our pistols raised. Ready for anything. When we rounded another corner, we stopped as our eyes took in the scene.

Mick and Rico were tied up and gagged, sitting beside piles of gold bars. Warren Beauchamp Sr. was at the bow, standing beside the droning winch along with one of his companions. Mick's dive boat idled nearby and had another armed man aboard it. Warren had an arm around Dorothy's body and a pistol pressed to her temple. She was squirming and fighting for every breath, tears streaking down her cheeks.

"Drop the gun, Dodge!" Warren shouted. "Or I'll blow her brains out."

She cried out again. Struggled to break free. Warren squeezed tighter around her neck, choking her.

I took a half step forward and to the right, giving myself a slightly better angle.

"Not another step, asshole!" Warren bellowed. "I tried to be reasonable with you. I ordered my men to leave you alone at first. But you had to persist. And now here we are. You killed my son, and now… now I'm going to kill her if you don't drop your gun."

I held my aim steady, knowing that if I did lower it, he'd not only kill me but Dorothy and everyone else as well. I was relieved, but also slightly surprised to see the three of them still breathing. Now that Mick had shown them the wreck site, Warren and his men no longer needed anything from them. They were extra baggage and loose ends. One way or another, he'd kill them. I was certain of it.

I held my aim. Patient. Ready.

"Okay, Dodge," Warren hissed. "This is how it's going to be? Okay. I'll—"

He froze as a distant siren cut across the air. Warren's eyes momentarily darted toward the sound, which was coming from the north. My eyes didn't. The only part of my body that moved was my right index finger. A tight, sudden flex. Everything else was motionless.

The 9mm round burst from the chamber, blasting away the upper part of Warren's skull. The man flew back, letting go of Dorothy and his weapon as he flailed, his corpse crashing to the deck.

A second gunshot tore across the air just after mine. The guy beside Warren barely had time for his face to react to his leader's head being blown apart before he fell victim to a similar fate. Ange, knowing that I had the better angle on Warren, had targeted the sidekick, and the guy had gone down, crashing to the deck never again to get up.

Following my rapid trigger pull, I dropped and turned, taking aim at the criminal on Mick's dive boat. The guy managed to fire a sporadic round into the pilothouse behind me before I put two bullets into his chest. He shook backward, teetering over the rail of the Whaler and crashing into the Caribbean.

I lowered my weapon, rushed across the deck and caught Dorothy as the terrified girl nearly collapsed from the intensity of the moment. Her head fell into my chest and I told her over and over that she was safe now.

Ange arrived and took over, holding the woman tight and looking over her wounds. I removed my knife and rushed over to Mick and Rico, removed their gags, then went to work on the ropes securing them to a row of deck cleats.

"Logan," Mick gasped, blinking in the brightness.

His forehead was cut up and bruised and covered in sweat. He looked exhausted and dazed.

Ange brought Dorothy over, and she fell into Mick's arms. She cried and shook. And he and Rico held her tight.

"How did you know?" Mick said, once he was able to speak.

"Let's just say you guys have a lot of friends on the island," Ange said. "Word got to us and we flew back right away."

"Is that all of them?" I said, staring into Mick's eyes. "We took down three in the water. Two at the stern. Then these three. That's eight in all."

"I think so," Mick said.

We did a quick sweep inside the pilothouse before returning to the deck.

"I'm sorry, Logan," Mick said. "They threatened to torture Dorothy. I had no choice but to tell them the wreck was here."

I placed a hand on his shoulder. "You did what you had to do, Mick. No treasure is more valuable than family."

Then I glanced toward Warren Sr.'s dead body. Both corrupt father and corrupt son dealt with. Good riddance.

"Fortunately, things worked out," Ange said.

Mick nodded. "Fortunately you two showed up out of nowhere and saved the day."

I shrugged. "I did what any good friend would do."

I looked up, gazing to the west toward the sirens as the police boat grew bigger on the horizon. Grabbed a pair of binoculars and spotted Officer Ramirez standing on the bow, along with another officer at the helm and three guys wearing civilian clothes. They were flying toward us at over fifty knots.

Striding to the starboard side, I vaulted onto Mick's dive boat, headed straight for the cockpit, and unlatched and cracked open the paneling just below the helm. Removed the wire to the starter, then sealed it back up.

"What the hell are you doing?" Mick said, wincing back the pain.

Then I placed a tiny tracking device in a cockpit locker and jumped back over to the workboat, where Ange and I untied the lines securing Mick's boat.

"What's going on?" Rico said.

"You've got to trust us," I said. "This isn't over yet."

When *Craic of Dawn* was free, I gave it a solid push. The current quickly carried it around the workboat's side, and it drifted along, heading north.

The police boat closed in, and Ange and I ushered the trio to the port bow. We grabbed weapons from the deck and gave one to Rico.

"Just follow my lead," Ange said to the others, then gave me a nod.

Seeing that she had it under control, I slipped away from the group and headed aft. Kneeling beside my gear bag still resting at the stern, I pulled out my sat phone then zipped it back up and left it there against the bulkhead.

Once in the pilothouse, I held up the phone and punched in a number. After relaying information to Scott's and my contact, I ended the call. Stepping to the forward bulkhead, I watched intently through the cockpit window as the police boat closed in.

THIRTY-SEVEN

Officer Ramirez stood at the bow of the police boat as it slowed. Seeing a group gathered on the main deck, he pointed for the pilot to ease up to the workboat's port side.

"We'll tie off there," he said.

Ange and Mick waved, then they cast the lines and secured them. Ramirez grabbed a line and one of the other officers followed suit.

"Boy, are we glad to see you guys," Ange said.

Ramirez climbed across first, landing on the workboat's deck and pausing for a moment to take in the scene.

"Holy crap," he gasped. His eyes swept over the deck, starting with Warren and the other criminal's mangled corpses. Then the tower of gold bars. Then his eyes narrowed. "Any more of them?"

Ange shook her head. Another officer climbed over, followed by three men dressed in civilian clothes.

"These are agents from the mainland," Ramirez said, seeing Ange's confused expression. "They're after Beauchamp. Boys, it looks like your job's been done for you."

Ange helped Mick forward. "He's hurt," she said. "He needs to get to the hospital immediately, and the dive boat drifted away."

Ramirez nodded. "The police boat's faster anyway." He motioned to the other men and they helped Mick off the workboat. Dorothy and Rico followed, the young man still clasping a pistol in his right hand. Ange still had her weapon out as well.

"No need to be armed anymore," Ramirez said. "It's over. You're all safe now."

Ange nodded but maintained her steady grip on her Glock.

The lawman's eyes scanned over the deck again. "Where's Logan?" He was flustered a moment, then added, "Is he…?"

"He's fine," Ange said. "He's in the pilothouse. Soon as we're gone, he'll weigh anchor and cruise around the island to Puerto de Abrigo."

Mick groaned again.

"We need to go, now!" Dorothy exclaimed. "He's still bleeding out."

Ramirez thought a moment, then motioned to the three men. "We'll stay here. Clean up and help Logan. Officer Garcia, take these people to Last Frontier. I'll call in to have an ambulance meet you there."

Ange nodded, then the other uniformed officer climbed into the cockpit and fired the engine back up.

"Promise me that Mick here will get a piece of that," Ange pleaded, motioning toward the mountain of gold as the lines were untied and cast.

"I'll do everything I can to ensure things are handled fairly, Mrs. Dodge," Ramirez replied.

The two uniformed law enforcement officers shot each other knowing nods, then the police boat accelerated away, its dual 250-horsepower engines rocketing it up to speed in a flash.

Ramirez watched and waited until it was a couple hundred yards off, then gazed over the deck once more. Stared at Warren's bloody, lifeless body. Gave a satisfied smile. Wiped the sweat from his brow and turned his attention to the pilothouse.

"You three stay here," he said, then strode aft.

He walked up the steps, went straight for the forward door. Heaved it open and scanned over the cockpit. It was empty. He shut the door and strode around the port side of the pilothouse. Kept relaxed and steady, trying his best to hold back his excitement.

He rounded the back corner, then found himself gazing into the barrel of a Sig 9mm pistol.

THIRTY-EIGHT

I held my weapon with both hands. My mind and body steady. My eyes narrowed. My target just five feet away.

Officer Ramirez froze as he rounded the corner, stunned speechless at first, his mouth hitting the deck and air gasping from his lungs.

"Hey, easy," he said, holding his open hands out in front of him. "Logan, what are you doing?"

I remained silent. Just staring into his eyes.

Ramirez shook his head. "The fight is over. All our enemies are down."

I held my aim. Narrowed my gaze even tighter. My index finger ready on the trigger.

"I'm not your enemy," Ramirez said, his tone nervous and tense.

One of the men on the main deck called out, checking to see that everything was all right.

"Order them to stay put," I said. When he hesitated, I took a half step closer, my body still well out of the other men's view. "Do it, now."

Ramirez swiveled his head and did as instructed. The three men stayed.

After another brief silence, he shook his head, still playing the part of the confused victim.

"I just have one question," I said calmly. "All that crap you said about your father and how his service inspired you. And your sense of duty to return to your homeland and fight to make things better. Total bullshit?"

Ramirez's expression went from shocked to resolute, then warped to remorseless satisfaction.

"That old fool wasted his life," the officer snapped, his tone cold as ice. His face hardening. "Thirty years of service. Then he died two years into retirement."

I nodded. "So, you chose to waste yours murdering people."

"I chose to live a life unshackled by the elite," he said. "Instead of driving myself to an early grave for pointless causes."

"Cheating and torturing and murdering small business owners in your home country, all while pretending to be the people's hero." I shook my head. "I've met some vile men in my time, Ramirez. You're right up near the top." Keeping my pistol aimed at his head, I added, "It really is quite the little operation you've got going here. Borrowing money from big banks using false identities. Corrupting your way into control of waterfront communities. And when you get caught, like what happened back in the States, you had old Beauchamp to pin everything on. He takes the fall as the supposed face of the whole scheme. Serves time in exchange for a big payday by you, then you do it all over again."

I paused, letting the anger grow on his face.

"But what happened, Ramirez?" I said. "Why'd you get so careless all of a sudden? Why'd you get so desperate for cash that you murdered and robbed?" I narrowed my gaze even sharper. "Let me guess, something happened and the big banks suddenly got suspicious and called in their loans?"

The corrupt officer's face turned red. Then he sneered and said, "You speak as if you've beaten me."

He took a half step forward.

"Another move and you'll never walk again," I said, aiming at his knee cap.

He turned to look toward the three men. Smiled at them.

"You're forgetting that you're outnumbered four to one, Dodge. Are you sure you can take on all of us?"

He took another slow half step, then charged.

I opened fire, blasting a round into his chest. And then another. He grunted and shook but kept barging toward me. He crashed into me before I could fire a third, and we slammed to the deck and rolled. He tried to hold me down, but I was much bigger and stronger, and he was injured.

I flung him off me, hurtling him like a rag doll into the back of the pilothouse. He bucked, then reached for his weapon. I slid out my knife, grabbed his forearm to prevent him from withdrawing the pistol, then stabbed my blade just above his collarbone and the bulletproof vest under his police uniform.

I forced the knife in as deep as it would go, then ripped the crimson-coated blade free. His eyes shot skyward and he collapsed, dead at my feet.

Hearing heavy footsteps coming from just around the corner, I swiped my gear bag from the deck, lunged over Ramirez's corpse, and hurled myself over the rail. Splashing headfirst, I sank deep and pulled at the water, tearing myself toward the bottom.

The three men opened fire, pelting rounds into the sea, the lead projectiles slowing before they'd penetrated three feet and sinking lifelessly beside me as I fought the current. Reaching the bottom, I grabbed hold of a boulder, swung myself around, and removed a weight belt, dive mask, and can of Spare Air from my bag.

Donning and clearing the mask using air from the tiny canister, I tightened the belt and breathed in while letting the current pull me away from the scene. The dark hull of the workboat grew faint, then soon vanished entirely.

THIRTY-NINE

After five minutes of drifting, and with my air running low, I kicked for the surface. Breaking free less than a hundred yards from the coastline, I immediately slid down my mask and gazed to the south. The winding nature of the shore made it impossible to see the workboat. But less than thirty seconds later, I heard a humming motor and watched as the police vessel motored around a bend.

I spotted my wife right away, standing at the bow with a pair of binoculars pressed to her eyes and a smile on her face. Mick motored the boat right up to me and offered me a hand up over the side, and Ange threw her arms around me.

"Why do you always have to take on the harder roles, huh?" she said, looking me up and down.

"I'm fine, Ange," I said, hugging her again. "Made out better than usual. I'm guessing you handled your man easily enough?"

Dorothy pointed toward Ramirez's accomplice, the officer lying motionless and handcuffed on the deck beside the port gunwale. "She took him out with one quick strike."

I chuckled. "Nice to see you're healing quickly," I said, pointing toward Mick's exaggerated wounds.

"Now are you two going to tell us what's going on?" he said. "'Cause I'm pretty sure we just committed a felony."

"No, you didn't," I said.

"Ramirez was running the whole thing," Ange said.

All three of their mouths dropped open. It was Dorothy who finally got a single word out. "What?"

"Are you certain?" Mick said.

I nodded. "Positive."

"He's dead, right?" Ange said.

"Big-time." I turned to the others who were still in shock. "Ramirez secretly ran the entire operation," I explained. "Beauchamp was never in charge. He was just a fall guy. Just like for their con back in the States. He was the one who served time, not Ramirez. But Ramirez was always calling the shots. It was a nice little cover for him down here. I mean, who would ever suspect a near fifty-year-old low-ranking cop to be running a major illegal operation—conniving and murdering to maintain his little empire?"

The three were silent a moment, then Mick said, "How did you guys figure it out?"

"Logan did," Ange said.

"With a lot of help," I clarified. "From contacts of ours from over the years. It wasn't easy, though. Ramirez was smart. And brutal. Ran a pretty tight ship. But no operation's perfect."

I thought back to the moment on the plane when the realization had flashed into my mind. When I'd pictured Ramirez arriving at the criminal compound after the encounter, and the bruised and partly swollen knuckles of his left hand. Then I'd pieced them together with the marks Junior had had on his face prior to our scuffle. Cuts and bruises to his right cheek and chin—delivered by someone with a dominant left hand.

Then I remembered the dinner at Casa Mission. How Ramirez had kept his left hand in his pocket the whole time, not wanting me to see his damaged fingers and make the connection. And how he'd just stopped by for a quick visit, then left, supposedly needing to head to the police station for a shift.

But he'd already slipped up.

Once Ramirez became a potential suspect, more evidence of his being the head honcho flooded into my mind. How Junior had acted around the officer at the boat launch, even though he held a low rank. And how, looking back, Ramirez had been clearly striving to play the part of the battered, up against the world, saint. Then a call to the CIA revealed that he'd been lying about his identity, and his past in the states. The final nails in the coffin.

Ange accelerated us into deeper water so we could see the workboat in the distance. Then she zoomed in and focused on it with her binos.

"Looks like they're trying to weigh anchor," she said. "Three guys still aboard."

"It's a shame," Mick said. "After all this, they're still making off with part of the treasure."

"I wouldn't be so sure," I said. I shot Ange a smile, and when Mick looked at me for an explanation, I said, "I may have tampered with the windlass controls and the helm before my little rendezvous with Ramirez."

Mick laughed as best he could. "You two sure cover all your bases."

"Speaking of which," I said, spotting a ship motoring toward us on the eastern horizon.

FORTY

We retrieved Mick's dive boat, the Irishman taking station in the cockpit and following us as we motored toward a 255-foot Navy salvage and rescue ship. The USNS *Grasp* was one of the most versatile salvage vessels on the planet and had been utilized by Mobile Diving and Salvage Unit Two in various operations around the world.

Though she had been decommissioned in 2006, she had been transferred to the MSC for continued use. The MSC, or Military Sealift Command, is an organization that works in unison with the United States Navy to provide a full spectrum of support to our nation's warfighters during peacetime and while at war.

The *Grasp* and her crew had played major roles in

dozens of high-profile salvage efforts. And more recently, they'd helped me recover a Nazi biological weapon resting at the bottom of the Florida Strait off Key Largo. The weapon had been part of a secret last-ditch mission and had been fired from a lost U-boat that had run aground near where the torpedo was lodged in the rock.

"Friends of yours, I hope?" Dorothy said, gazing upon the vessel, which looked similar to an *Arleigh Burke*–class destroyer, with a long, narrow body and a bridge that rose fifty feet into the air.

Steering well clear of the shore, the *Grasp* anchored down in a three-point moor, its crew utilizing its port, starboard and stern anchors. As we closed in on the vessel, I shot off a quick message to Jack, requesting pickup.

"I'll get this bird back in the air right away, compadre," he replied. "Glad to hear you all made it out."

Ange eased us up along the starboard side of the ship, where an orange ladder was secured in place for us.

"Well, if it isn't Chief Dodge," Wade Bishop said, grinning at me while leaning over the gunwale.

He tossed a line and brought us in. Mick pulled up right behind us, and after we tied off, Wade tossed a line to him as well so he could secure *Craic of Dawn*.

I'd first met Wade back in 2000, while I was assigned as a temporary Underwater Ordnance Division Instructor at EOD school at Eglin Air Force Base in Fort Walton Beach, Florida. Wade had been one of my best students, and one of a small handful I'd gone recreational diving with after he'd completed his training.

"Good to see you, Wade," I said, climbing aboard and shaking his hand. "Putting on a little weight?"

The five-and-a-half-foot-tall Hawaiian glanced at his stomach, then laughed. "The treadmill on this thing's secured for maintenance."

"Looks like it's been secured for a while," I said with a chuckle.

Ange shook his hand as well, having met him back off Key Largo, and we introduced him to the others.

"Captain up in the bridge?" I said, motioning toward the superstructure.

"Had to see this up close for myself," a man said in a familiar Southern accent.

I peered up at Commander Sprague, the commanding officer of the *Grasp*. The lean, athletic man with thinning black hair gazed out toward the coast through aviator sunglasses.

"We heard the gunfire on approach," he said. "You want to fill us in on what exactly happened here?"

Wade motioned behind him, "Lots of coffee in the bridge. Let's settle in for some storytime."

We all gathered up in the main control center near the top of the superstructure. There was a wide spread of tall windows, giving us a wide view of the island and surrounding ocean. We told Commander Sprague, Wade, and other members of the crew everything that had happened, then gave them the rundown on the site—depth, current, visibility. Things like that. I also informed them about the C-4 I'd attached to the workboat's keel as a backup just in case things hadn't gone according to plan.

"So there are three guys still on that thing?"

Sprague said, pointing toward the workboat.

"I doubt they'd make a swim for the shore," I said.

Sprague nodded. "We'll see how tough they are when we motor on up with a dozen men armed with assault rifles."

I smiled at Mick. These were the right men for the job. The perfect blend of firepower, equipment, and skill.

"Scott and I have already gotten in touch with the Mexican Navy and Coast Guard," Sprague said. "They have boats inbound. ETA half an hour." Having heard enough, he turned his attention to Wade. "Assemble a boarding party. And bring whoever's on that workboat into custody."

"Aye-aye," Wade said, a big grin on his face. "I love parties."

As he rose, I turned to my wife. "I think that's our cue, Ange."

"You're not gonna stay for the salvage?" Mick said.

I looked toward Sprague, then said, "Sorry, Mick, but salvaging Spanish galleons isn't exactly the *Grasp*'s primary function. I'm sure they'll be off after everything's been cleared up."

"Duty calls off Georgia," Wade said. "Then hopefully we'll be back home in Virginia for at least a few weeks."

"But we'll do all we can to help you," Sprague said. "We've worked joint operations with Mexico before. And I have close relations inside the Mexican government. I'm sure once we've told them all that you've done, a fair deal can be struck."

"Thank you, sir," Mick said. "But it was Logan

and Angelina that pulled this off. We'd still be captives, and the gold would be in the hands of criminals were it not for them."

"And the wreck would've never been found in the first place were it not for you," Ange said.

The group migrated back down to the main deck and Wade relayed orders.

"Anything else you need from us before we take over from here?" Sprague said, eyeing Ange and me.

"Only that our names never be mentioned," I said.

Wade nodded. "Still evading credit like a pro, I see."

"More like evading attention."

My old Navy buddy laughed. "I get that. No problem, Chief. We'll make sure your names stay out of this."

"Oh, one more thing," I said, turning to Mick. "I think it might be the *Nuestra Señora del Juncal*."

He raised his eyebrows, and I explained, "She was a galleon that went down in 1631. Never been found. Her intended course was from Veracruz to Havana, and there was a big storm that year that would have certainly thrown her off course before she sank. I have it on good authority that there's a good chance it could be the ship you found, but I'll keep up the research."

Wade nodded, then Mick patted me on the back. "Remember when I said that you were an easy family to like? I think even that was an understatement."

"Likewise. Good luck with the recovery. If you ever find yourself in the Keys, feel free to reach out."

"And you have a second home in Cozumel if you're ever in the area."

I smiled. "Something tells me your shop's gonna get that long-overdue upgrade after all."

Sprague eyed Ange and me. "You two need a lift back to shore?"

As the words left the Navy commander's lips, the distant hum of an engine echoed across the air. Peering to the west, we spotted Ange's Cessna soaring over the island.

"I appreciate the offer," I said. "But we've got a ride."

The amphibious aircraft circled in front of us then splashed down near the stern of the *Grasp*. Jack saluted us through the pilot's window as we stepped out onto the deck.

"I'm not sure how I can possibly thank you two for all that you've done," Mick said.

"Just keep us in the loop, all right?" I said. "Pictures and whatnot. Let me know how the recovery goes."

"You sure you don't want to head to shore?" Dorothy said. "Maybe have dinner at Casa Mission?"

"Any other time we would," I said. "But we should be getting back home. And we'd rather not be here when the Mexican authorities show up."

I thanked Wade, Sprague, and the entire crew, then Ange and I said our goodbyes to Mick, Dorothy, and Rico.

"Make sure you all visit again soon," Dorothy said, wrapping her arms around us.

Mick nodded. "Who knows, maybe we'll all find another wreck someday?"

Ange and I climbed down to the police boat, then hopped over to the Cessna's port float as Jack eased her past. We held on to the wing strut and climbed inside.

"Thanks for the lift, Jack," I said as we nestled in.

"Anytime." He grinned. "Ange, you mind taking over? Something about all these heroics just leaves me beat."

We laughed as Jack crawled into the back and sprawled out while Ange settled into the pilot's seat.

"How'd you end up passing the time?" I asked while Ange brought us up to speed.

"Found a nice margarita bar near the marina."

Ange's eyes bulged. "You drank before flying my—"

"Just kidding," he said, waving her off. "I just topped off the gas tank, then took a nap. What happened to all your gear?"

We told him, and his only reaction was to laugh. "You guys lose more dive equipment than anyone I've ever met."

"Well, next time I'm in a shoot-out, I'll put a higher precedence on gear retention," I joked.

We held on as the craft splashed over the slightly whitecapped sea, then lifted into the air. Within minutes, we were cruising over the shore at a hundred feet up.

"Thanks for coming with, Jack," I said.

He shrugged. "It's nice to get away. Take a break from marina life for a bit." He peered out the window at the beautiful island fringed in turquoise water below. "It's just a shame we came all this way and didn't get to drop down for a dive. Or at least I didn't."

"We'll just have to come back someday," Ange

said. "When we're not hunting down a bunch of armed criminals."

The sun began to set over our left shoulders as we soared out over the Gulf. Ange kicked on the autopilot and propped her bare feet up on the instrument panel, then I inched closer and she rested against my shoulder. For the first time since Benny had called me at the marina earlier that day, I let out a long sigh and felt my body relax into the seat back.

FORTY-ONE

Even in the dark, the archipelago's lights glowing a skinny lazy J in the surrounding blackness, it felt as if our islands had never looked so good. Home had never felt so good.

After an enjoyable, laid-back jump across the Gulf, Ange brought us down into Tarpon Cove just after midnight. A trio of silhouettes waited for us as we approached her slip in the dock. I climbed out to tie us off, and Atticus nearly fell into the water as he leaned over the edge and greeted me with a happy succession of licks. Sometimes I felt like he knew when we'd been through a difficult ordeal. That the intuitive pooch could sense it somehow. And he was showing each of us even more love than usual as we climbed down.

Lauren threw her arms around Jack, and my beach

bum friend swept her off the planks, locking his lips to hers.

Scarlett jumped into mine and Ange's arms.

"How are they?" she said.

"They're just fine," Ange replied, knowing who she was referring to. "Dorothy sends her thanks and says she already misses you."

"And Beauchamp? You guys got him good this time, right?"

"He won't be causing any more trouble ever again," I said. "Though it turned out he wasn't the one calling the shots after all."

"Really? Who was it?"

We grabbed what stuff we hadn't left behind at the wreck site, locked up the Cessna, then told our daughter the PG-13 version of all that had happened while making for the parking lot and driving to Jack's house. He lived on the same street as our property just down the channel from us. His place was closer than the marina, and he'd offered to have us all stay there for the night since it was so late. Being a school night, we unfolded the living room sleeper sofa for Scarlett as soon as we entered, then Ange and I said goodnight and migrated to the guest bedroom.

Ange ran a bubble bath in the adjoining bathroom while I nestled into a wicker chair out on the balcony with Atticus at my feet, taking a moment to wrap my head around all that had transpired over the past few weeks. As usual, the thing that amazed me the most was how fortunate I was to have such a solid team watching my back. I could never have figured out what was happening, or taken down Ramirez and his men, were it not for Ange and Scarlett. Not to mention Jack, Scott, and Wade and his team. And our new Cozumel friends, Benny and Armando. And of course, Mick, Dorothy, and Rico.

Though the whole thing hadn't quite been the relaxing getaway we'd had in mind, it sure hadn't been boring.

It started to rain, and Atticus followed me into the living room, then, sensing it was time for bed, nestled up beside an already passed out Scarlett.

"Rest up, boy," I whispered, kneeling beside him and petting the top of his head. "You're joining me on my run in the morning."

His tail wagged a little, then he licked my cheek and dropped his head onto the comforter.

Ange was still in the tub when I entered the guest bedroom, her head and toes the only parts of her visible through the thick blanket of bubbles.

"You should really join me," she said, keeping her eyes closed. "The Epsom salt feels good."

Requiring no persuading, I stripped down, and she giggled as I dropped into the heat and cozied up beside her. The smell of eucalyptus and coconut oil filled the air. The hot water felt amazing, but far better was the sensation of my body being pressed against hers. And I wondered for what felt like the millionth time since we'd married how I'd gotten so lucky. What wave of hypnosis had come over her that had caused her to say yes when a woman like her could have anyone she wanted?

We stayed in until her hands were pruney, then climbed out and patted ourselves down. The rain had intensified—thick sheets smacking against the roof and windows. We were still damp as we got lost in each other's embrace, crashing onto the bed and putting the perfect exclamation point on the evening.

EPILOGUE

Things settled back to normal after that. Scarlett turned her focus back on school and working part-time at the marina. Ange and I helped Jack and Lauren out at as much as we could, ticking most of the big maintenance items off the list and working on various other small projects. We balanced our time between the marina, our property to oversee our new build, and taking our boat out on the water. The end of lobster season loomed on the horizon, and Jack and I were hitting up some of our favorite secret spots to fill up our fridges with the sweet, succulent meat.

We stayed in close contact with Mick, and just a couple weeks after leaving Cozumel, he informed us that he'd secured the salvage rights.

"The government's agreed to an eighty-twenty

split so long as I don't drag it out," he said over the phone, his voice sparking with excitement. "Looks like the shop's getting that face-lift after all."

Running the numbers in my head was mind-boggling. When we'd found the Aztec treasure, we'd only managed to get four percent of the haul. And we'd ended up splitting that four ways. With Mick's twenty percent slice of the pie, he was looking at a potential nine-figure payday.

"I'll say," I said, laughing through the phone. "Just don't let all that go to your head."

"Dorothy and I have talked it over, and we've already agreed to donate most of it to local charities here. Orphanages. Homeless shelters. And Cozumel's reef restoration teams. This treasure's gonna do a lot of good for the island."

He ended the call by thanking me again for all my family had done, and reiterating that if we ever needed anything, he was just a phone call away.

January seemed to fly by, and on a nice evening in early February, the Dodge clan drove into a packed parking lot at Salty Pete's for his long-anticipated fortieth-anniversary celebration, commemorating the day he'd first opened the restaurant back in 1972.

The place was packed tighter than a can of sardines. Familiar faces and new acquaintances. Pete had friends all up and down the islands, and some of his old pals had even flown in from half the world away to help commemorate the event and pay homage to one of the most beloved characters on any island anywhere, let alone Key West.

Jane Verona, Key West's chief of police and a longtime friend, was there, the Latina making a rare appearance in civilian clothes. With her was Officer Colby Miller, a man who'd been gunned down by an old nemesis of mine. Though the injury had resulted in his needing a wheelchair, he was still on the force, working out of the main downtown station. Harper Ridley, a writer for the local *Keynoter* and longtime friend, was also there.

We sat around our favorite table on the balcony, our family squeezing in between Jack, Lauren, and his nephew Isaac on one side, and Jane, Colby, and Harper on the other. Taking in the lively atmosphere, we led off with appetizers and cold drinks and exchanged sea stories.

Pete was even livelier than usual, the jolly proprietor bouncing from person to person like the social butterfly he was, going from one smiling face to the next. It amazed me how one man could have such an impact—such a large sphere of people he'd influenced over the years.

Cameron appeared through the crowd just before the entrées arrived, the young man greeted by Scarlett nearly tackling him to the deck. We'd saved him a seat, and as he approached, I noticed that he was wearing a new ball cap. It was blue with an orange bill and had a cartoon alligator logo on the front. We exchanged knowing glances, then I shook his hand.

"I think you made a good choice," I said.

Scarlett noticed the hat, then exclaimed, "You're a Gator?"

He nodded, and she threw her arms around him again. Kissed his cheek.

I was glad he'd chosen to go with his dream school. That he hadn't been deterred by the fear of heavy competition. From a selfish perspective, I was also happy not to have to travel out of state to watch some of his future games.

"Let us know when you're playing and we'll be there," Ange said.

Mia and another waitress arrived with our entrées. Oz had outdone himself for the big night, conjuring up seemingly endless spreads of grilled pompano, hogfish, and lobster tails. Along with a huge batch of mouthwatering conch chowder.

Pete pranced over to our table, then patted me on the back.

"Thought you might need another," he said, handing me a commemorative mug. "Just don't go breaking this one."

We both laughed, reminiscing the time months earlier when I'd used a prototype of the mug to knock out a troublemaker in the restaurant's parking lot. Then glasses were handed out, and we all toasted with champagne to Pete and his years of business.

"Never thought I'd be drinking champagne at Pete's," Ange said to me.

Halfway through dinner, Pete made his way onto the outdoor stage to a chorus of cheers. Going against his character, he remained silent a moment, taken aback by the company, the claps, the hollers, and the resounding support. For a moment, I thought I caught a glimmer of moisture in the conch's eyes, but he swiftly wiped it away.

"Welcome, island family," he said. "It warms this old man's heart to receive such a great welcome. As I look around at this sea of friends, both from old days and recent, I can't think of much else to say other than thank you. From the bottom of my heart. And I can't imagine a luckier man in the world."

He choked up a little, then continued. "We first opened our doors in 1972. It was a Tuesday. Rainy and windy. And I think we may have had a dozen or so lost tourists and close friends of mine stumble in that first evening. And though the island has seen many changes in that time, this place remains. And it's all thanks to the support I've received. The love I've been shown by all of you." He raised his glass. "To great friends. To forty years of saltiness. And to Cayo Hueso. May our slab of ancient coral act as a haven for wandering seafarers and rambling oddballs forever."

The gathered crowd let out emphatic cheers and splashed down gulps of the sparkling wine. After kicking back half his glass, Pete wiped his mouth and smiled as he held up a hand, reclaiming everyone's attention.

"As you all know," he continued, his level of enthusiasm amping up even more, "live music has become a staple here. And these walls have heard some of the best island and folk-rock musicians to ever sing a tune or strum a chord. But on the day we opened, we had a special young man stroll in to play for us. He sat right over there on an upturned crate. And though he played for little more than a handful of people and two stray cats, he put on a show like he was performing at Madison Square Garden. His words were idyllic and pure. His melodies milk and honey for the ears. And his voice echoed the heartbeat of the islands. The soul of Cayo Hueso. That stormy night, this place fell under the spell of this pirate poet washed ashore with his guitar. And though his golden locks aren't what they were back then—yes, time has had its humor with me as well—his enchantments are as powerful as ever. Ladies and gentlemen, it is my honor to present to you, the one and only, James William Buffett."

A thunderous surge of applause, cheers, and whistles erupted through the night air. Unlike anything I'd ever heard and borderline painful to the ears. Like a spontaneous, raging storm had just howled in and settled right over the balcony.

Then the man himself appeared into a sea of wild Parrotheads. Ambling up onto the stage was Bubba in all his glory.

"Pete's just full of surprises," Ange said.

After a friendly hug with the man of the hour, Jimmy grabbed a crate from behind the stage and switched it out with the stool. They both got a good laugh at that, then the King of Island Escapism settled in with his acoustic.

After giving a quick thanks to Pete and a greeting to everyone gathered, he led off with a familiar riff, then dove into the lyrics of "A Pirate Looks at Forty." More cheers and hollers filled the air. And Pete's cranked up wilder than I'd ever seen it before.

I closed my eyes, relishing the experience as Jimmy rocked along his set, leaving me in awe of the music's power on the soul. To take you places in your mind, to make you feel things and to conjure up emotions. It's not just the rhythm or the lyrics or the strings. It's beyond that. A language of the heart and soul. As primal and ancient as the wind. And few conjure up those emotions better than the man on stage.

For one evening, we were the kings of the universe. And there was no place in the world I'd rather be.

The excitement and passion were palpable. And no one wanted the evening to end. I met up with Pete during the chorus of "Come Monday" and leaned against a corner railing beside him. We were both silent for a while. Just listening to the music. Feeling like I was in a trance and that if I pinched myself it would all fade away.

"Camelot," Pete whispered again.

He nodded, and when I looked at him, I saw a man consumed with love and emotion. I patted him on the shoulder. Though Jack and I went further back, it was Pete who'd first really brought me in and welcomed me into their island family. And I was just grateful to be a part of it.

Both Ange and I were too far gone by the time the party wrapped up, so Scarlett drove us to the marina. I lumbered down the dock with my arms draped over the women of my life, then sprawled out on the sunbed when we reached the Baia.

Ange and Scarlett snuggled up beside me with a blanket and animatedly relived the high points of the evening while Atticus lay at our feet. I just listened. Happy and utterly content. As they spoke, I thought over Pete's words. Turned them over in my mind, and then smiled.

It didn't matter how long Camelot existed. The important thing was that it did. However brief its place in time, the moment was there.

It's here, I thought, looking at my family and

trying to wrap my head around the beautiful irony of my life.

And I cherished it and smiled and knew that it would never end. Not really. That it would live on and be with me always. And I was forever grateful for that.

"Saturday tomorrow," Scarlett said, nudging me from my thoughts. "After a good sleeping in, we should dive the *Cayman Salvager* wreck. I've never seen it before, and it looks incredible from pictures."

I nodded, then leaned back and exhaled in that satisfied manner that stems from moments of pure contentment.

"Sounds like a plan, Scar."

THE END

Note to Reader

It's hard for me to believe this is the 15th Logan Dodge Adventure. For those of you who've followed along with Logan, Ange, Jack, and the rest of the island crew since the beginning, I thank you from the bottom of my heart. And for those first dipping your toes into these sea stories, I hope you liked it, and that you enjoy the rest of the adventures as well. It's been a fun ride, and one that wouldn't be possible without your support, reviews, and recommendations of my stories.

Cheers to many more adventures,
Matthew

LOGAN DODGE ADVENTURES

Gold in the Keys
Hunted in the Keys
Revenge in the Keys
Betrayed in the Keys
Redemption in the Keys
Corruption in the Keys
Predator in the Keys
Legend in the Keys
Abducted in the Keys
Showdown in the Keys
Avenged in the Keys
Broken in the Keys
Payback in the Keys
Condemned in the Keys
Voyage in the Keys
Guardian in the Keys

JASON WAKE NOVELS

Caribbean Wake
Surging Wake
Relentless Wake
Turbulent Wake
Furious Wake

Join the Adventure!
Sign up for my newsletter to receive updates on upcoming books on my website:

matthewrief.com

About the Author

Matthew has a deep-rooted love for adventure and the ocean. He loves traveling, diving, rock climbing, and writing adventure novels. Though he grew up in the Pacific Northwest, he currently lives in Virginia Beach with his wife, Jenny.

Made in the USA
Columbia, SC
12 April 2022